I0687549

A Red, Red Rose

by

Susan Coryell

This is a work of fiction. Names, characters, places, and incidents are either the product of the author's imagination or are used fictitiously, and any resemblance to actual persons living or dead, business establishments, events, or locales, is entirely coincidental.

A Red, Red Rose

COPYRIGHT © 2013 by Susan Coryell

All rights reserved. No part of this book may be used or reproduced in any manner whatsoever without written permission of the author or The Wild Rose Press, Inc. except in the case of brief quotations embodied in critical articles or reviews.
Contact Information: info@thewildrosepress.com

Cover Art by *Tina Lynn Stout*

The Wild Rose Press, Inc.
PO Box 708
Adams Basin, NY 14410-0708
Visit us at www.thewildrosepress.com

Publishing History
First Faery Rose Edition, 2013
Print ISBN 978-1-62830-181-6
Digital ISBN 978-1-62830-182-3

Published in the United States of America

Holding the candle at arm's length, I crept forward, a step at a time, my other hand grasping at the air in front. I felt like a blind person without a guide dog.

My fingers brushed across a grainy surface, and crumbling powder dusted my fingertips. Instantly, I recognized the metallic smell of rusting screens. I knew then I must be on the ancient screened porch tucked between the wings of the house, the crumbling porch with the antique rocking chairs. The music had led me here. Again the strains wafted over and around me, holding me captive as I stood, shivering, gazing at the dim light of my flickering candle.

The music stopped as abruptly as it had begun. Struggling to clear the cobwebs of sound spinning in my brain, I took a deep breath and looked around. I sensed, rather than saw a movement in my periphery. When I turned, I became aware of one of the rocking chairs. Gently, so as to be barely perceptible, the chair rocked itself back and forth as though someone invisible sat in it, enjoying the languorous, rhythmic motion. Rocking, rocking, rocking, without any sound at all.

Not conscious of moving, I found myself standing beside the ancient rocker, now motionless, dusty, the seat sagging within inches of the floor, as though it had not moved in a hundred years. I had not dreamed it. The chair had rocked itself, and someone or something had led me here to witness it. Led me with the music. I had the evidence. On the decaying cane seat lay a single fresh rose just out of the bud.

Praise for *A RED, RED, ROSE*

*Nominated for a literary award
with the Library of Virginia, fiction division, 2013*

"The mystery and love story drive the plot but there are so many thought-provoking elements in the mix—from adoption to sibling rivalries, race and class. I read it while traveling. It made the time go by quickly and left me with much to think about."

~Keya Chatterjee, author

"*A RED, RED ROSE* has everything: a rich and haunting ambiance, a mysterious ghost, a sweet bit of romance and a captivating sleuth who guided me through the thrills and chills of a clever plot—then left me breathless and wanting more."

~Nancy Means Wright, author

"A beautifully crafted story redolent of the languorous atmosphere and brooding evil of the old South. Ashby, a modern girl with a cell phone and Internet access, comes into intimate contact with her staid and tradition-bound ancestors and eventually aligns herself in their common cause. The fast-paced tale weaves contemporary characters, Southern charm and Gothic mystery into the historic setting all the way to its violent, shocking and yet fitting end. The story evokes some of the same emotions as Carson McCuller's *The Ballad of the Sad Cafe.*"

~Peter H. Green, author

Dedication

For the grandest kids:
Shannon, Holly, Jack, Ashby, Verily, and Lizah
whose lively imaginations
take story-telling to dizzying heights

Acknowledgments

Special thanks to my helpful and understanding family, especially my husband Ned who never complains when I retreat into my writing shell and to my daughter Heidi Coryell Williams and daughter-in-law Valerie Coryell who are invaluable readers and editors.

For my sons, Ted and Derek, and for the magnificent children who call me Granny, all of whom inspire the writer in me in different ways, I am grateful.

Finally, I acknowledge the influence of my ever proud and supportive parents, Noble Ashby and Emilie Robb McDaniel, profoundly missed in this world.

Prologue

Dear Diary,

Serendipity! Summer at Moore Mountain Lake! Aunt Monica and Uncle Hunter live in historic Overhome, on the lake, and they've invited me to be an au pair for my cousin Jefferson. Of course, at first Dad resisted the idea of my traveling alone. You might say he's a tad overprotective. Then, Mom and Dad won an around-the-world cruise for two this summer. How lucky is that? Since my parents would never think of leaving me at home alone for so long, their cruise ticket was MY ticket to Virginia.

Dad has a lot of bad vibes about the old family estate. He left Overhome after college and never went back. Some kind of family feud or something. So, that happens, even in the best of families. Now I hope to reconnect, to find the answers to a lot of questions there.

I know only the basic facts. Three Overton sons were born on the estate—Madison, Washington and Hunter. Washington and Marian, my birth parents, were killed in a car accident when I was two. Then Madison and Helen adopted me. I really dig the funny, old-fashioned names they use in the South! Madison, Washington, and Hunter, descendants of generations dating back before the Revolutionary War. Now only Hunter is left at Overhome—lord of the manor—so to speak.

They mean well, but Mom and Dad just don't get it. Never returning to Overhome, never talking about my biological parents. I mean, what's the big mystery? Why the secretiveness? Okay, they made a safe and loving home for me, but they've deliberately kept my entire life completely separate from the reality of my birth.

I don't remember my natural parents, and being adopted has never been a problem. I've always loved Mom and Dad, and they me. But, there's a primal feeling in every adopted child, I think. A need to know where you came from. I sometimes dream I'm drifting at sea in a little rowboat. I realize I am tied, by a long rope, to a larger ship. This quiets my fear, yet I still feel my little dingy wobbling and bobbing, while I clutch the sides, hoping to sight land. Looking back at my Psych 101 class, I think Freud would say the line represents the umbilical cord, the ship my adoptive parents. I'm floating in a sea of unanswered questions about my heredity. Certain things just cannot be ignored. Or forgotten. I am shaking with desire to see, to feel, to know, to connect with my mysterious self. Anything less is a form of blindness. Overhome is the perfect place to dig up my roots, learn about my ancestors, find out all I can about the family history.

For the record, Mom thinks the old family conflict has gone on long enough. Mom's all about trying to promote harmony. She's stayed in touch with my aunt and uncle at Overhome and kept up with the progress of my cousin Jefferson, who's going on eight. Mom says I will be an ambassador of goodwill. I admit that worries me some, but I'll do my best. Hey! Nobody's perfect.

Anyway, I have an ulterior motive. I've always wanted to be a writer. That's one reason I'm keeping this diary. "Journaling," my creative writing prof calls it. "Write about your life, your thoughts, feelings, impressions, as often as possible. Think of it as a lifetime assignment. It's all grist for the mill."

I admit I am a romantic, fascinated with the South, especially the old South. Mammoth, white-columned houses surrounded by ancient shade trees. Laid-back aristocratic sons and daughters of the Confederacy sipping mint juleps on the verandah. Ahhh! Virginia, I am ready for you, and every nerve in my body says you are prepared to offer up some good old Southern hospitality—not to mention the setting for my first novel. I feel my muse calling me home.

So...Overhome, Moore Mountain Lake, Old Virginny—here I come, ready or not! Who knows what's in store for Ashby Overton? I sense invisible strands stretching back over the centuries tugging at me, pulling me into a new-old world. Bloodlines, Dad would call them. Lifelines from my point of view. Mine and Freud's, that is.

Chapter One

The pickup fish-tailed through a dizzy S-curve, then straightened and clattered over the planks of a narrow bridge. One more. *Just one more bend in this roller coaster road and I'll hurl.*

"You okay?" The driver gave me a sideways glance from under his well-worn ball cap with Born to Fish embossed on the brim. He'd told me his name when he picked me up at the bus stop, but his accent threw me off and I wasn't sure whether he'd said it was Duke or Luke. "You're lookin' kinda pale."

"It's been a long trip. I am not a fan of bus rides." I realized I sounded whiney. "It feels like I left civilization days ago."

"Civilization?"

"You know, like…New Jersey? I caught the midnight Greyhound at Penn Station from Newark. I rode all night and all the next day. Today, that is. It's like forever to Virginia. The battery to my iPod actually went dead." When I received no response, I added. "My first trip to Virginia."

"Well, I guess we have our own li'l civilization down here." Doffing his hat to reveal flattened, straw-colored hat hair, he peered straight over the steering wheel without so much as a glance my way. I squirmed at his sarcasm. He appeared not much older than me, probably in his mid-twenties, but he was certainly

4

nothing like my Jersey boys. I was off to a lame start for my summer in the South.

Reaching into my purse, I retrieved my cell phone and flipped it open to shoot a text to a girlfriend at home.

"Forget it," the driver said, still without looking at me. "There's no signal down in these valleys."

"You've got to be kidding! You mean I'll spend the whole summer in a dead zone? No communication whatsoever? How'll I connect with my friends?"

"Oh, you'll prob'ly get a signal at th' house. Overhome's on a cliff, y'know. Above th' lake."

I hoped he was right. My cell was my lifeline. "So, what's it like? I mean, life at Overhome. At Moore Mountain Lake? I'm going to be a *companion* for my cousin Jefferson this summer."

There was a slight hesitation. "Well, you'll like Jeff. He's a good sport—has a lotta energy."

I thought for a moment about how to phrase my next question. "And my uncle and aunt? Hunter and Monica? Do—do you know them well?"

He chuckled. "Sure do. They pay me t' work for 'em. An' I've lived on th' grounds all my life."

"Sorry. I should know that. I think I'm sort of, you know, really stressed out right now. My dad is Madison Overton. He left Overhome after college and never went back."

"I've heard my grandpa talk about Madison," he said with a nod.

"Dad wasn't too happy about me coming here. Thank God for my mom. She's watched this, I dunno, this growing fascination I have with my Southern heritage. You know, the old family estate, the long, involved history, all the Spanish moss hanging from the trees. Together we convinced Dad it was a good idea for me to spend the summer here." I did not add that Dad and I had shared some hot words about my being an adult now and capable of navigating on my own. My rational side knew that living at home while attending community college hadn't helped my case much, but I needed the financial security. Dad still saw me as his little girl.

"Yer outta luck with th' Spanish moss. It grows further south. Sounds t' me like y'been readin' too many romances."

"Uh-huh. That's what my mother thinks." What he didn't know is I'm always composing romance novels. It doesn't take much to set off the writer in my mind.

With the onset of twilight, the sky had turned the color of dull pewter. The tingle of an approaching storm recharged my exhausted senses. The trees and grass shone green and bold in the waning light. Vegetation in my native New Jersey was never this lush and healthy. The Virginia countryside is so rich and colorful. Primitive. I would not be surprised to see a brontosaurus prowling around.

Snapping back to reality, I felt a pinch of—what? Excitement? Anxiety? I was a long way from home. Sure, with my shiny new associate's degree in hand, I considered myself, at long last, self-sufficient. I admit my independence often appeared as full-on stubbornness. My high school guidance counselor once wrote on a college recommendation—Ashby Overton is a high-achieving, goal-oriented student. Dad was less kind. To him I was his bull-headed daughter. So, how could such a strong-willed woman of the twenty-first century already be homesick?

Shutting out the twang of country music blaring from the truck radio, I stared out the dust-streaked window. Heavy clouds folded into the darkening skies, spilling onto the horizon. Mom and Dad. They'd be stepping up the gangplank of a swanky cruise ship this very moment, claiming their sweepstakes prize.

"Looks like we're in fer a real gusher," my driver said, peering into the gathering gloom. "It's not much further. Maybe we c'n beat th' storm." He stomped on the gas so that the tires squealed above the soulful steel guitar on the radio. Squeezing my eyes shut, I grabbed for the arm rest. *Hold on, stomach. We're almost there.*

"Here we are," Duke, or Luke, said at long last. He slowed before turning into a narrow, steep driveway with a ceiling of thick trees. Gray stone gateposts topped with carriage lights marked the entrance. Above them the trees laced their branches together like fingers, so that the effect was that of a tunnel, a living, breathing green tunnel.

I shivered, but not from fear, my thirst for adventure renewed. Silently, I thanked Uncle Hunter and Aunt Monica for inviting me to spend the summer. With my twenty-first birthday looming, I was ready to spread my wings, take a little time to explore my options and to earn some money for tuition to State. What a great way to head into real adulthood, to be on my own for the first time in my life! I felt grateful to my mother, who was determined to heal the rift in the Overton family. Rift? It was more like a chasm.

At last the truck came to a halt. Looming in front of me was the old house itself. Dumbly, I stared. The ghostly whiteness of the clapboards shone against a dark background of clouds and trees. Black shutters framed endless rows of windows, and a massive slate roof rose so steeply that I could not determine where it ended and the gloomy sky began. A half dozen dormers thrust forth from the peaked roof, their window glass as opaque as the night. In graceful symmetry, four magnificent stone chimneys punctuated the sweep of roof before disappearing into the trees. The lines, the bulk and harmony of the place, the mixture of dignity and informality, age and timelessness, left me speechless. My racing mind had already framed the setting of my own gothic novel; I'd found my muse.

"Better get in the house quick." Mr. Born-to-Fish retrieved my bags from the back.

I slid from my seat and stepped down, straightening my rumpled clothes as best I could. Again, my eyes swept upwards, probing the heights of the house for a dividing line with the sky. A gun bolt of thunder rattled my ears and lightning forked the sky. I jumped as a deluge of rain flooded from the heavens.

"Hurry! You'll get soaked. This way." I followed his long strides up the flagstone walkway to a vestibule that housed the front door. Pushing the door inward, he ushered me into the tiny space where a slender, elderly woman stood. "This is Miss Emma Coleville. She'll show you around." He looked at the old woman sheepishly. "Afraid we got a li'l wet," he apologized. "This is—"

"Ashby," I filled in quickly. "Ashby Overton." I extended my hand. "I've heard so much about you, Miss Coleville. May I call you Miss Emma?"

"Everyone does," she said. White hair formed a pale halo around a colorless, aging face, and she wore a light dress covered with a white apron. She looked for all the world like a tall tallow candle.

Dad had told me about Miss Emma Coleville. She had been an employee at Overhome since Dad himself was a child. She'd served as housekeeper and nanny, but also as a companion to my grandmother. "Miss Emma and my mother were very close," Dad had said. "She and Mother grew up together. I think the Colevilles had money once, but I only knew Miss Emma as a servant. She always kept candy in her apron pockets for us boys. She used it to bribe us to behave ourselves."

Miss Emma looked at me with sharp eyes. Did she welcome me, or not? The old girl was certainly giving me the once-over. "You can leave the suitcases here, Luke," Miss Emma said, clearing up the question of my driver's name. Then she turned to me. "Your aunt and uncle are out for the evening. I'll show you to your room."

Out? Were they to return soon? I hadn't expected this. Curious about their appearance and personalities, I'd looked forward to meeting them when I arrived. Swallowing my disappointment, I followed Miss Emma through the door and along an entrance foyer that opened up into a cavernous room with a massive, vaulted ceiling. High, wooden catwalks, reached by identical pairs of stairs, hung like decorations facing each other from opposite walls. A fireplace as tall as a man gaped wide from the far wall. The perfect balance of the oversized room somehow soothed the eye, while warm red-and-gold Persian carpets and small furniture groupings softened the huge space. Rich oil paintings, gilt-framed mirrors, and brass sconces stood out against the walls. One entire wall was devoted to formal portraits of men and women dressed in period finery. One bewhiskered fellow looked both official and forbidding in his gray uniform. The overall effect was one of timeless wealth and luxury, though I could not imagine anyone actually living in such a formal space. While I felt like I was touring a museum, my writer's mind recorded all the details for future use.

"This is the oldest part of the house." Miss Emma ushered me to the left-hand staircase which we ascended slowly to the top landing. "The house was built about 1740. Originally the structure was a barn— the only two-story barn in these parts, I understand. Later it was converted to a manor house. Francis and Emilie Overton lived here then."

I looked over the railing to the room below, and my stomach lurched. Heights and I do not get along. Instantly, I grew dizzy. I clutched the railing and shut my eyes until the vertigo passed. Miss Emma seemed not to notice my discomfort, however, and she warmed up as she talked about the room below. She and Luke shared the same lilting drawl, but her enunciation was perfectly clear, except for the strange way she said "oat" and "aboat," for out and about.

"The living room looks much as it did a hundred years ago. The Overtons consider it their duty to preserve the traditional furnishings." Indicating the portrait wall, she said, "These are all paintings of the Overton family." She would have lingered at the picture wall, I think, but finally sensing my uneasiness, she pressed on. I was afraid to trust myself looking over that balcony for too long.

As we passed through a narrow hallway and down

two steps, it seemed like the ceiling was closing in on us. I had the uncanny feeling I was growing taller—like Alice in Wonderland. We came to the last room at the end of the hall. Choosing a big, old-fashioned iron key from the chain at her waist, Miss Emma inserted it into the keyhole and unlocked the heavy door.

"W-why do you keep it locked?"

She replaced the key on her chain. "It's safer," she said without looking at me. The cast iron hinges creaked as she pushed at the arched, wooden door. Obviously, it had not been opened in a long time. "Here it is, Miss Ashby—your room. Your aunt and uncle thought you would enjoy the privacy. And the view." Curiously, my sense of adventure increasing with every heartbeat, I looked around the square room with its low ceiling and floors polished with age. The walls were stucco, whitewashed and trimmed in dark wood moldings. Pushed against one wall was a four-poster bed. A worn but still beautiful carpet covered the floorboards, its thin, yellowed fringe silky against the dark floor. Opposite the bed stood a heavy chest of drawers made of age-dark wood. Attached was a small oval mirror that tilted. Its glass, though pitted and thin with age, reflected my features without distortion.

The housekeeper moved to the outside wall, where she satisfied herself that a pair of leaded-glass French doors were secure. "There. Everything's in order. I hope you'll be comfortable."

"It's very…old." Funny. It was not what I'd meant to say. Exhausted and keyed-up at the same time, I felt an unsettling, smothering sensation. It had begun in the claustrophobic hall and intensified with every step. Now, within the room, I had an odd sense of enfoldment, like someone had wrapped me in a warm down quilt, comforting, but restricting, too, like I was in the dark cocoon of a scary dream, knowing I would wake up safely in my own bed.

Soothed by the steady thrum of rain on the slate roof, I walked to the double doors and looked through the glass. A railing outlined a balcony, but beyond that everything was black, until a branch of lightning lit up the grounds below, and my eyes swept over the back yard. To the right, near a thick line of trees were what looked like stables, a riding ring, and a small house, a guest house, maybe. In the distance, to the left, all was flat-black. The lake.

Sensing the housekeeper stirring behind me, I turned and watched her click on the bedside lamp.

"I'll bring a supper tray up directly. It's too bad your aunt and uncle are out for the evening. You can meet them tomorrow."

I didn't try to hide my surprise. "Tomorrow? You mean, I won't see them at all. Tonight, I mean? They knew I was coming. It's been planned for weeks."

Miss Emma's face softened then. "Please, don't take it personally. They're at a charity ball. It was planned long before they knew about your trip here. They're spending the night at a hotel in Roanoke." When she saw my disappointment, she added, "Your aunt and uncle have many social obligations."

"Oh. But my cousin—could I meet my cousin?"

"I'm afraid he's sound asleep. Jefferson is an early riser. He tried to stay awake to greet you, but it was an unsuccessful struggle. It's late for him, and he's such a sound sleeper, I doubt even this storm could rouse him." She walked to the door, opened it, and looked out into the hall. "Ah, Luke has delivered your bags, I see." Bending, she moved my suitcases into the room, hefting them with surprising agility. "Now, I'll leave you to unpack while I get you some food." For a moment she paused like she had more to say, but she wrenched the creaking latch and let herself out.

The atmosphere felt heavy—that blanketing, smothering sensation again. Stripping off my damp clothes and buttoning on a bathrobe from my suitcase, I puttered around the room, touching the furniture and getting a feel for my new space. I wanted to keep moving, to stir the stagnant air with activity in this room which seemed to have stood empty for a long time.

A light rapping at my door made me jump. Miss Emma stepped into the room carrying a tray with sandwiches and chips and a pile of obviously home-made chocolate chip cookies, along with a tall glass of iced tea. "You'll want a candle." Placing the tray on the dresser, she pulled a slim, new taper from her apron pocket. She removed the cellophane wrapper before slipping the candle into a blue china candle holder resting on the dresser. Then she reached into the same pocket and brought out a box of matches, which she laid alongside the candle.

"A candle? Why a candle?"

She hesitated slightly. "The lights. They go out frequently around here."

"You mean, because of the thunderstorm?" I became aware again of the rain drumming on the roof.

"Storms." Miss Emma searched for words. "And other times, too." She looked at the candle. "Especially in the old part of the house. Especially in this room."

She looked away like she wanted to avoid further questions.

"Miss Coleville—Miss Emma—whose room is—was this?"

Again, that hesitation. "Why, this was Rosabelle's room." Her voice was so low I could barely hear.

"Rosabelle?" My eyes widened in the oval mirror. "Who was Rosabelle?" If she was an Overton ancestor, Dad had never mentioned her. I would have remembered such an unusual name.

But Miss Emma had already retreated, leaving me standing before the mirror wondering as the old door latched shut. Oh well, I'd question her later, when I wasn't so tired. She seemed to be an expert on anything having to do with the history of Overhome.

Without thinking, I removed a match from the box, struck it, and held it to the wick. How many candles had stood in that very same blue candlestick on the old dresser over the years? What other Overton ancestors had occupied this room, and why had the housekeeper called it Rosabelle's room? Had Rosabelle been the first occupant? The last? I felt totally drained. Reaching for the tray, I carried it to the night stand and climbed into the bed. Plumping the pillows against the high wooden headboard, I leaned back to enjoy my late dinner in this fascinating, totally foreign place.

Hungry as I was, I took my time savoring the food while settling into the mood of my retro surroundings. When I had finished the last crumb and inhaled the last drop of sweet tea, I placed the tray on the nightstand, then leaned back to close my eyes and open them again, checking to make sure this wasn't all a dream. I had, after all, spent a good many years of my life dreaming myself into the past lives of literary heroines and movie idols. All I had to do was tour a historic home or watch a period costume show and I would find myself right there—mingling with the locals—no matter how along ago. Well, this was no drama. This was real. A whole summer to absorb two hundred years of Overton ancestry—their lives and loves and secrets. Especially their secrets.

Rosabelle. Rosabelle. Rosabelle's room. The syllables rolled off the tongue like poetry. My thoughts returned again and again to the melodious name; a feeling of contentment wrapped around me, and I felt myself drifting off to sleep, lulled by the rhythm of the rain. Without warning, there was a sharp slap of thunder, then the lights snapped, leaving the room dark except for the flickering flame from the candle. My heart thumped wildly as I sat up in bed, but I lay back, calming myself. "It's a good thing the lightning woke me. I could've burned the house down falling asleep with a candle burning," I told myself. For a while I watched the flame dance and jump and make wavy shadows on the dimpled walls, until I could feel my eyes drooping once more.

A pistol crack of thunder lifted me again, and I realized the taper had gone out, snuffed by a puff of damp air, probably. Well, it saved me from getting out of bed. The room was silent and black as a cave. Gradually, my beating heart slowed to lullaby rhythm. Before I slipped into sleep, I was conscious of yet another strange sensation. I smelled the light sweetness of roses. I dreamed I was in a garden.

Chapter Two

I awoke to the loud chatter of birds on the balcony. Propping myself up against the headboard, I struggled to remember where I was. Morning light streamed through the leaded glass doors, casting trapezoids of sunlight onto the wine-colored comforter of my bed. The bedside lamp was on. I had gone to sleep in the dark room in the midst of a storm, forgetting to turn off the lamp when the lights failed. I remembered, too, the warm, protective feeling of last night, but in the shining dawn the mood was different, almost playful. It made me feel like a kid ready for recess, energized, expectant, prepared to take on the world. And, believe me, I am so not a morning person. Can a room have a personality? I could still smell roses in the air as I threw off the covers.

I peered into the old mirror. Tousled by sleep, my hair was a mess of honey-blonde with gold highlights. Mom and Dad had told me my biological mother had been a beautiful blonde. Too bad her light hair is our only genetic link. The rest of me is pretty much Overton. My blue eyes are lighter than what Dad calls the "Overton navy-blues," which are so dark as to appear black at first glance. High cheek bones, a straight nose, a decisive chin with a tiny cleft looked back at me from the old mirror. I smiled a bit wanly. "Toothy smile and pale skin," I told the mirror, shifting to catch my profile. "But I suppose I could have come out worse." I turned from the dresser, looking for a hairbrush.

Unlocking the French doors, I looked out upon a clear, jewel-bright day. The birds perched along the wooden balcony like they were performing on a balance beam. A rising sun cast ripples of chrome onto the blue-black water of the lake. Last night's storm had washed the air clean and the endless green acres behind the house glittered with dew. Near the stables was the riding ring. Horses. Fascinating creatures. My thoughts flashed back to five years ago at summer camp—riding lessons—where I'd learned to respect horses but also to fear them. They're big and unpredictable and they have heavy feet, believe me.

Dad was a great fan of horses. "Overhome is horse country, Ashby. A person's worth is judged by her equestrian skills. When it came to horses, my mother—your grandmother—was top of her class." I'd heard that many times. And yet, my Grandmother Lenore died in a riding accident. Dressing in cargo Capris and my new sandals, I mulled over my as-yet-unmet relatives, Uncle Hunter, Aunt Monica, and my cousin, Jefferson. What if I don't like them? What if they don't like me? "Oh stop being so self-centered," I reprimanded myself. Quietly, so as not to awaken anyone, I slipped from the house into the yard. Part of me longed to head down the steep steps to the dock and the lake, but I found myself, instead, following the cobbled path to the stables. I was surprised to see someone stalking down the path in my direction.

It was an old, old man, in his eighties, I figured. Large-framed, with stooped shoulders and pure white feathers of hair ruffling from under a battered baseball cap. His face was as creased as a cauliflower, with years and years of weathering. Wearing denim overalls and strong, muddy boots, he pumped steadily toward me. Though he must have seen me, he made no effort to get out of my way on the narrow path. All I could think was, so, maybe I'm in his way, but what the heck? What the heck is this all about?

The old guy came to an abrupt halt directly in front of me, squaring off to block me from passing him. Lifting his head, he rasped into my face, "Didn't y'see th' signs? NO TRESPASSIN.' This here's private prop'ty. Now, git!"

"B-but…I'm Ashby."

"Don't care who y'are." He flailed his arms. "Go on. Git!"

"Abe, wait. She's th' niece. She got in late last night." Luke, my truck-driving chauffeur, ran toward us shouting. Catching his breath, he laid a hand on the old man's shoulder. "It's okay. This is Jeff's cousin…" When Abe's face remained blank, Luke persisted. "Y'know, Lenore's granddaughter. She's here for th' summer."

The wrinkles creased into a scowl. "Lenore's granddaughter? Hmmm. Well, I don't see no resemblance."

"It's all good. Go on back to th' stables. I'll take care of this." Luke's voice was patient—like he was talking to a child. He turned away from me to watch his hobbling departure.

I was pissed, and not just because of Abe's reaction. I admit I was stinging from the old guy's assault, his rejection, unexpected as it was. I was actually shaking. I mean, I have every right to be here, to walk the paths and breathe the air. I don't need an old bully pushing me around from day one. But it was Luke's words, "I'll take care of this," that really set me off. Like, I'm some kind of problem to be solved! I took a couple of deep yoga breaths while counting to ten. I'd heard Dad talk about Abe, who worked with the horses and, like Emma Coleville, had been here since time immemorial. I took the moment to look at Luke. In sunlight he had a pleasant enough face, very tan. His lively nutmeg eyes were brown and spicy, but his straw pile of hair was as messy as ever.

"Sorry 'bout my grandfather," he said, once he was satisfied the old bulldog was gone. "I hope y'don't take it person'ly. He's always on th' lookout for trespassers. We've had some vandalism."

The soft drawl I had noticed yesterday, the curious slurring of syllables, somehow didn't go with the muscular frame. He grinned then, and I realized he was good-looking, in a rugged sort of way, with a firm jaw, even, white teeth and eyes that danced when he laughed. "The Murley family's worked here for three generations—my grandpa, my parents, and me. Abe an' I live in th' house behind th' stables. He's caretaker here at Overhome, an' I'm in charge of th' horses."

"You mean…you're the stable boy? I didn't realize there are still places where stable boys work. I thought they only existed in old romance novels."

Luke's look told me to get real. "Like I said yesterday, we have our own li'l civilization here in th' South." He gave an ironic laugh. Lifting a brogan, he inspected the sole. "Well, us stable boys muck aroun' in a lotta…sh—manure." Dropping his foot to the ground, he gave me a hang-dog look. "Shucks, ma'am. If I'd a known we was gonna meet agin', I'd a dressed up."

His boots were actually quite clean, as were his jeans and T-shirt. I bit off a retort. "There aren't many stables where I come from." I shrugged. "I guess I have a lot to learn."

A half-smile lit his face. Luke Murley apparently had a better handle on our meeting than I did. "Tell me again. You're from…"

"New Jersey. Newark, New Jersey."

"Oh. Right. That'd be up North."

"So, call me a Yankee," I replied.

"Well, y'know what we say about Yankees here in th' South?" Without waiting for my answer, he continued, "We say there's Yankees an' then there's damn Yankees."

"Okay. I'll bite. What's the difference?"

"The damn Yankees are th' ones who stay." A grin lit up his eyes.

Luke Murley sure could pull off the hick act. I mean, I knew I deserved the put-down. "Touché," I said. But I couldn't resist adding, "And I only know two things about the Civil War."

He raised an eyebrow as he waited for the punch line.

"It's over, and we won."

He smiled. He got it. It was time to move on. "So, you're an equestrian," I said lamely.

"Hoo-boy! I like th' sound of that! E-quest-ri- an!" He accented the first syllable. "It sounds a lot classier than stable boy."

I wanted to tell Luke Murley he could knock the chip off his shoulder. He looked like he wanted to say the same thing to me, then, abruptly, he changed the subject.

"So, you on a school break or somethin'?

"I just graduated from community college. I plan to take a gap year and then go for my bachelor's after that. Study to be a writer."

"College." Luke gazed off into the distance for a moment. "I'd like t' think someday I could get away from here—go t' college myself." He paused a second before adding, "But Abe needs me t' help full time. This place's too big. It's too much for 'im. There's other workers, of course, but I guess it's hard t'get good help these days, 'cuz fer sure me 'n Abe do most of th' work." Again Luke shifted gears. "Have y'met Jeff yet?"

"I haven't met anybody yet. I mean, except you, of course, and—and—"

"Abe. Call him Abe."

"Okay. Abe. And Miss Emma, as you know."

Luke nodded and chewed on his lip for a while. All the humor had gone out of his eyes. "Well. I think you're in for a very, um…a very interestin' summer," he said. "I've gotta get busy. See y'later." With a wave of his hand, he turned and trotted back to the stables.

As I meandered around the grounds, my mind rolled over my encounter with Abe Murley and his grandson. Were these guys for real? Or am I the weird one here? I had never met anyone like either of them before. This place was offering up one surprise after another.

The house, I decided, was even more imposing in the daylight. The sun mellowed the antiquity of stone foundations and chimneys and vaulted roofs. I had the feeling that Overhome had always looked old. Situated on a knoll, the house stood guard over rolling hills and emerald pastures fringed by dense forest. A creek cut through high banks along the border of trees, occasionally jutting out into the cleared areas. Near the bottom of a gentle slope behind the stables was an arched wooden bridge. It was a scene worthy of any writer's imagination.

On impulse, since it was still early, I decided to take a look at the lake. I made my way down the steps to a large dock where a big, slick boat sparkled in the sun. Cream-colored and wrapped in a ribbon of teal-painted stripes, it hung suspended on the lift like a ginormous birthday gift. Cool. How fun would it be to tool around the lake in that sweetheart? The covered dock was bright with ceramic pots of red geraniums. Blue and white-striped cushions on the lounge chairs completed the jaunty, nautical look. The sun brushed the shimmering waters with strokes of orange and pink. A band of green foothills ascended to two mountain peaks, one higher than the other, then tapered off again, circling the lake like a wreath. Though a gentle morning breeze cooled my face, nothing stirred the mirror surface of the lake.

A slight movement on the low floating dock stopped me in my tracks. A huge bird—it was almost a yard tall—stood like a sentinel on the wooden planks. Gray-blue in color, with a snipe neck and a prominent beak, it balanced on one foot like it was practicing yoga. Then, slowly and deliberately, it latch-stepped its way across the length of the dock and back. Mesmerized, I held my breath and watched. How could anything so large and ungainly-looking move so fluidly? I must have stood there, without moving a muscle, for ten minutes or more, afraid I'd startle the creature into flight. Finally, it lifted into the air like a graceful kite.

The distant purring of a boat motor rose. The bird had flown off when it sensed the intruder—a ski boat gliding into view from around the point. Behind the boat, a slalom skier swayed from side to side, carving sets of smooth parentheses onto the jeweled waters of the cove. I looked longingly again at the boat up on the lift. Surely water skiing was another adventure to look forward to this summer. With the skier's wake sloshing against the floating dock, I turned to retrace my steps to the house.

The balcony leading off my room perched a good thirty feet above the ground, I judged, what with the slope of the back yard. Well, I'd just have to get over my acrophobia when using it. There were no steps, and I liked the feeling that my little balcony was all my own, that it could only be entered from my room. Very private, indeed. Letting myself in the door, it occurred to me that in all my explorations something was missing. There was no sign of a garden. There were no roses anywhere.

Chapter Three

Miss Emma served brunch in the formal dining room. It was weird. I mean, only three people eating at a long banquet table heavy with silver and china and antlers of candelabra. I swear it could easily seat twenty-five.

"More tea, dear?" Aunt Monica asked in a breathy voice. "Your uncle left for Bradford earlier. Bradford is our county seat. He will be back late tonight. Some pressing business with the lawyer. It was simply not to be avoided." She reached for an ornate, gleaming teapot, which rested on a large silver tray with matching cream and sugar containers. Raising an eyebrow, she asked again, "Tea?"

I tried not to stare at Aunt Monica's arresting face. The long, slim neck, very white skin, and jet black hair curled up in an elaborate style made her look like a painting of a Greek goddess I'd seen in one of the New York galleries. Just as goddesses are ageless, so was Aunt Monica, though she was probably in her mid-thirties. Then, there was the way she used her hands, the gestures designed to show off her long, lacquered fingernails and jeweled rings. But it was her articulation that really got me. Had she been taking lessons to eradicate a Southern accent? She enunciated every syllable slowly and deliberately, the way somebody might speak to a non-native. I was reminded of Eliza

Doolittle in *My Fair Lady*, trying to get rid of her cockney accent by saying, "The rain in Spain stays mainly in the plain," over and over.

My seven-year-old cousin Jefferson sat beside his mother. His little elf face was framed with copper-colored hair, streaked with sunny highlights. Freckles made a tiny footpath over his nose. Overton blue eyes, several shades darker than mine, hinted at a spirited and curious mind. Looking to be bubbling over with things to say, he was, instead, quiet as a turtle. Was this an exhibition of upper-class manners or something? Children should be seen and not heard? Jefferson fidgeted and kicked at the rungs of the chair, and once he opened his mouth to say something, but promptly closed it again, holding his lips in a barely-controlled line.

"Well, Jefferson," Monica turned to him at last. "What plans do you have for your cousin on this glorious Saturday?"

He exhaled loudly and his eyes flickered with excitement. "We can swim in the lake and explore the woods and ride the horses…"

His mother sighed softly. "Now, now, Jefferson. You must stay off the horses. You know how your father feels about that." She turned her languid gaze onto me. "While we want Jefferson to enjoy all the wonders of his world, we do have rules—life vests before jumping in the lake; don't go into the woods alone, and stay off the horses without an experienced rider along."

Jefferson made a face his mother could not see. "Aww. Jeez. We just wanna have fun." He squirmed in his seat as his mother turned the conversation back to her own doings, something about a late luncheon at the club and how she hoped my uncle would be home in time to attend.

"By the way, Ashby. How are your parents? Are Helen and Madison enjoying their trip? Have you heard from them yet?"

"They only left yesterday, Aunt Monica," I said, suppressing a nervous giggle.

"Yes, of course. You know, I only met them briefly, at our wedding in Charlottesville years ago. Still, your dear mother has been a wonderful correspondent. I can always count on hearing about you in her letters." Delicately she patted her lips with her linen napkin. "Well, you two run along now. Get to know one another. I am so glad you are to be with us this summer, my dear. I'm quite sure we have a lot to learn from you." Gracefully she pushed her chair back and rose from her seat.

What could my aunt possibly hope to learn from me? I found the woman totally baffling. As the tapping of her heels faded, my cousin's smile broadened until the freckles jumped off his face. "Let's go see the horses!" Slipping from the high-backed chair, he grabbed my hand.

I felt a thrill as the small, warm hand pressed into mine so trustingly. I'd always wanted a younger brother or sister, and even though I was puzzled by his behavior at the table, I already liked him.

I tried to follow along as he zigzagged from one point of interest to another. He stopped to watch a butterfly on a bush and knelt down to divert an army of ants from attacking a dead grasshopper. Cocking his head, he observed, "I love Saturday!"

"Saturday? You have the whole summer to play, Jefferson. What's so special about Saturday?"

"Call me Jeff, please. And I do *not*. I mean, I don't have the whole summer to play. My mother's got me planned…" He paused and searched for a word. "She's got every minute *programmed*. It's worse than school."

"Programmed?"

"Monday, Wednesday, and Friday it's day camp." He ticked off the days on his fingers. "Tuesday is French lessons. Thursday's piano." He made a face. "I *hate* piano. I'm the only boy in the class."

I tried to hide my surprise. Then what did they want me here for? It's hard to be a companion for a kid who's completely "programmed."

Jeff continued on his way, chattering as naturally as he breathed. "But they only last till lunch time, all of my programs. Me and you can play afterwards." He grinned widely. "I finally talked ole' Emma out of afternoon naps."

I laughed in spite of myself. "I'll bet your mother wouldn't like to hear you talk like that, Jeff."

He made another face. "Yeah. She's tryin' to make a gentleman out of me. It stinks. You should see the kids at camp." He rolled his eyes. "The way they act…my mother would freak out."

Jeff didn't talk; he emoted. After watching the way his mother operated with him, I figure he had to let it all out while he could. The idea endeared him to me on the spot. "So, who all goes to this camp of yours?"

"My friends." He blew on a dandelion that had gone to seed and chased the flying debris with his hand. "Lake people." He gestured in a wide circle.

"Lake people?"

"That's what they call us. We're the lake people. Then, there's the locals."

This got me thinking. Did somebody tell Jeff his world was divided up like this? Did he figure it out by himself? Maybe the camp counselors were "locals" and they let the kids know, either subtly or outright, that "lake people" are different.

It hit me then that my cousin and his friends were separated by acres of land and water. It was nothing like where I grew up, with the crowded row houses and bungalows crawling with kids. No wonder his parents sent him to day camp and lessons galore; otherwise, the kid would spend the summer in total isolation from his peers. On the other hand, maybe they were trying to get rid of him. You know, have somebody take him off their hands so they could be free to do whatever it is lake people do. My aunt seemed the type to have a lot of things going for herself.

"All the campers go to my school," Jeff continued his stream of thought. "Lake Country Day School. Luke says they're spoiled brats. He went to public school and he says he learned good enough for anybody." Jeff shrugged. "Luke's teaching some of 'em to ride. He's a great riding teacher."

And Luke's a local, I thought, but I kept it to myself. "So, what do you play at camp?"

Jeff bent over and picked up a handful of stones, which he began throwing at fence posts. "Well, we take swimming lessons, archery, croquet, badminton. Stuff like that. We have a nature center where we learn about plants and birds and stuff. It's okay, I guess." He aimed a stone and hit the wooden post dead center. "There's way too many girls," he finished, as though that explained his lack of enthusiasm. "I'd rather ride my horse. And fish. Hey, Ashby, do you like horses?"

We had reached the stables. I looked for Luke Murley, but there was no sign of him. "You want to know the truth, Jeff?"

He looked at me from under his lashes, then nodded.

"Well, I took lessons a long time ago, but I never was very good. Actually, I did quite a lot of riding one summer at Girl Scout camp, but I had a bad fall—broke my arm. It left me—well, I guess it left me afraid of horses."

Jeff snorted. "Oh no. Are you gonna be like my dad?"

"Your dad is afraid of horses?"

This got a good laugh. "Not for himself, silly. For me. He's afraid I'll get hurt."

Because my uncle's mother died in a riding accident, I thought. I mean, it made sense, but it didn't seem possible to keep a free spirit like my cousin from doing what he wanted most. I hadn't met Uncle Hunter yet, but I was already getting vibes about my role at Overhome. Did my uncle expect me to be the heavy with Jeff because Aunt Monica is a fluff-brain?

Luke rounded the corner of the stables. "Hey, Luke!" Jeff gave a delighted squeal and jumped up to give him a high five. "Can we go for a ride?"

"Sorry. Gotta take care of somethin' right now." Luke looked genuinely disappointed. When he saw Jeff's young features fall, he reached out a hand to pat his shoulder. "Tell y'what, Jeff. Wanna go with me to check th' bridge? Abe found a broken board right in th' middle of th' bridge. Could be dangerous."

"Cool! Do you think it's the Night Riders?" Jeff's cheeks flushed.

"Maybe. Maybe not." Luke looked at me. "Night Riders. It's a gang of local guys. Bad boys with too much time on their hands. They get wasted an' roam around th' countryside at night playin' pranks."

"Oh man! Do they make Abe mad," Jeff put in. "Hey, Ashby. Come with us."

Over Jeff's head my eyes locked with Luke's. He gave a quick nod, telling me he would watch out for Jeff if I wanted to beg off.

"How about I join you after I change my shoes," I said to Jeff. My new leather sandals were already showing signs of abuse from the day's walking. Tromping around shopping malls at home could not compare to the stones and gravel and farmland I'd hoofed it over today. "I'll meet you in a bit."

Jeff waved, trotting off in the direction of the rustic bridge I'd seen earlier.

I ambled back to the house. My thoughts returned again to the idea that my uncle had invited me here for a purpose. Well, it was okay by me. It might surprise Uncle Hunter to know I had a purpose of my own. This summer was a perfect chance for me to find out more about my birth parents, and about Dad and the rest of my Overton ancestors, too. Not to mention the age-old mysteries lurking in the shadows of an authentic Southern estate. Why had Dad left me in the dark about his own past here?

All I knew was he had left Virginia over a disagreement with his father, something to do with Dad's refusal to return to Overhome after college, which somehow led to his being disinherited. His father had left the entire estate to the youngest son, Hunter. Suppose Dad had inherited Overhome? Would I have grown up here? What would it be like to grow up wealthy in rural Virginia? To be a lake person?

In my room again, I rummaged through my suitcase for my well-worn Nike sneaks, when I spied a new bottle of sunscreen Mom had thrown in. "Don't get too much sun on that fair skin of yours." I heard her voice clear as day. I fished out my baseball cap and jammed it on my head. "I'm safe now, Mom," I muttered, smoothing the SPF 30 on my cheeks and arms. My laptop rested beside my suitcase. I was in the habit of using my computer to keep a diary, my own log of memories to draw from for my writing.

These few hours I'd spent at Overhome were already full of promise. I reached for my laptop. It did not take long to realize that wireless would be a dream only for the distant future at Overhome. Finding an outlet beside the bed, I plugged in the computer, only to discover that the Net had not yet found its way to Overhome either. So much for Facebook for the summer. Icing the cake, my cell phone, for some reason, was a complete no-go in my room, though I had yet to test it elsewhere on the estate. Talk about a dead zone. No hope of any nearby cyber cafes, either. I was totally bummed.

At least my nifty remote control travel radio should work. I hit the scan button, searching for a decent station—a little rap, some alternative. "A.B.C. Anything but country," I mumbled, as I scrolled past bluegrass, gospel, and some station that called itself, "the best country in the country." Finally, settling for light rock, I propped myself against the ancient headboard and took to the keyboard.

Where to start? My experiences here could lay a solid foundation for a great historical romance. Already, I was writing settings and forming scenes in my writer's mind. A mystery, perhaps. A romantic masterpiece. An American version of a Victoria Holt novel or a Mary Stewart trilogy, two writers whose styles I fell for in middle school and tried, without much success, to imitate. How I admired their vast vocabularies and sweeping sentences and remote, exotic settings. I had read every novel Mary Stewart ever wrote. *The Crystal Cave* blew me away. Of course, *Jane Eyre* by Charlotte Bronte was like my Bible. I'd brought it with me for my annual re-read. The same for her sister Emily's *Wuthering Heights*. I am a sucker for gothics.

****

Dear Diary,

Believe it or not, there's a hottie down in the Boondocks! His name is Luke, and he looks to be in his early twenties. Tall, dark, and handsome, he's not, but pretty hunky, nonetheless. We didn't exactly get off to a great start. In fact, he shows no interest in me at all. Luke talks and acts like a redneck, but I detect some deep currents beneath that macho surface. Could be interesting, eh?

Technology is in the Dark Ages here. What irony! I mean, I wrote "Ashby is going dark," on the Wall of my Facebook before I left NJ. Little did I know HOW dark! It looks like I'll have to depend on local color for fun. Stay tuned. I think it's gonna be a long, long summer.

Oh, apologies to Victoria Holt and Mary Stewart and my dear Bronte sisters for the hormone-induced entry. Remember, I am gathering raw material here. There's plenty of time to write my masterpiece! Muse, stay with me!

I closed my laptop with a snap and a silent promise to write more soon and went to search for Jeff. With any luck, he and Luke would still be tracking down the bad guys and I could join the both of them. I definitely wanted more face time with the stable boy.

Chapter Four

The music woke me; it was a song I'd heard long ago. *Da-Dum Dum, Da-Da Dum Dum*. I couldn't tell where it came from. Low, melodious strains drifted around my head, like somebody above me sprinkling notes on the air. I looked up, but saw only stucco walls and wood moldings. A piano? No, it didn't sound like piano. It didn't sound like any instrument. It was more of a voice. A hollow, haunting voice without any words. Eerie as it was, the music didn't frighten me. The melody was so pleasant, and that warm, protective feeling I'd experienced my first night in this room wrapped around me like a muffler. While I dressed, the song wafted its melody, but not until I stood before the oval mirror brushing my hair did the words come to me.

"*Flow gently sweet Afton, amang thy green braes.*" That was all I could remember of the lyrics. Dad used to sing the song as a bedtime lullaby when I was very young. "*Flow gently, sweet Afton.*" Softly I sang the words, lilting over the Scottish accents as Dad used to do. The old tune made me smile at myself in the mirror. I hadn't thought of it for years. What had brought it back to me?

"It's this room!" I startled myself by saying aloud.

I began to think up all sorts of romantic plots. Somebody named Rosabelle had lived here and she'd sung the song to her children as she rocked them in an old oak chair. Or maybe a woebegone young suitor standing below on the lawn had serenaded a teen-aged Rosabelle standing at the French doors. Or, perhaps someone named Rosabelle had died in this room and her loved ones had sung the song at her wake. The last was too morbid, even for my writer's imagination, and I shivered. I was in a hurry to get out of the room.

Memories never die in a place like Overhome. They just swirl around in the molecules until somebody breathes them in and they live again. The thought pushed into my mind as involuntarily as the music.

Still thinking about the music that drifted down from the sky like snowflakes, I headed for the dining room for breakfast, my mind moving over yesterday's events. Jeff and I had spent the afternoon swimming and paddle-boating in the lake, and then, since Uncle Hunter had not appeared, my aunt had gone to their club alone. Miss Emma had thoughtfully let Jeff and me barbecue and scarf down our dinner on the flagstone porch instead of subjecting us to that mausoleum of a dining room again. Then we'd played Chinese checkers until we both nodded off over the board. I never did get to the stables to see the horses, but Jeff seemed to be having such a good time, he didn't notice.

"Well, well," a modulated voice broke into my thoughts as I entered the dining room. A tall, slim man stood up from his chair, smiling. He looked nautical in a crisp blue polo shirt and khaki chinos.

"Ashby, so nice to meet you, at last." He reached out his arms and drew me to him in a hug. "I'm your Uncle Hunter. Welcome to Overhome. I'm sorry it's taken me so long to welcome you. First a charity ball, then a boring meeting with my attorney. Boring but necessary. These days man cannot live by horses alone."

My uncle looked so much like Dad that I felt I already knew him. I'd seen some old photos, but they hadn't shown such an amazing similarity. Dad's youngest brother could have been his twin. They both had the same lofty forehead and cheekbones riding high and prominent in the narrow face. Even their dark hair was similar, curling a bit at the temples and the neck. Despite the seven years difference in their ages, they were startlingly alike. Except for the eyes. Uncle Hunter's eyes were dark blue and deep-set. Overton eyes, yes, but Dad's eyes crinkled and danced with subtle humor. My uncle's glittered, hard as diamonds.

"Hi," I said when I got my voice under control. I tried not to stare. "You and Dad look so much alike."

My uncle smiled. "People have always said so. How nice it is to have you with us, Ashby." He reached for the teapot and poured a cup for me and then for himself.

"Ashby. What a lovely name. Lovely and unusual. You were named for Marian's grandfather, Ashby Noble. I was not sure Ashby was an appropriate name for the little blonde cherub you were, but I must say it fits you perfectly." He smiled again. That is, his lips smiled, but his eyes did not. "I'm glad Helen was able to talk my stubborn brother into putting his seal of approval on your visit with us for the summer. Just because Madison decided to leave Overhome forever, he shouldn't pass that sentence on to you."

"Did you know my birth mother, Uncle Hunter?" I could have kicked myself. It was an awkward way to begin a conversation with an uncle I'd only just met.

But he was the one who'd brought up my being named for my maternal grandfather. He didn't bat an eye.

"Marian. Yes, Marian. Well, to tell you the truth, she and my brother Washington never wanted to bother with a kid brother tagging along. They were high school sweethearts, you know. She was very pretty and Wash was crazy about her. I used to spy on them making out in the parlor. They moved away from Overthome shortly after they were married. We didn't see much of them. And then—" He stopped, clamping his lips into a line.

He was silent for a long moment. He couldn't say the words—"Then they came back to visit one night and were killed in a car accident." We both knew how the sentence should be finished, but my uncle's lips seemed frozen shut.

"Tell me about yourself, Ashby," he shifted abruptly. "Are you involved in any sports? What are you studying at college?"

"I want to major in writing. Now that I've finished all my gen ed courses at CC, I plan to go on for a B.A. Maybe a Master of Fine Arts degree." I rattled this off like one of the old electric typewriters in the business lab at school. "Oh, and in high school I was on the track team, and I did gymnastics. Plus, I was editor of the literary magazine." I was sure he was just being polite. I mean, why would he be interested in the everyday life of a typical suburban girl from New Jersey?

Rapid footsteps approached, and then Jeff poked his head inside the door.

"Jefferson! Come in. So, you've met your cousin Ashby, have you? And what do you think? A good pal for the summer?"

I cringed. Nothing like putting the kid on the spot, but Jeff was swaddled in his own thoughts. Taking a deep breath, he exclaimed, "I'm old enough to ride by myself, Dad. And good enough, too. Luke's teaching me."

"Whoa. What's this, son?" His tone had changed. "I'll be the judge of when you may ride solo. Horseback riding is the best sport in the world, but it does have its dangers."

Jeff turned his look onto the floor.

"All in good time, son. When you're ready, you'll ride to your heart's content. When and where you like. But for now, unless Luke," he faced me, "or Ashby, is willing to oversee, you will *not* ride the horses without my permission."

"Aww, Dad." Jeff looked miserable. "Luke's too busy." He looked at me. "And she says she don't like horses."

"She *doesn't* like horses," he corrected. "My decision stands. You'll get your chance, Jefferson, I promise." He sounded jovial again. "Who knows more about horses than anyone else? Who's the best rider in the state of Virginia?"

Jeff looked resigned. "You, Dad. But…"

"No more now. You're my only son, and I won't have you endangering yourself. Now, come along to breakfast and tell me everything that happened while I was gone."

Talking, Jeff took his seat. "There's a board broke, I mean broken. In the bridge. Luke thinks it might have been…" He searched for the word.

"Deliberate?" Uncle Hunter supplied.

"The Night Riders again," Jeff said.

My uncle nodded. "There. You see what I mean about danger. What might happen if you were to ride a horse over that bridge, Jefferson? It could throw you, maim the horse." He shook his head.

Just then Aunt Monica floated into the room. "Hello, darling," she said to her husband, her voice breathy as always. "Remember the bridge party at Six Gates this evening. I believe the Taylors are planning to be there."

Jeff's face went flat as the family soap opera played out before me.

"Yes, of course, Monica. But first, I'd like to show Ashby our lake." He winked at Jeff. "And Jefferson and I must have our canter, of course."

Jeff's expression changed yet again, and he looked at me with a barely perceptible twitch at the corner of his lips, then lowered his lashes, all in an instant. The competition for Uncle Hunter's attention between my aunt and cousin was alive and well. And Jeff was just as adept at the game as his mother. What I couldn't figure out was where I fit in with all of this. But, for the first time, I knew what I wanted from my cousin Jeff. I wanted him to like me—to like me the same way he seemed to like Luke Murley.

****

"Isn't she a beauty? A bow-rider with an inboard and plenty of horsepower." My uncle lounged behind the steering wheel, one arm propped on the gleaming teal-and-cream freeboard as he idled the boat out of the cove. Jeff and I settled back against the seats, as soft and plush as whipped cream.

The cove buzzed with watercraft of all kinds, colors, and sizes. The sunny wind brushed my cheeks and blew my hair back from my neck. "Wow! Lots of little water bugs," I said, noting the darting, jumping, circling one and two-person jets buzzing in every direction.

"Look dead ahead, there, Ashby. That's Moore Mountain. People say the mountain looks different every day," Uncle Hunter said. "The shadows, the sun, who knows what makes it change from green to blue to purple. Any way you see it, it's beautiful."

I let my gaze follow the height and width of the heavily forested rock fingers that creased the mountain face like a gigantic green fist. I'd been impressed by Moore Mountain when I saw it from the dock on my first early-morning pilgrimage. By water, it was even more imposing, a study in natural contrast. The soft and gently rounded top gradually descended to a stark, rocky base, which plunged, sharp as a knife, into the water. I found my eyes traveling from top to bottom and back again.

Uncle Hunter rolled the craft smoothly into the main channel. "Let's take a spin up to the bridge. We'll dock at Port Plaza."

I was all eyes trying to take in the vast beauty of Moore Mountain Lake. Peering deep into a secluded cove on a slice of sandy beach, I spied a tall, blue-gray bird. "Oh, look! That bird! I saw one just like it on the dock."

"Magnificent creature, eh?" My uncle turned to Jeff. "Do you know what it is, son?"

"A great blue heron," Jeff answered without hesitation. "We learned that at the nature center at day camp."

"Bird-watching?" his father asked.

"I'd rather be fish-watching," Jeff said, so seriously that both my uncle and I had to laugh.

We passed a fascinating house situated all by itself on an island and then the state park, its wide expanse of beach polka-dotted with sun-bathers and swimmers. Skimming along at a fast clip, my uncle slowed for the NO WAKE markers as we approached the bridge. After docking and securing the boat with lines and protective buoys, we climbed out and ambled along the wooden walkway. I felt like a tourist.

"Let's feed the carp!" Jeff cried.

The shallow waters lapping against the dock boiled and bubbled with hordes of slippery carp, their greedy, gaping mouths vying for popcorn and other goodies thrown to them by onlookers. "Look at big-mouth there." I pointed to a carp with jaws large enough to gulp down a good-sized human baby.

"They're ugly and harmless," Uncle Hunter said. "And thick enough to walk on." We moved on.

Jeff's excitement rose with every step up the multi-tiered plaza. "Can we play miniature golf? And I want to do the rock climb! Oh! Can we stop at the Ice Cream Parlor?"

"No, no, and I guess a single scoop won't ruin your lunch," Uncle Hunter replied. "Much as I'd like to show Ashby around, we really do have to get home, Jefferson. We'll come back when we can spend more time."

Jeff's face fell. I felt his pain. Port Plaza reminded me of the boardwalks on the Jersey shore, a smorgasbord of colorful, congregating teens and upbeat music, all mixed with the smells of pizza and popcorn and sun screen. Uncle Hunter looked my way and commented, "Port Plaza is our major source of honky-tonk at the lake." He'd read my mind.

On the way back, Jeff pointed out a massive bird's nest atop a channel marker. It looked as if an inner tube made of twigs had washed up onto the buoy. "An osprey nest," he told me. "They're huge. See that big bird on guard? That's his wife's head poking out of the nest. She's sitting on the eggs."

"His wife?" I asked.

"Osprey mate for life," Jeff said. "I learned that in my bird watching class, too."

"If we steer too close, he'll fly out and try to detour us," Uncle Hunter said. "They're very protective of the nestlings."

At that moment, the creature did, indeed, lift his wings and dive at us with a loud "Chee! Chee! Chee!"

"Occasionally you'll see osprey at our dock," my uncle said. "And I understand a few bald eagles have been spotted hereabouts."

As we rounded a point, I recognized the dock at Overhome. "Thanks for the tour," I told my uncle. "Awesome lake. Incredible mountain. Port Plaza reminded me of home."

"My pleasure, Ashby. We'll go again. I promise." Jeff and I watched while my uncle docked and hoisted the boat. Then we climbed the steps to the house.

****

Dear Diary,

A quick note from a teary-eyed Yankee chick. A boat ride to civilization today made me homesick for the Jersey shore. Hip-hop music, greasy food and cool dudes with tattoos and earrings strollin' and chillin'. I was all set to stick around and soak up the atmosphere, hang out and dig the action. Nature and history and ancestry are all good, but fun is fun, and I felt major separation anxiety when we had to leave.

About nature. This is the most naturally phenomenal setting, everywhere you look. But I sometimes feel like I'm in Jurassic Park. Just now, only a few feet away, a bevy of bluebirds is huddled on my balcony. Don't you love alliteration? I swear they look like they're plotting something. I can't help but think of that DuMaurier short story, "The Birds," and Hitchcock's spooky movie, same name, about the creepy, foul fowl out to get the humans. One or two of my balcony birds have braved it as close as the French doors to peck at the colored glass. It's like they want something. Maybe I should feed them, bring back some scraps from lunch. Well, at least the birds have distracted me. My homesickness for the Jersey Shore is gone. My tears have dried!

Chapter Five

Jeff sat amiably at my side. Apart from his mother, he was a different child, relaxed, full of chatter, everything I could hope for in a cousin-companion. I wanted to squeeze him until his freckles hopped. "I *love* fried chicken." Jeff licked his fingers noisily. "And I *love* picnics. You don't have to have manners at picnics." He jumped up, then pulled at my hands. "Let's go check out the horses!"

"Oh all right. I guess I can't put this off any longer. Are you sure you don't want to go for a swim instead?"

"You can ride, Ashby." My cousin's look was earnest. "Hey! I know! We'll get Luke to teach you. Luke teaches lots of people to ride. Let's ask him! Come on, Ashby."

"Hold on, Jeff. Let me get my hat." I scooped up my baseball cap, then grabbed his hand.

He dragged me behind him as he ran. "When you're good enough, you 'n me can go riding together and Dad won't have to worry."

"I'd rather learn to water ski." But I had to laugh at my cousin's determination.

Stepping inside the stable was like entering another world. Instantly, I was back five years ago at summer camp, inhaling the same earthy smells, hearing the nickering and snorting and grunting from the shuffling animals in their stalls.

Jeff led me to a stall. "This is Sunshine, my palomino pony."

From his stall, Sunshine eyed Jeff. The dark eyes shone and the silky mane lay like gold on his neck.

"He wants a treat, don't you, Sunshine, old boy?" From his pocket Jeff drew a peppermint candy, which he held to the eager, nibbling lips of the golden horse. Instantly, the red-and-white disk disappeared. Sunshine pushed his muzzle against Jeff's empty hand for another treat. I watched this boy-to-horse bonding with a new appreciation. This was obviously a well-loved ritual between my cousin and his pet. "Wanna try, Ashby?" He handed me a candy. "Give Sunshine a treat."

"Will he bite?"

Jeff threw his head back and laughed. "What a wimp. Here. Hold your hand flat."

"Better be careful. Sunshine's been known t' nibble on fingers," a strong voice intruded.

I turned and faced the square frame of Luke Murley.

Jeff hopped up and down. "Luke! You'll teach Ashby to ride, won't you? Huh? Please?"

Before Luke could answer, from behind, something pushed my hat until it fell over my eyes. Tipping the cap back into place, I whirled to face Sunshine. He flapped his wet lips right in my face—a horse kiss, I suppose. More likely, he wanted another peppermint. I jumped, blurting out the first thought I could articulate, "Don't you feed this animal anything? He's trying to eat my hat!"

Luke and Jeff exploded in laughter.

"What's so funny?"

"Aww, Ashby," Jeff said when he'd regained his breath. "Chill. See, Sunshine only does that to people he likes. He's trying to get your attention is all."

I backed away from the omnivorous horse and watched Jeff turn his persuasive powers on Luke again. "Luke, y'know, if Ashby learns to ride good enough, she can go riding with me when you're too busy." His eyes flickered from Luke to me and back again. "Anyway, I want you guys to be friends."

Luke hesitated, then gave a casual shrug of his shoulders. "Okay with me. I c'n work with her, if it's all right with your Dad."

Jeez. Is my uncle that controlling? I wondered. Do I have to have his permission to put one foot in front of the other, just like Jeff does?

Opening my palm, I held the candy under Sunshine's lips, then jumped as the horse wet-lipped my hand.

Oh, what the heck. I'd conquer my fear, learn to ride again, just to show Luke Murley that a city girl can take to horses. Anyway, it might be fun. And it would be a good way to get to know Luke. I stroked the horse's nose. The warm, soft hair felt pleasant under my fingers.

"When do we start?" I asked.

Luke handed me the rubber curry comb. "How 'bout now? Jeff keeps Sunshine squeaky clean, but Sasha, here, could use a good brushing." He pointed to a dappled gray horse in the next stall. "Sasha will be a good horse for you t' learn on. He's gentle, but spunky enough fer fun." Luke led Sasha out of his stall and put him in crossties, then tapped the curry he'd given me. "Use circular motions. Rub hard. All over. When you're done, use this soft brush. I'll be in th' tack room when you're through." He looked at my cousin. "You c'n help her."

Jeff nodded. "I'll show her how to comb Sasha's mane and tail."

"Thanks." Luke turned to me again. "Oh, be sure t' talk t' Sasha so he can get used t' you and th' sound of your voice."

"Okay Boss," I saluted. "When can I ride him?"

"Y'got some things to learn before that. First, y'gotta learn your parts."

"Parts?"

"Parts of the bridle, parts of the saddle, and parts of the horse." I must have looked disappointed, because he added, "You'll get your seat in th' saddle soon enough." With a flicker of a smile, he turned and left.

"Do you also teach water skiing?" I called after him.

Luke stopped and turned slowly. "I'm a man of many talents," he said. I thought I heard him laugh under his breath as he walked away.

"See!" Jeff exhaled. "I told you Luke is a great teacher. I'll help you. I know how."

With Jeff by my side, I put all my energy into working over every inch of Sasha's spotted coat, being careful to pull my hair back into a pony tail and well away from his mouth, just in case. As long as he was secure in the crossties, Sasha would be less likely to step on me or kick me, so there was no need to be afraid.

The currying was darn hard work, and I found myself pausing to wipe the sweat from my brow. Jeff and I kept up a steady rhythm. The reward was Sasha's shining, silky coat. Luke himself couldn't do a better job.

Continuing to fuss over Sasha's grooming, under my breath I found myself singing, "Flow gently, sweet Afton."

Chapter Six

Dear Diary,

So sorry I've been neglecting you. It's past midnight, but I don't feel a bit sleepy and so am back at my laptop. Part of me feels like I've been at Overhome forever, but I haven't even scratched the surface. Life here is decades deep. I need to record my whirling thoughts, while my senses breathe in the essence of Overhome.

Every morning Luke gives me a riding lesson—very early before he starts his round of chores. Everyone rides English saddle here—hunt seat to be specific—a flatter saddle than the Western type I learned on—with no horn. I sucked the first couple of times I tried it, but I've gotten the hang of it. I'm not crazy about wearing jodhpurs, but Luke says they're better than shorts, and I hate the helmet, which makes a mess of my hair, especially when I get sweaty hot. Ugh.

But OMG! My lessons with Luke are incredible! He cannot help but touch my hands as he teaches me how to deal with the reins. And when he holds onto my leg to help me position my body on the horse, I can feel the heat of his touch tingling all the way to my scalp! Nonchalant as he is, I feel his eyes on my body all throughout the lessons. I am in heaven! I've picked right up on my old riding skills and, best of all, the fear is gone. I love the excitement of controlling a huge, powerful animal. Luke has me riding the ring and beyond. Could my Jersey friends understand the thrill I feel every time I climb onto Sasha?

In the afternoon I meet Jeff at the bottom of the drive where his vanpool du jour lets him off. We walk through the green tunnel—that's what we call the canopied driveway—and have lunch. Then it's play, play, play! We swim, throw the football, play croquet or board games, and, of course, visit with Sunshine and Sasha. No, my gal pals back home just wouldn't get it. I'm even surprised myself; playing like a kid can be awesome.

Lacking e-mail and having to search for a cell phone signal makes it hard to stay connected with friends at home. Even for a wannabe writer, letters seem agonizingly slow and archaic compared to IM-ing and text messages. And none of my friends would ever write a letter back to me. I'm going to have some explaining to do when I go home. Of course, it's impossible to reach Mom and Dad without e-mail. I look at the gorgeous postcards they mail me from various ports of call and know they are having an amazing time. That makes me happy.

My aunt and uncle remain swathed in mystery. Okay, so I'm being over-dramatic. I mean, I don't feel I know them at all. Monica is totally wrapped up in her social life. It's all she talks about, but sometimes I feel her enigmatic eyes searching me, like she is trying to figure ME out. And Uncle Hunter is all about business, both on and off the estate. Whenever they appear together, we go through the cat and mouse act with Jeff.

To his credit, Hunter makes it a point to ride as often as he can with his son. The only other thing so near and dear to Jeff's heart is when Luke takes a break from his work to throw the football with us on the back lawn. As a feminist, I like to think I hold my own with the boys, and I throw a mean lateral. But I have to admit watching Luke play is half the fun.

****

Putting my laptop aside and turning off the light, I pulled the bedspread up under my chin and gazed across the room in a pensive mood. Pale streamers of moonlight filtered through the French doors. "Rosabelle's room," I whispered. Did she gaze at these same glass doors fifty years ago? A hundred? I reached to turn off my light rock radio program. Oddly, every time I turned on my radio, it was on some country music station, even though I, myself, had never switched stations since my first night here. When I asked Miss Emma if she'd been tuning in bluegrass while cleaning my room, she got all pissy and told me she had no idea how "that contraption" works. Oh, to quiz her on Rosabelle's and my room, yet I admit I'm more than half-afraid of the response I might get. And Marian and Wash, my birth parents. Not a mention of them since my first talk with Uncle Hunter. Well, I know it's time I started digging for my roots. I drifted into dreams.

I came abruptly awake. A chill swept over my shoulders and face. Afraid to move, holding my breath, I looked around my room with wide-open eyes. Nothing unusual. The moon had moved higher in the sky, altering the slant of moonbeams through the glass doors; otherwise, nothing had changed since I'd fallen asleep. Wait a minute. Was one door slightly open? Or was it merely an optical illusion created by the deceptive moonbeams? I had to check it out.

Sliding from the bed, I made my way to the French doors. They had been locked securely, of that I was sure. Scaredy cat that I am, I checked them every night before getting into bed. My room was warm as ever, yet a shiver began at the nape of my neck and ran the length of my spine. As I reached the doors, I saw that one of them was unlatched, open about an inch. Hypnotized, I watched my hand reach for the knob to let myself out onto the balcony. The night air was mild and still and not the least bit chilly. An almost-full moon glowed halfway down the sky, throwing golden slices of light onto the dark lake surface and casting shadows from the barn and guest house onto the yard. Not a breath of air stirred. I looked over the balcony. All was quiet below.

Raising my eyes to the moon in the deep night sky, I wondered if I could possibly have imagined the chill. Had I been dreaming? A light breeze brushed my face, wafting a sweet perfume all around me. Roses. The unmistakable fragrance of roses in the air. I looked down again at the yard, but all was undisturbed. Then, something caught my eye. The table I had pushed to an out-of-the-way corner earlier in the day. Old, made of wrought iron, it must have stood on the balcony a long time, with its peeling, rusting paint. I remember how the finish crumbled when I pushed it aside to clear the view of the stables. Okay, I admit it, I moved the table to get a better view of Luke at his work. But something was different. I moved closer. In the center was a glass bud vase. It was the old-fashioned kind of glass, thick and crackly. It held one perfect rose, a deep-red rose just emerging from the bud.

I froze, trying to make sense of the scene. The vase. The rose. They had not been on that table before I went to bed. I reached for the heavy vase and brought it to my face. The petals brushed like perfumed velvet against my cheek. For a long time I stood there, feeling the summer night wrapped around me, breathing the soft rose smell. At last, I went in, latching the doors from habit. I placed the vase in front of the oval mirror beside the blue candlestick, thinking, a red rose is a symbol of love. Who could be brave enough to climb a very tall ladder, place the vase on my balcony table, somehow open my locked door, and then slip silently off into the summer night? I sank into the soft mattress, but it was some time before I slept again. My last thought was, "It's this room. Rosabelle's room."

****

Next morning, I sat up, rubbed my eyes and shook my head in utter confusion. I couldn't believe what I saw. On my dresser, the crackle-glass vase stood empty, and beside it, the candle was burned down to a nub in its china blue holder. I remembered the events of last night—the blast of cold air, the opened door, the budding rose in the vase on my balcony. It was not a dream. The vase was proof of that, empty though it was. Still in a daze, I moved to the dresser and picked the vase up. With the crackles imbedded deep in the thick glass, it felt cool and smooth in my fingers. I turned my attention to the candle, the very same candle I had used only once, ever so briefly my first night in the room. Candles don't burn themselves down. Or do they? The French doors were still latched.

"Okay. This is beyond weird," I said to my reflection in the mirror. "I've gotta talk to Miss Emma.

Get some answers about Rosabelle and her room."

From the sideboard in the dining room I helped myself to tea and toast. I was up early for my riding lesson with Luke; the dining room was empty. I decided I would take my breakfast to the sun porch where I could think. Before I could move, as if by magic, Miss Emma appeared at my elbow. "Shall I scramble up some eggs for you?"

"Oh, no. Thanks. Tea and toast will be fine." She was turning to leave, when I asked, "Miss Emma, could I ask you something?"

Her face was colorless, closed-in, her eyes wary.

"Miss Emma, my first night here you told me I might need a candle in my room. You said that the lights frequently go out in the old part of the house. Do you remember?"

The old lady looked at me and nodded. A stripe folded itself between her eyebrows.

I hurried on. "The candle you gave me? This morning I found it completely burned down, but I didn't light it. I didn't touch it." I drew a quick breath and plunged on. "And there's this old tune I keep hearing, it comes from nowhere…and a rose…"

She jerked her head toward the gilt-framed mirror which hung above the sideboard. "Not here," she whispered through tight lips. "Not in this room." Every feature of her ashy face reflected terror. Hurriedly, she turned and left me standing with my mouth open.

Now what was that all about? What could cause such abject fear? Moving slowly toward the porch so as not to slosh my tea, I mulled over the encounter. Was she totally whacked? Dad had always talked of her as the salt of the earth, but, then, he hadn't seen Miss

Emma for a long time.

My cell vibrated. So, the porch was good for a signal, at least for today. It was a text from a friend back home. SUP? KIT. Any other time I would have welcomed the buzz, but I was so totally absorbed in Miss Emma's response, and in my unexplainable situation, I couldn't think about anything else. TTYL, I text-messaged back with a half-hearted vow to call my friend later when I could get my mind off all the woo-woo. For a nanosecond, I considered calling her on the spot. Running the whole story by her. On second thought, I realized she would think I'm under an ancient voodoo curse or something. She'd try to get me to come home and take me to see a shrink, whisk me back to the real world. Funny—before Overhome, I'd been tied to my cell. Finding no bars, no signal here, well, it totally bummed me out. Today? Today my cell phone seemed more of a nuisance than a comfort. How quickly things can change.

Pulling my chair close to the porch table, I ate while I ran over Miss Emma's furtive look and jack rabbit response to my innocent questions. No answers emerged. In frustration, I picked up a local garden magazine and began thumbing through it. Though Virginia could be called lush by any standard, many of the plants here are also native to New Jersey. My home was not called the "Garden State" for nothing. Mom and I had worked long and hard to coax our little plot of land into a showpiece of many of these same perennials: boxwoods, azaleas, ivy. The mountain laurel was new to me, as was the Virginia creeper, but I could relate to the ground covers. Periwinkle and pachysandra. We planted both everywhere we had a blank spot. Of course, there were roses galore splashing the glossy pages with a full pallet of color.

Sipping my tea and picturing our garden at home with nostalgia, I heard something in the yard. Somebody was hurrying up the path from the stables. It was Luke. "Luke, Luke!" I waved. I trotted out to the yard.

He stopped and waited for me to reach him. "Hey," he said. I could tell instantly that something was wrong.

"What is it, Luke?"

"I'm just back from th' north pasture." He gestured. "Abe sent me. Seems th' Night Riders've been at it again. A waterin' trough's been beat up an' we need t' fix it right away."

"Night Riders. What's up with them, anyway?"

"They just get off on causin' trouble." Luke looked distracted.

"So, who are they? And why does Abe think they did it, wrecked the watering trough?"

"Nobody's sure. I've got a few ideas, but…we're gettin' mighty tired of it."

He shook his head. "They like t' leave their sign. Confederate flag. This time they spray-painted it on th' barn." He frowned. "So, that's gotta be cleaned up, too. Looks like we'll have to put off your ridin' lesson this morning. Sorry."

He was sorry? Did he have any idea how sorry it made *me*? I loved these early lessons, riding atop my dappled gelding in the cool morning brightness. Just Sasha and me…and Luke. My face must have shown my disappointment

Luke looked at me as if he'd just discovered I was present. "We'll make it up. I'm free tonight. We can use th' lights for th' ring. Maybe Jeff can join us." I loved the way his grin warmed his face all the way up to his eye brows.

"Okay. Tonight, then. Hope there's not too much damage in the pasture, or on the barn, or wherever."

Waving, he moved off at a trot. I watched him with mixed emotions. There was something I couldn't get about Luke. He seemed to enjoy giving me riding lessons, but he was such a teacher. So detached. It just wasn't natural. He had to sense that I had more than a passing interest in him. Why didn't he return that interest? Maybe he doesn't like blondes. Or, worse, he already has a girlfriend. Somebody very horse-y who's grown up on the land like him. I'll bet she's no damn Yankee, either.

Let it go, I thought. I have the whole morning to myself and I'm not gonna waste one second of it mooning over Luke Murley. Reading the flower magazine had already set my mind on gardening. Well, I'd spend the found-time exploring the grounds again. But this time, I would look for a garden.

Chapter Seven

Gardens need sun and an eastern exposure. The front grounds were overhung with trees. So I branched off the path and headed for the backyard. As I passed the house, I was surprised to see, tucked into a corner between two wings, a small screened porch that was obviously not used. The musty smell of rusting screens made me sneeze as I moved in to get a closer look. Ancient wooden rocking chairs, their paint a bare memory, their woven bottoms sagging like moldy waffles, were the only furniture on the porch. I thought of the people, now long-dead, who must once have rocked in those chairs, a creepy thought. Why had this one part of Overhome been left to molder and decay? I stood soaking in the antiquity of the scene until the chill prompted me to move out into the sun again.

I passed the ruins of some outbuilding. Small rock foundations, with here and there tumble-down fireplaces poking up like tombstones, were remnants of plantation life, no doubt. Following a low stone fence that rolled down the hills of the extensive grounds, I came to a set of stone gateposts similar to those at the main driveway. A rusted wrought-iron gate stood between the posts, flanked on both sides by metal pickets. Lifting the latch, I stepped gingerly down several steep, narrow rock steps covered with creeping greenery and moss. The air was somehow cooler here.

Damp. It just felt, well, it felt *old*. I was surprised to find myself in what must have been, at one time, a formal, fenced garden. In the center a mass of boxwoods, untrimmed, and tall as a man, branched out every which way. It was several minutes before I realized there must have been some sort of pattern to the labyrinth. A maze? On all sides patches of lilies, rhododendron, and mountain laurel mingled with English ivy and the Virginia creeper I'd just seen in the flower magazine. Near the back, in the corner, stood a small, weathered gazebo with a pointed roof. Once white, it was now a peeling gray. It looked like something in an Andrew Wyeth painting.

Following a healthy path of periwinkle, I stood gawking at the tumbles of rose bushes on both sides of the crumbling gazebo. Approaching the thorny tangle, leaning over to pluck a fragrant blossom, I stopped midway at the harsh sound of a man's voice. "What're y'doin' here?"

I jumped, stabbing my finger on a thorn so that it bled. "Ooh!" I gasped.

"State yer business." Abe Murley hefted his stooped frame from behind the gazebo.

"I-I'm…I was looking for roses," I stammered. My pulse beat double-time in my throat. Damn. Luke's grandfather again. Would I have to tangle with him every time we met?

"Give me yer name agin'. I don't remember things like I used to."

"Ashby. Ashby Overton. I'm here visiting my uncle…"

His old eyes were bright, hard beads. "Lenore's granddaughter."

I nodded vigorously

"Lenore died too young." Abe's tone had completely changed—from confrontational to dreamy.

Well, what was I to say to that? "The roses…they're beautiful," I choked out.

Abe appeared not to have heard me. "Lenore loved roses. She loved the gazebo. We used to sit here sometimes." Leaning over, he cupped a rosebud in his calloused palm. At length he raised his head and looked at me. "Yer grandmother was a wonder. Thar wasn't a horse alive she couldn't ride. Ride like a queen. What a beauty Lenore was. She jes' died too damn young." He plucked a bud from a stem and handed it to me. "Roses was special to yer Grandma Lenore."

I swallowed hard. "Special? Why?"

He looked at me without seeing, the light fading from his eyes. "Oh, it was because of Rosabelle, I expect."

"How so?" I began eagerly, but he was already leaving. "Abe, come back. Please! Come back!" I didn't mean this in a purely physical sense. Right before my eyes, he had faded into another world.

He loped toward the gate, shaking his grizzled head and mumbling. I heard snatches of his voice, "Too young. Too damn young."

For a while I sat in the gazebo, taking in Abe's tantalizing sound bites. Though I remembered every word, what played and replayed in my mind was the short phrase, "Because of Rosabelle."

I wandered from the weedy remains of garden back along the stone fence. Roses. How did they manage to bloom in the overgrown garden? If Abe worked them in deference to my grandmother, he had done a crappy job of it. Was my midnight rose plucked from the gazebo garden? Deep in thought, I almost bumped into Miss Emma, who was sweeping the back walkway to the house.

"What's that in your hand?" she asked without preamble. "Where'd you get that rose?"

Taken aback, I spluttered. "I... Abe gave it to me. At the gazebo."

She sniffed, but she sounded sad when she said, "Abe Murley is an old fool. Filling your head with his nonsense. Did he recall quaint, romantic tales about him and your grandmother? Well, you can't believe a word of it. His people were nothing but dirt farmers before he hired on at Overhome. And he, always dreaming Lenore felt something special for him. Well, he's wrong. Lenore was the kind of woman who made everybody she knew feel they were her best friend."

"Miss Emma, Abe said roses were special for my grandmother because of Rosabelle. Do you know what he meant?"

The old lady gently took the rose. "Oh yes. I know." She turned it over several times, then brought it to her nose. "Just the smell of this beautiful thing brings back so many memories. Wonderful memories. And sad ones." She gave me a far-away look.

I was on the verge of getting down on my knees and begging her to spill everything when she dropped a bomb. "But, I have to remember my promise, my dear. My promise to Lenore just minutes before she died. You see, *I* was Lenore's best friend. I didn't just *think* I was."

"So, my grandmother made you promise, what?"

"Not to tell anyone." She snapped out of her

reverie. "Not until I knew it was time." She replaced the rose in my hand. "Just don't believe everything Abe Murley tells you." Without another word, she hurried into the house.

Rose in hand, I walked in the direction of the stables, pensive. I'd gone in search of answers this morning but found more questions than I'd started with. If I was going to unravel the strands of this complicated plot, I knew where I would start. I'd learn all I could about my grandmother, Lenore Overton, the one who died too damn young.

Chapter Eight

I curried Sasha, one eye on the doorway, hoping for a Luke-sighting. Luke had a terrific workload. I knew that now. He was no stable boy. Not only did he care for a dozen horses, but he also maintained all the books and accounts having to do with them, ordered feed and equipment, and oversaw the boarding business. He was in charge of breeding, showing, and general sales of the horses. On top of this, he gave riding lessons to children from neighboring estates, ran the 4-H Club, and organized horse shows. Maybe, just maybe, he was too busy to take much interest in a visiting Overton relative. Then, again, there was always that possibility of a girlfriend of long-standing. Absorbed in my thoughts, I was startled by a noise from the small room off the stalls. Luke called it his "office," and it was where he worked on and kept the books and ledgers, but I had never been inside.

Whispering a promise to Sasha to come back soon, I returned my horse to his stall and peeked in the door, hoping to find Luke. Instead, I looked straight into the uncompromising cobalt eyes of my uncle.

"Well! Good morning, Ashby. What a nice surprise."

"Currying Sasha. I thought Luke might be in here. Sorry."

"Don't be sorry. I've been wanting some one-on-

one time with you. Sit down. I've just finished my work here." He shut the large accounting ledger and patted it. "Luke's records. Impeccable as always."

From where I sat, I could see Sasha in his stall. I threw him a kiss.

My uncle caught my gesture. "It seems you've developed a real love affair with that horse."

"What's not to love?"

"My sentiments exactly." My uncle nodded. "Horses. They're in our blood."

"You sound like my dad." My eyes went to the row of trophies and cups on the shelf hanging behind the desk where he sat. There must have been a hundred ribbons attached to a tack board. "Wow! That's a lot of trophies. Yours, Uncle Hunter?"

"Actually, it's the horses who win the trophies." He turned and looked over his shoulder. "Some of these beauties go as far back as my mother's time." Standing, he reached for a dusty, tarnished loving cup and removed it from the shelf. "Old Dominion Horse Show. Grand Championship. Capitola," he read. He handed it to me. "Cappy was my mother's favorite horse—an exquisite Thoroughbred and a wonderful show ring hunter. Cappy and my mother were so in tune with one another, many people believed that my mother could merely think commands and Cappy would follow through without a hitch."

"My Grandmother Lenore." I touched the darkened silver. "I wish I could have met her. Dad told me she was an amazing horsewoman." I looked at my uncle. "Uncle Hunter, my birth father, Washington, did he ride, too? Are any of those trophies his? I mean his horse's?"

"Washington was…he was a rider of a different sort." My uncle gave a slight frown. "His passion was race cars. The faster the better. Actually, Wash became quite a skilled driver. Today he might well have been a NASCAR champion. Our father never approved, though. He could see no parallel between horseback riding and race car driving." He looked back at the trophy shelf again. "No. None of these trophies have anything to do with Wash, although I believe he did have quite a trophy collection of his own. From stock car races." His look brightened. "Yes. I know where they most likely would be. In the trunk with Marian's things. Their trunk in the attic. It was sent back here after, well, after the accident—the accident that killed them both. I'm sorry. It must distress you hearing about this. They were your mother and father, after all."

"Oh no. I mean, I want to know everything about my birth parents."

"Then, I suppose you'd like to see the contents of that trunk, eh?"

Dumbly, I nodded.

"I'll have Miss Emma show you the attic. I'll tell her right now, in fact. I have to go up to the house to change before I leave."

"Oh, thank you, Uncle Hunter. Please understand, I love Mom and Dad. They've been wonderful parents to me. They're the only parents I've ever known, but I've always been curious about my past."

"I quite understand, my dear. No need to explain. If you have questions, any questions about anything, please ask." He gave me a curiously piercing look and I had the sudden thought that Hunter Overton would be a hard man to keep a secret from. "Just ask," he repeated.

He rose from his seat and escorted me to the door. "By the way, Ashby, I want to tell you how pleased your Aunt Monica and I are with the way you've taken on Jefferson. I believe he is absolutely smitten with you. He talks about you constantly."

Flattered and surprised at his praise, I felt myself blush as I watched him stride purposefully away. Not until he was out of sight did I realize I'd lost an opportunity. Why hadn't I told him about the rose on my balcony, the strange music in my room, the self-burning candles? And why hadn't I asked about Rosabelle?

"Hey!" a familiar voice broke into my thoughts. "I've got some downtime. Wanna work on your canter?" Luke moved to Sasha's stall and knelt to examine my horse's hoof. "Sasha needs a hoof pick here. Know how t' use one?"

"I was just going to take care of Sasha when I found Uncle Hunter in your office." I was tired of waiting for Luke to move on from the teacher-student role. Enough, already. Couldn't we just be friends?

Luke didn't even look at me. "Warm up with a trot aroun' th' ring. Then we'll have time for a canter." He readied his horse for a ride.

I tightened Sasha's girth and led him from the barn. I wanted more than horse talk with Luke; I wanted a real conversation, a date, a night out. Surely, even in the sticks young people had *some* kind of social life besides horses. As much as I was enjoying my summer, I was getting itchy spending all day every day with old people and a seven-year-old. There was no denying my growing attraction to my riding instructor. How could he be so oblivious? Of course, I knew that Luke drove off some evenings. That inescapable date with the phantom girlfriend, I thought ruefully.

In the ring, I buckled on my helmet, ran down the stirrup, and then stepped into it. I slung my right leg over the horse and eased my butt into the saddle. Posting with the trot, I followed Sasha's outside foreleg, admiring his strength as we rode in unison. It happened every time. Once astride Sasha, I forgot everything else, especially my fear. After a good warm-up in the ring, Luke led us on a brisk canter over the fields. Cantering is heavenly, my favorite gait. The gentle rocking sensation, with the wind and sun on my cheeks and the good smells of summer grass and trees—it's absolutely exhilarating. Aware of the smooth, sensuous rhythm, I moved in sync with the horse under me. I was in the zone! Ten minutes later, I wiped the sweat from my brow and patted Sasha's flanks.

Luke reined his horse beside me and gave me a half-grin. "You're an awful fast learner, for a city girl."

"Thanks. I'll betcha I could even learn to water ski, with the right instructor."

"I hear ya'. But, one thing at a time, okay? Are y'plannin' to enter a tri-athlon or somethin'?"

Not exactly, I thought. Just trying to monopolize as much of Luke Murley's time as possible. I flashed my brightest smile.

"Anyway, I'd say you're about ready for th' trail."

"Whoa! Now, that's good news. Jeff will be thrilled." I hesitated a moment, before adding, "Thanks for the lessons, Luke. Jeff's right. You are a great teacher."

Making all sorts of plans in my head, I led Sasha

back to his stall. I'd completely forgotten about the trunk in the attic.

****

Strolling through the green tunnel to collect Jeff that afternoon, I couldn't wait to tell my cousin I'd been declared fit for the riding trail.

Without warning, a thunderous crash in the underbrush broke the quiet; a snarling growl electrified the air. What appeared to be a huge, gray wolf bounded from the woods into my path. I screamed, then froze, as I stood staring down the barrel of wolf-muzzle, paralyzed at the sight of slavering jaws and pointed teeth and wildly flickering eyes of an odd, clear blue. The beast continued to growl low in its throat. Flecks of foam flew about its mouth; it poised for the jump. I knew I was a goner as the light funneled inward and I felt myself go limp. My throat closed. Darkness sucked up the light until only a pin-point remained and I felt myself slump to the ground.

I awoke to confusion. Luke leaned over me, his face close to mine. Jeff held my hand, patted my cheeks. They both wore worry on their faces.

"W-what happened?" A shaking voice broke through my consciousness and I realized it was my own. Struggling to a sitting position, I stammered, "The animal…d-dog…wolf? It jumped at me."

"Dog? Wolf?" Luke looked around. "I didn't see any animals, but I sure heard y'scream. Time I got here, you were passed out cold." He peered into the trees on both sides of the green tunnel. "Wolf. Blue eyes? Dark gray? Huge?"

Weakly I nodded. "Bolted out of the woods. I must've fainted." I inspected my limbs and touched my neck and face. "I was sure it was going to tear my throat out."

Luke kicked at the ground and stewed. "I know that animal. It's a crossbreed. Half shepherd, half wolf—an' it's mean. Belongs to Eddie Mills."

"Who's Eddie Mills?"

"Mills' property, or what's left of it, borders Overhome. Eddie an' me went to high school together. He rode with a rough group, then, an' I suspect he's leadin' th' Night Riders, but I can't prove it."

Jeff watched us with big eyes. "What're we gonna do, Luke? He can't get away with scarin' Ashby like that."

"My guess is it was an accident. Most likely he was in th' woods on a recon mission. Gettin' ready for another evenin' of fun with his Night Ridin' buddies. Maybe I'll just do some night work of my own. Make a neighborly visit after dark. I've been itchin' for an excuse to take Eddie on. Him and his mongrel."

Luke reached for my arm and helped me up. "Better let Miss Emma take a look at you, just t' make sure nothin's broken."

I shook my head. "I'm okay, Luke. Really. I fainted from fright." Shakily, I began to walk, and Luke put a strong arm around me.

"Sure?"

Nodding, I felt myself go giddy again, but it had nothing to do with the wolf-dog's attack. It was Luke's touch that made my knees weak this time.

Jeff ran ahead, calling for Miss Emma, who met us on the porch steps.

"There. Miss Emma will take care of you." Luke delivered me over to the housekeeper, who, in turn, put her arm around me and led me to the chaise on the sun porch.

She sent Luke and Jeff on their way, then examined me in great detail, lifting my eyelids, taking my pulse, feeling up and down my arms and legs for tender spots. "Looks like nothing is injured" she said in the most feeling voice I'd ever heard her use. "But you're pale as paper, child."

"Really, Miss Emma. I'm fine. I've never done that—fainted from fright. It's totally not me."

"Well, you've had a real scare. I'll just sit here with you for a while."

It was the opportunity I'd been hoping for. The last time I'd asked about Rosabelle, Miss Emma'd backed away like a crab. This time, I wanted some answers. I sat up on the chaise. But the first thing that emerged from my lips was about my uncle's promise to let me see Marian's trunk. My body might be unscathed, but my mind was a real scramble. "Uncle Hunter said there's a trunk of my mother's and father's things in the attic. He said he'd speak to you about it."

"Oh, yes. He did mention that trunk. I can show you the attic. But…are you sure you're up to it? I mean, do you really want to go dredging up the past?"

"They were my birth parents. I've never known anything about them. Dad and Mom felt there was no need for details. I'm the one who feels the need. Can you understand where I'm coming from?"

The old woman sighed and sat on the foot of the chaise. "Yes. I can understand your need. My own family heritage is very important to me. But there's so much you don't know, dear. There's so much you probably shouldn't know." She looked at me then for a long, silent moment. I remembered our first meeting my first night here. It was the same appraising look.

Apparently, she came to some kind of decision. "I've been putting it off, but I realize now I can't hold back any longer." She readjusted her weight and sighed again. "Do you know how much you look like your Grandmother Lenore, sitting there?"

Oh, God, I thought. She's running off the track again.

But she continued. "Lenore and I were best friends as far back as memory serves. We shared everything, and when she died, it was me she called to her deathbed. Not Thomas, her husband, and not Abe Murley. It was me, Emma Coleville."

"Please go on," I urged.

"You see, Lenore trusted me. I told you before that Lenore made me promise to fulfill her dying request. But, actually, there were two things she asked of me at the time."

I nodded encouragement, afraid to break her stream of consciousness by speaking.

"First, Lenore asked me to look out for Hunter, to take care of him and bring him up to be a fine gentleman. The other two boys were older and less vulnerable, but Hunter was her baby, really, just a child when the accident happened. Lenore was thrown from her horse, you know. Lenore, who never fell off a horse. A freak accident. She hit her head and was in a coma for days. One night, she revived, just long enough to call for me. Then poof! She was gone. Just like that." She snapped her fingers.

"And the other request, Miss Emma? What else did Lenore ask of you?"

The old woman turned her eyes on me then. "She asked me to watch for you, Ashby."

"Me?" A chill coursed through me. "Why me? I-I wasn't even born. How could she possibly ask you to watch for me?"

The housekeeper wagged her head from side to side. "Oh, I'm making a mess of explaining this. I knew it would be difficult." She took a deep breath and went on. "Lenore said to me—I remember every word as if it were branded on my brain. She said, 'Emma, when I die, Rosabelle will go away. But she'll come back. You know Rosabelle only comes for the women, and you know the signs as well as I do. You must be on the lookout. You must be prepared to explain everything.'"

I stared at Miss Emma, too flabbergasted to say anything.

"You see, Lenore knew Rosabelle would come looking for you…that she would be waiting for you…or someone like you."

"But, you say Rosabelle comes for the women? What about my mother, Marian? Or Monica?" I asked.

"Oh, no, no. Neither of them. There was never a sign of her return. Until you got here, of course."

At last I found my voice. "Rosabelle?" I reached over and clutched the housekeeper's thin hand. "Miss Emma…who *is* Rosabelle? I've got to know."

She hesitated so long, I was sure she'd lost her focus. At last she spoke. "You know, at first, I thought it was only Lenore's wild imagination. She was such a fanciful young girl. I was always the pragmatic one. She was the dreamer. But there were signs, all kinds of things that happened at Overhome, that could only be explained by… Why, even now, now that Lenore's been dead lo these many years. I've seen her in the dining room mirror."

Seen who? Rosabelle? Lenore? My mind was tangled with confusion.

"Don't you know there's all kinds of spirits, Ashby? Good ones...bad ones. How am I to sort them out?"

"Then, you're telling me that Rosabelle is a spirit? A ghost?"

Miss Emma lifted her delicate frame from the chaise. "You said that, Ashby. Not me. I've never voiced it outright like that." Slowly, she shook her head. "I'd be real careful what I say, if I was you. You never know who might be listening." Leaning over, she felt my head, to check for fever; instead, her hand encountered a wash of cold sweat. "You'll be all right now," she said. Without waiting for my response, she walked into the house, leaving me to stare at her retreating back in awed silence.

Chapter Nine

By dinnertime I'd put Miss Emma's confidences of the afternoon in my memory bank to bring up and think over later. While Uncle Hunter, Jeff, and I waited for my ever-tardy aunt to make her appearance, my uncle used the opportunity to give me a history lesson on the house.

"This room and the keeping room next door are what we consider the original house, though they were actually part of a barn." He pointed up. "Your room, Ashby, is right above us. That barn was built back in the eighteenth century. Overtons have lived on this land for over two hundred years."

I took in the floors covered in carpet and the walls papered in silk. For sure it did not look like a barn, but things somehow sounded different and felt different in this room. I wondered if Miss Emma felt the same way. I couldn't help but think of her terrified look at the mirror over the buffet when I asked her about the weird stuff going on in my room. I jerked back my attention to my uncle.

"...and by the mid-1800s, Overhome was a thriving Southern plantation. The 'great house' had been expanded from the barn, and the slave quarters, kitchen house, and sheds fanned out behind. Some of the ruins of these buildings still exist out in the yard."

"Slave quarters? Did you say slave quarters?" I

asked.

"Well, yes. In order to survive at the time, Overhome depended on a small cadre of slave labor, as did all the plantations. I believe at one time there were as many as several dozen slaves living and working at Overhome."

"B-but slavery?" I could not wrap my mind around the idea that my own family had been slave-holders.

"It was a deplorable practice, no question about it. Nonetheless, slavery was the basis for our Southern economy then."

"Oh," was all I could muster. Of course, I'd studied U.S. History. I knew about slavery in the South, but it was a completely abstract idea. The professor lectured, the text described. It was too long ago and too far away to be real. "If I had thought about it, I guess I would have realized…" I trailed off. "It's hard to visualize people sitting in this room being served by slaves. I…I just find it hard to accept."

"The War Between the States ended all that, thankfully. Though no one can be proud about slavery, we Overtons still hold our Confederate warriors as heroes. My great-great grandfather, Colonel Burwell Overton, reigns resplendent in his Rebel grays in our portrait gallery." My uncle pointed toward the portrait wall. "Burwell served with Jubal Early. I believe Abe Murley still salutes that painting every time he enters the house." A half-smile escaped Uncle Hunter's lips. "But the Overtons were able to stay solvent, actually to prosper, after the war, with the coming of the railroad in the early 1900's and the booming economy that flourished around Samson's Ford."

Jeff sat patiently listening to this history he must

have heard many times before. "Then they built the dam, right, Dad? Flooded the rivers and sank all our out buildings—the old slave houses and the family cemetery and everything." He made a swooshing sound and a plunging gesture to illustrate his point. "There's all kinds of buildings and roads and trees and stuff way down at the bottom of the lake." He blinked his eyes in excitement. "A whole underwater town! Kinda spooky, huh?"

"The lake changed everything in these parts. When the Moore brothers settled in the 1740s, I'm sure they appreciated the picturesque mountains surrounding the rivers and streams meandering through the valley." Uncle Hunter glanced at me to make sure I was following the story. I nodded, and he continued. "Not until a pump-storage combined with reversible pumps was perfected some two hundred years after the naming of Moore Mountain was a workable dam possible. There was a lot of resistance to the idea of a hydraulic dam. Folks were afraid that the natural beauty of the three-mile gorge would be forever destroyed. Many people were forced to sell their land, for considerable compensation, mind you. Because Overhome is on high land, we were able to save the main house and enough farm land to keep the horse business alive."

My uncle paused to take a breath. "Oh dear. I hope I haven't bored you to tears, Ashby. I can get too wound up on one of my favorite topics." He looked at Jeff, as if to make a final point. "Of course, all of our family graves were moved to a local church cemetery on high ground before the land was flooded."

Jeff nodded. "One time me and Dad went to the Baptist churchyard and looked for our name on the old tombstones. We used charcoal over paper." He pantomimed a brushing motion.

At that moment, my aunt arrived. Her entrance matched the elegance of the room, the flowing, pastel caftan tacking like a delicate sail as she walked, her jeweled earrings glittering like Christmas ornaments in the candle light. "How are you?" she enunciated, with a fluid rotation of her long neck. "What an upsetting...what an un-unfortunate incident, t-to be attacked by th-that creature."

I was surprised to hear the stammer interrupt my aunt's usual oh-so-careful enunciation.

"Hunter, we simply must do something to prevent this ever h-happening again." She seemed extremely agitated, fussing with her caftan and blinking her eyes rapidly.

"Now, Monica, I can assure you we'll see that Ashby is protected from further attacks by marauding dogs. I've already taken preventative steps. Don't worry about it any further. So, what's going on at the club tonight? I can see you're dressed for something festive."

Jeff had sat silent as long as he could. "Dad! Luke says Ashby is good enough to ride the trails now. Isn't that awesome?"

Uncle Hunter turned his gaze on me. "Is that so? I must say, you are a fast learner, Ashby. I told you riding is in our blood."

"Thanks," I said. "I had some lessons a few years ago. It all sort of came back to me."

"Dad! That means me and Ashby—"

"Ashby and I," his mother corrected.

"Ashby and I can ride together now. We don't *need*

to wait around for you or Luke to go along." He cocked his head to one side. "'Course, we'll still have our rides together, huh, Dad?"

"I wouldn't miss our rides for the world, Jefferson," he said gravely. "And I'll consider your proposal for your riding the trail with your cousin, as long as she's amenable." He eyed me again. "I thought you were looking especially energized and fit, Ashby. Riding does that. Good for the health, good for the soul."

I liked what he said, but I found myself wishing he would smile more often. It would make me feel easier about him. Another contrast with Dad. Dad was jolly, always smiling, joking. It lightened his whole expression. Uncle Hunter's seriousness weighed him down. The only time I'd seen him let down his hair was when he was driving his ski boat.

Under the table I reached for Jeff's hand and gave it a squeeze. We shared a secret look of triumph.

The talk floated through the flickering distortion of candles as I allowed the sense of the ancient room to flow around me. Generations of my family had sat at this very table, their conversations ebbing and flowing, and settling into the porous barn wood where the rise and fall of their voices, their very words, were trapped forever.

****

Dear Diary,

Another unbelievable day in Oz. When I came to bed, I found the radio tuned to country music, yet again. And so my thoughts turned to the original resident, Rosabelle. I'm beginning to think she waits here for me, whiling away her time listening to the soulful sounds of bluegrass in our room.

On that topic, I'm getting nowhere. I need a confidante. Good word, huh? Somebody I can trust, somebody to run over all the data with, sort out fact from fiction. Since I can't seek out my pals in N.J., who to trust? Luke? Luke, the mystery man. I can't be sure about him. Why is he so reserved? Abe, who lives in romantic dreams of yesterday? Hunter or Monica? I'd sound like a hysterical lunatic, certainly unfit to oversee their child, "See, there's this old lullaby and roses which appear and disappear by magic and a candle that melts without being lighted and a radio that tunes itself." The rational mind would say, "Impossible."

Talk about your gothic settings! And Overhome has one helluva dark and gloomy history, even without the Spanish moss. But then Miss Emma tells me there are SIGNS! And it all begins to make sense, which is the scariest thing of all. All I know is, as I sat there at dinner tonight in that museum of a room, I felt a kind of immortality where nothing is ever lost, where nothing dies, and nothing changes. If I have a muse, surely she resides in the dining room.

My uncle says there's a trunk in the attic. A trunk full of memories collected by my birth mother and father. Miss Emma says I shouldn't stir up the past, but I am on a mission—I must know.

Chapter Ten

My eyes were wide open, as though I had never slept, but my lighted radio showed three a.m. The music again. "Flow gently, sweet Afton, amang thy green braes. Flow gently, I'll sing thee a sing in thy praise." The lyrics coursed clearly through my consciousness. Gingerly, I placed my bare feet on the carpet, moving automatically toward the French doors. Latched, they creaked when I tugged them open. Tip-toeing across the rough floor of the balcony, I looked up into a night sky, overcast and starless. I peered blindly into the yard below, but nothing stirred. Only the muted sounds of night fell on my waiting ears; the music abated as suddenly as it began.

For a long while, I stood, expecting, what? I did not know. To hear, to see, to feel something in the heavy darkness. But all was quiet. As I turned back to the doors, rubbing the chill from my bare arms, I felt something brush against my foot, something soft and thin and weightless. Bending to rake my fingertips across the spot, I lifted a feather-soft object to my face. It was a single rose petal. Whirling to look again at the shadowy yard below, I discovered nothing. This remnant had been dropped by some unseen hand. With one last look, I threw the petal over the railing and entered my room.

Latch the doors. Lock out the night. Settle into the

comfort of the old bed and let the blanket of sleep smother the confusion of thoughts. Think of something pleasant. Something soothing. Flow gently, sweet Afton, amang thy green braes.

I awoke next morning to the sound of birds whacking themselves against the window. Leaping out of bed, I ran to the French doors as a wash of blue wings swooped into the atmosphere. What's up with these birds? Shaking my head, I stepped out onto the balcony. Then, I became aware of the sound of voices outside. Hurrying out, I saw in the distance the backs of three people standing on the dock, their voices rising and falling with their excited gestures. Luke, Uncle Hunter and Abe, who spoke most loudly. When he moved to the side, I spied the object of their conversation. Lying still and wet on the floater dock was the wolf-dog that had attacked me in the green tunnel, obviously dead.

My stomach lurched. Luke had said he would take care of the creature. Was this the result? Even so vicious an animal as that deserved better. Dressing hastily, I flew through the hallway and down the stairs to the back door. Out of breath, I arrived at the dock to find the men kneeling over the sodden form. Silent now, they all wore puzzled expressions.

Abe was the first to speak. "Y'see? I told you this animal didn't drown." He reached for the neck and straightened it, flipping the jowls from side to side. "It's done been strangled, see? Somebody shaved the fur right off'n th' neck in a perfect circle. This here animal never knew what hit 'im."

Nervously, I looked at Luke, but he appeared as genuinely mystified as the others. Luke shook his head.

"Funny thing is I went out lookin' for th' wolf-dog last night. About midnight. I snuck into th' kennel at Eddie Mills' house. It was full 'a hounds, but no wolf-dog. I just figured Eddie kept it in th' house nights. Short of breakin' and enterin' there was nothin' I could do, so I came home and went to bed." Luke looked at the others. "But how the hell did it turn up on th' dock?"

"Well," Uncle Hunter said. "There'll be no more trouble from this animal." He gave Luke an apologetic look. "Distasteful as it might be, Luke, would you mind doing the dirty work here—returning the body to the Mills family?"

"They're not gonna be happy about this. Eddie raised that animal from a pup. Granted, he trained it t' be an attack dog. But he loved it for its loyalty. An' its power, I reckon."

"Are you thinking what I'm thinking, Luke?"

"Y'mean that Eddie might try to get even?"

"We all know what they…what he is capable of doing." Uncle Hunter paused. "We may have to step up our surveillance. Are you interested, Luke? A little more night-watching?"

"No problem," Luke did not hesitate. "My pleasure."

"Thanks. I don't know how we could run this place without you. Now, I must be off. Let me know if you need anything, in the way of help." With a nod to me, he turned and climbed the steps to the house.

Luke turned his eyes on me for the first time. "Jeez, y'look shook up."

I stared at the sodden hulk. "Even dead, it still looks terrifying. B-but I just hate to see any animal die like that." On the verge of tears, I felt my voice quiver.

"But part of me is thankful. I mean, what if the wolf-dog were to attack Jeff? And me—big wimp, falling down in a dead faint. I couldn't protect him…completely worthless." My eyes filled and tears trickled down my cheeks.

Luke's expression changed curiously. "Y'know, I had you figgered all wrong." He paused. "From day one, I thought y'were another spoiled rich gal, y'know. One more Yankee snob just here for th' adventure." Again he stopped, locking eyes with me. "But it's clear, now. You're serious; y'really care about Jeff." Then he blinked and added, as if he'd just thought of it. "No wonder th' kid is so crazy about you."

I wiped my face. "Spoiled? Rich?" I sputtered. "I live in a puny two-level townhouse on a crowded cul-de-sac and went to the most middle-class suburban high school you can imagine. My dad is a public school chemistry teacher and my mom is a kindergarten aide. In high school I pimped French fries at McDonalds to pay for my clothes and my cell phone. If I want to drive to the mall, I have to borrow the family car, and I've worked my way through community college selling undies at Lindy's Lair while living at home. Of all my faults and shortcomings, rich and spoiled have never even remotely qualified."

"Whoa! Your face is bright red!" With a sheepish look, Luke touched my arm. "I said I was sorry, or I meant to, if I didn't. Look, why don't y'come have breakfast with Abe an' me. In all th' excitement, we haven't eaten yet."

The gruesome death aside, Luke's offer was a nice turn of events. Well, I suppose his false impressions about me could explain his aloofness. And I had been a pain in the ass on more than one occasion, seen from his point of view. Could we be in for a happy change in our relationship? I stood out of the way while Luke and Abe dragged the corpse off the dock and onto the grass and covered it with a canvas tarp. Then the three of us trooped up the steps and across the lawn to the tiny guest house where they lived.

Once inside, I looked around with curiosity. Compact and cozy, the kitchen had every modern appliance imaginable, including a dishwasher and microwave oven; it was tidy and well-organized. Sunlight sieved through gauzy curtains at the open window behind the table, glancing off china mugs and a matching teapot. Luke put the teakettle on to boil, then sat at the table with me while Abe whipped up an omelet.

"Your house is so tidy!"

Luke laughed. "Without a woman's touch, y'mean? It's a wonder, eh?" Miss Emma had told me Luke's parents were both dead and I wondered if I would ever learn the details. As if reading my thoughts, he offered, "My folks were killed in an airplane crash. I was ten. Plane went down in th' Blue Ridge on a foggy return flight from their first holiday in years. It didn't seem fair—still doesn't—but Abe an' me, well, we had t' keep on livin'. So we just stayed here and went on with th' life we know best. I guess I got used t' being an orphan."

"My parents, my birth parents, were killed in a car crash. An awful coincidence. I guess you could call it that."

Abe placed three loaded plates on the table, then turned to take the whistling kettle from the stove.

Carefully, he poured the steaming liquid into the teapot. We ate silently for a while, then Abe spoke in his usual growl. "I don't want t' spoil breakfast, but I think I know who killed th' wolf."

Luke and I both looked at him in surprise as he reached into his pocket and displayed the contents before us in his open palm. "I found these on th' dock, picked 'em up before you and Hunter got there, Luke."

Luke craned his neck. "Wha-a-t? What's that, Abe? I can't see it."

"Rose petals. Y'know what that means. Rosabelle. She's here. Again." Delicately, he dropped the crumpled red shards in a little heap on the table.

"It means nothin'," Luke said. "It's nothin' but old superstition, pure bull." He frowned and shook his head. "Abe has th' lame idea we've got ghosts or somethin' around here. Spooks going boo! in the night. Can we get real? It's the twenty-first century, for God's sake."

Surprised at my own feeling of calm, I placed a light hand on Luke's. "Please, Luke. Let him talk."

"Fine. Talk all y'want. I'm tired of hearin' it, myself." He stood up, clearing the plates in one swift movement from table to kitchen sink before he strode out of the room. He muttered, "Everybody in this freakin' place is livin' in th' past. Doesn't anybody think about th' future?"

Abe paid not one whit of attention to his grandson's outburst. Pulling a pouch of tobacco from his pocket, he took his time filling his pipe. After some moments of tapping and puffing, he was ready to talk. "Y'see, Thomas Overton, your grandpa, was a hard man. He run Overhome with a iron fist. He run his own fam'ly th' same way. Th' three boys, well, they was all a'scairt a him, him and his razor strop. Neighbors took pains to stay out'n his way, too. In these parts Thomas Overton got whatever he went after."

For a while he puffed reflectively. When he began again, it was in a different voice, dreamy and soft, the same voice he'd used in the gazebo when he spoke of my Grandmother Lenore. "But Lenore, she was diff'rent. I taught her to ride. Did y'know that? Lenore was born an' raised at Overhome. She married her own cousin, Thomas, that's the same Overton fam'ly but many times removed. They was distant cousins. It was him come to live here after they was married. His branch of the Overtons hadn't done so well after th' Civil War. I reckon, livin' on th' grand estate here musta went to his head."

For a long time Abe sat veiled in a mist of his own thoughts, but at length he continued. "'You'll always have a home here, Abe,' she used t' say. 'You belong at Overhome, you and yers.' She was like that, Lenore was. A magnificent woman. A real looker, too. An', oh boy! Could that lady ride a horse." He stood, then, and I was afraid our talk was over, but he had other plans. "I wanna show you my scrapbook. Be right back."

I poured us each fresh tea, watching steam curl from the mugs as I waited for it to cool. Tapping the cup with my fingernail, I let my eyes circle the bright room, wondering what life could be like here for Luke and Abe, wondering about the grandmother I would never meet, and, as always, wondering about the roses. I was halfway through my tea by the time Abe returned with a worn-looking scrapbook in his hands. Plunking it in the center of the table, he began turning yellowed pages. Focusing on one of the pages, his expression soured. "Emma Coleville," he barked. "Uppity woman!"

"Oh, may I see, Abe? She must be very young there."

He turned the crumbling page so I could see the blurry and faded image of a coltish young girl leaning against a fence, laughing at her look-alike companion. I would never have recognized her as a young Emma Coleville.

"Too good for her own good, Emma Coleville," he growled. "Always puttin' on airs. She tried t' turn Sarah against me. Tried but never even got close."

"Sarah? Who is Sarah?"

"She's th' one standin' next to Emma there. She an' Emma was sisters." He pointed. "Sarah Coleville Murley, my wife. She passed on some years ago. Died in childbirth with our only son. He was Luke's father, y'know."

"I'm really sorry, Abe."

He appeared not to have heard me. "Emma jest couldn't get over her sister 'marryin' down' as she called it. And after Sarah died, why, Emma took it upon herself t' tell me how t' raise my own son. 'Do this, Abe. Do that, Abe. Teach 'im manners and raise 'im up to be a man of worth.' Then she got on a toot about sendin' 'im to college. That damn woman hounded me fer years about savin' money fer college. But I was agin' it. I knew if my son left th' land he'd never come back. Th' land Lenore wanted us Murleys to live on. So what if we started out as poor tenant farmers? We was always smart. Proud, too. And we was never too good to git our hands dirty like them uppity First Family of

Virginia Colevilles. So, I put my foot down 'bout college. I never got past fourth grade m'self. A high school diploma was good enough for my son, an' it's good enough for my grandson. I'll swanny if that old crow, Emma, ain't tried to sneak th' college idea into Luke's head, too."

Luke returned in time to hear this last remark. "Oh, please. Don't get 'im goin' on my Aunt Emma. I swear she's as psycho about this ghost crap as Abe is." Giving me an annoyed look, he pointed to the scrapbook. "Well, have y'seen enough?"

"Actually, I haven't seen my Grandmother Lenore yet." I spoke in my sweetest voice. "It would mean a lot to me, Luke."

"Oh, go ahead. But there's a lotta work to be done around here, y'know." He clomped off again.

Unperturbed, Abe began turning page after page, offering a running commentary on each fragile newspaper clipping, fuzzy photograph, and moldering program bill from horse shows long since over. There stood Abe in one picture, a much younger, taller, and handsomely smiling Abe, alongside a pretty, dark-haired woman, my grandmother. With perfect posture, her figure slim and vibrant in a flawless riding outfit, she stood holding a loving cup between them. "She always insisted I be in th' winner's photos," Abe said dreamily.

Something slid from the back cover, given its freedom, perhaps, from age-dried tape. I bent to the floor to retrieve the fragment of newspaper clipping. "What is this, Abe?"

Abe's face fell. "Oh, that. I never could bear to paste that one in permanent," he said after a minute.

I read the headlines. "Barn Burns on Colonial Estate. Overhome Hit with Double Tragedy."

"It happened soon after Lenore died." Abe sounded tired.

Silently, I read on. "Exactly one week after the tragic death of renowned equestrian Lenore Overton, the barn at Overhome, the family estate, burned to the ground in a fire of suspicious origins."

Abe spoke from the hollow of his chest. "Fer days she laid there, still as death. It was a turrible fall, a fluke. Without warnin' and for no reason, her horse shied, then run her under a tree limb. She fell—hit her head—an' she never come to, except for a few minutes th' night she died. And then th' fire. Th' barn went up in flames. All th' horses escaped, every ridin' mount, except one. Lenore's horse, Capitola, th' one she was on when th' accident happened. It was burnt to a crisp. Dead. Just like Lenore."

No wonder Dad was so close-mouthed about his family's history. And Miss Emma had urged me not to stir up the past. Such haunting memories. Such sadness.

"Investigators never turned up no clues as t' what started th' fire. But I knew." Abe appeared to be talking to himself now. "It was Rosabelle. Rosabelle burned that there barn down. It was her way 'a gettin' even fer Lenore's death."

"Getting even? What do you mean, Abe? I'm not following you."

"Lenore saw Rosabelle as her guardian angel. Rosabelle killed Lenore's horse to get even. Don't ya see? That horse had no call to run Lenore under th' limb. So, Rosabelle, well, she jest took care of it. Rosabelle could be like that. A good protector takes revenge when revenge is called fer."

"And you're sure it was Rosabelle who started the fire because…"

"I found it th' next day. The rose. The one she left, like always. Oh, it was Rosabelle, all right."

I was a long time finding my voice. "D-did you ever see her, Abe? Did anybody see Rosabelle?"

Abe gave me a sad, distracted look. "Well, Luke don't believe it neither." He rose, shutting the scrapbook gently. "There's some things y'jest know, is all. It don't take no college degree to recognize th' truth when it's right in front of yer face." He turned, then and went into the next room, shutting the door, decisively.

My glance zeroed in on the crushed rose petals Abe had taken from his pocket. "Right in front of my face," I whispered.

Chapter Eleven

Aunt Monica and I faced each other over the glass-topped table on the covered deck. Linen napkins, creamy china, a vase of fresh flowers on each table, and a stunning view of Moore Mountain Lake completed the picture of posh luxury my aunt and uncle enjoyed at their country club.

"Carole Norton and her daughter will join us shortly," Monica said. "The Nortons live in Northern Virginia, but they summer here at the lake. Tiffany Norton is a bit younger than you, Ashby, but I think you will find her compatible." My aunt looked absolutely at home in this regal setting.

Taking in the vista of golf greens and lake, I could easily imagine the swishy "summer home," my aunt's club friend might live in. No sense being negative, but what could Tiffany Norton and I have in common? Uh oh. That's exactly the same attitude Luke had held about me.

"I told Hunter we simply had to get you away for a little R and R. After such a dreadful morning. That animal, drowning like it did." My aunt shivered. "Hunter was more than happy to spend the day with Jefferson while you and I took a breather. They can be such good pals."

My aunt's tone was wistful. "Hunter is a good father. And Jefferson adores him, but..." She trailed

91

off, fiddling with her napkin. Taking a sip of her iced tea, she gazed over my head. "But Hunter is frequently so intense, so controlling. I worry that he might curb some of that wonderful spirit I so love in our son." She stopped as though finished, then added, "You know, I think Jefferson actually is afraid of his own father, sometimes. Because of that intensity."

Wow. This was way too much information. I kept quiet.

As if she'd forgotten me, Monica continued her monologue. "Oh, I know I drill Jefferson on his manners. Sometimes, I think that is all I am good for. It is the way I was raised. By my nanny, of course. My parents were far too busy, socially and otherwise, to pay me much mind. Consequently, Nanny and I were quite close. Such a warm and loving person Nanny was. My mother insisted Nanny work on my etiquette. It was politeness and manners, at all times."

My aunt teared up. "Oh, I never intended to tell anyone this, Ashby. I cannot imagine why I even began... Something to do with that creature attacking you and then t-turning up so—so horribly d-d-dead. It is s-so upsetting."

"Aunt Monica," I found my voice at last. "It's all right. I'm all right. Really."

She waved my words away as she dabbed at her eyes with her napkin. "You do not understand, dear. The scare with the wolf—it was a catalyst. Whenever I become upset, really upset, I...m-my flaw—m-m-my glaring flaw returns. They, my parents, they dismissed Nanny, sent her packing when she could not erase it. They sent me to that horrid b-boarding school to be...to be fixed."

"What do you mean, fixed?"

"C-cured of my c-condition." She wiped her eyes again. "You see, I stuttered. It is caused by a neurological glitch between the brain and the vocal cords and lips, the ability to produce speech. This I learned much later, but only after I suffered years of embarrassment. I cannot think of those years without reliving the humiliation of not being able to answer questions in class or the paralyzing fear that I would be called on to read aloud. Even now, n-now that I only stutter when I am under s-stress, I still feel the pain of that rejection."

So that explained Monica's curious enunciation. Still, I was shocked at her unloading on me like that. I mean, all of our conversations around the dining room table at Overhome had been so formal, trivial and dry.

She took few deep breaths and shook her head several times, then reached across the table for my hands. "Please forgive me. What I really want you to know is how happy I am with the way you relate to our son. I wanted you to be a companion for him, yes, but not just anyone would do. I knew you would be perfect, another only-child of the Overton family, just like Jefferson, but having a solid family upbringing, and a mother and father who adore you, without pampering, in your growing-up years. Parents who would never banish you to a boarding school. I feel I know you from Helen's letters, know you to be well-rounded, happy, energetic, self-sufficient, all the attributes I never had the opportunity, or the wherewithal, to develop for myself, or to impart to my child."

She pressed my hands. "You are making my dreams come true. I have seen so much evidence already—how you are bringing out all the good qualities in Jefferson—the independence, the spirit, the love. You are such a positive family role model…I cannot thank you enough."

I murmured something incoherent. I was relieved Aunt Monica had ceased to stutter.

"Neither Hunter nor I had much experience with motherly love. I often feel guilty spending time at the club, leaving Jefferson at home, just as my mother did to me. And Hunter. He was so, so deeply affected by his mother's death. Perhaps too deeply. Your uncle has a dark side. A side most people never see. He…"

We were interrupted by the arrival of Carole and Tiffany Norton, a bright mother-daughter couple who looked more like sisters—petite, blonde, and bouncy as cheerleaders. Monica patted her hair and sat up straighter, holding her head at a regal angle.

"What fun!" Carole chirped as she gave me a little hug. "The more young people who come to the lake, the happier we all are. After lunch, you can go waterskiing with Tiff and some of her friends, if you like."

Tiffany cocked her head and gave me a look that said, Only if you want to. I liked her immediately for that.

"Sure! I've been dying to learn to ski, if somebody is willing to teach me." I cut my eyes toward Tiffany. "Uhhh…understand, I'm a complete rooky. I hope I won't be too much of a drag on your party."

"My friends and I love to get people up on skis for the first time," Tiffany assured me. "We take pride in every conquest." She gave her mother a cheerful smile. "Let's order lunch. I told everybody we'd meet them at the dock at two o'clock. Drew's got his family's ski boat for the whole day."

"Sweet!" I heard myself say. But my mind was only partly focused on the long-awaited opportunity to learn a cool, new sport. The other half kept mulling over the odd puzzle pieces of information I had already learned today, about Luke, my Grandmother Lenore, my aunt and uncle. And about Rosabelle, of course.

****

Dear Diary,

Where to start? First, I must say I was shocked to find that Tiffany Norton and her friends remind me of my buds back home when we were a couple years younger. Tiffany and Drew and Jordon, and the others are my newest country-clubbing amigos. Okay, so they're as used to the high-life as us peons are to breakfast, all enrolled in or planning to attend Ivy League colleges, but they must've left any snobbery back home. And...they know how to teach a total klutz to ski in one easy lesson. Well, make that a whole day of lessons. Drew himself, who skis on the Lake Team, admits the sport is not a one-shot deal. But by day's end I was getting up with every pull and staying up until my legs felt like linguini. That's on a pair, of course. (See, I've even picked up on the ski-lingo). Everyone agrees a gymnastics background helps with the old balance, though, and they're sure I'll be hanging out on a slalom ski before long. We parted with plans to ski again soon.

Aunt Monica is one needy chick, as I discovered from a long tête-a-tête (Thank you, Mary Stewart for that lovely term) with her today. Just getting out of the gloomy, old rooms at Overhome freed her up and loosened her lips, is the way I figure the deluge of tears and confessions. Okay, so I'm getting some insight into the psycho-dynamics of this dysfunctional family, but, for the life of me, I see no evidence of my influence on Jeff. Monica is all gushy about me making a positive change in Jeff's attitude—yada, yada, yada—but he's still playing his mom and dad against each other for all he's worth. Have I missed something here? Maybe instead of studying writing in college, I'll go for a psych degree. If anything, Jeff has made me *change for the better. I feel like a big sister who's all grown up and learning to take responsibility for somebody other than Ashby Overton. I mean, the whole time I thought about my visit to Overhome, it was all about me—my roots, my adventure, a background for my writing, and, hey! They're still high on the list. But that little freckle-faced kid has added a whole new dimension to life. And I never saw it coming until it hit me in the face.*

More good news...when I draggled in after hours of skiing and boating in the punishing Virginia sun (Yes, Mom, I slathered on the SPF 30 and I reapplied), Miss Emma came knocking on my door. She promised she'd usher me into the attic first thing in the morning. At last! A chance to glimpse a real slice of my mother and father's life, their short, happy, life, as they say in literature.

Oh, I almost forgot. Talk about short and happy. For a brief moment Luke and I were on the same wave length, but the illusion was shattered, oddly enough, by rose petals.

Chapter Twelve

Miss Emma sorted through her fist of keys until she found the right one. Though the attic door looked like any of the other doors in the long hall, it opened to a steep set of unfinished wooden stairs. Stale air that heated up with every step pushed into my face until I reached the top and surveyed the area. The attic and everything in it was powdered with a fine layer of dust that made me sneeze. Where to start? Crammed full, it looked like an abandoned museum, or possibly a fun house, preserved and waiting for someone to re-discover it. I moved on, stepping around ancient cradles, a wooden rocking horse, an old treadle sewing machine, a phonograph, several dress mannequins, dolls in a little wooden bed, and a host of other forgotten and discarded objects. By the time I finished my survey, there wasn't much of the attic left unexplored. At last, I located the trunk that had, no doubt, been sitting there some eighteen years, ever since the accident that had sent my parents to their grave and me to live with my adoptive mother and father. Someone had written with a black marker that was fading to gray, "Marian and Washington."

Two lives in a trunk, I thought. This is all that's left. It was a depressing thought.

A little choked up, I watched my fingers shake as I raised the creaking lid that protested my invasion of its privacy. Looking over the top layer of neatly-organized items, I spied a tuft of tissue paper. Opening it up, I found a filmy wedding veil covered at the crown with delicate seed pearls. Next to it was a glass jewelry box containing a string of matching pearls. My mother's wedding veil and pearls. Shouldn't they be handed down to me to wear when I become a bride? Another tissue tuft revealed a carefully-folded white baby's dress, probably a christening dress, but whose? Mine? My mother's? I picked up the garment and held it to my face. It smelled of cedar and moth balls, not at all like baby smells. But it was as soft as summer air against my skin. Gently replacing the tiny dress, I next lifted a silver-framed photograph showing a sweetly-smiling, dreamy-eyed bride, who stood alongside a handsome groom, looking sharp in his tuxedo. My birth-parents' wedding day, caught forever in time. She with the flowing, light hair, the slim neck encircled with pearls. He sporting the same patrician bone structure, dark hair, and cleft chin as his brothers, the unmistakable genetic imprint of the Overton clan. What would my life have been like had they lived?

Lifting out the upper layer divider, I encountered a small paper-wrapped bundle, which, with much unwinding, turned out to be a lovely antique cup and saucer. Its delicately scalloped edges were outlined with hand-painted pink roses. Most likely a family heirloom treasured by my parents. Putting the pair gently aside, I continued to sift through the assortment nestled in the lower part of the trunk. Piles of medals embossed with race cars, some attached to red-white-and-blue neckbands, a tangle of trophies similarly adorned, a book of dried and pressed corsages that smelled musty, and a silver baby cup, tarnished with age and engraved, simply, WASHINGTON OVERTON. I lifted a cigar box on which was written "My Memory Box." It contained ticket stubs, prom photos, a high school football program, a fine lock of light hair and a packet of envelopes tied with twine, which, when untied revealed a dozen greeting cards, everything from valentines to birthday cards, each signed "I love you, WASH."

Underneath the memory box lay a high school yearbook. A quick glance inside the covers showed me how some things never change. The signatures under the photos, the tidbits of advice and humor were not much different from those in my own yearbook. Below his picture someone named James Poole had written, "Go for the gold, Wash!" While, right beside him Rusty Porter had penned, "Forget the gold, buddy. Go for Marian!"

I flipped through the pages until I found, in the Senior Section, my father's young and smiling face, with the ambition "To win the Indy 500" printed underneath. Laughing eyes, old-fashioned haircut, my dad looked so full of life, but he was so dead. A heavy sadness tightened my throat. Life. Death. Both seem terribly unfair sometimes.

It took a while to find Marian's picture, since I could not remember her maiden name. I located her in the M's. Marian Mills. Mills? Where had I heard that name before? Of course. Eddie Mills. Luke had said Eddie Mills was the owner of the now-dead wolf-dog. Eddie Mills was, Luke thought, the leader of the Night Riders, the gang that vandalized the countryside. Were Eddie Mills and my mother related? Mills is a common name, but I would not be surprised since it seems everybody around here is somehow related. "To live, love, and laugh," was her senior ambition. It was too ironic to dwell on. I snapped the book shut. Too painful. Too futile. All my discoveries only intensified my sense of loss.

In the very bottom of the trunk was a packet of letters bound with a faded pink ribbon. Probably love letters—so private. Did I dare read them? Was it a violation beyond my privilege as only child of Washington and Marian Overton? I'll read just one, I decided after some thought. From the middle, I selected a blue-gray envelope addressed to Marian Mills, with the return address of the University of Virginia, the alma mater of all three Overton brothers.

"Hi, Marian," the letter began. "College is a groove! Of course, it would be so much better if you were here to share it with me, but I won't get on that old saw again, I promise. I know your folks don't believe in higher education for their women, and I DO realize you have to work to help out your family. Look, do you think you can get away for Homecoming here? It'll be a rad weekend—football against you-know-who—our biggest rival. Lots of parties and bands dishing live music at all the frat houses. Madison can drive down to get you and you can catch a ride back easily enough. What do you say? I hope you'll say yes!

"Speaking of Madison, he's gotten into a scrape here. He has to go before the honor court for alleged cheating. We know who set him up—can you believe one of his frat brothers? It's very complicated, but he is absolutely innocent. Problem is Dad will NOT believe Madison was framed. He insists he leave school, come back home and work the farm and pay penance or something. At the very least, Dad is cutting Maddy off financially. With only a semester left to go. What a stubborn SOB Dad can be! Madison is furious and I doubt he'll ever forgive Dad for this one. He's determined to finish and graduate, despite Dad, even if it takes another year to do so.

"So, how's everything at home? I miss the mountains and the lake and I miss you. I know your father and mine think this separation will make us forget each other, but they've forgotten that absence makes the heart grow fonder. My heart is bursting and I can't wait to see you again, Sweetheart. I love you, Wash."

I rocked back on my knees. I'd just learned more about my family and natural parents and their past than anyone had told me in my life. The Mills and Overton families both opposed the relationship between Marian and Washington. It also looked like there was a good-sized difference in the economic status of the two clans, so this was no Romeo-Juliet scenario. And my adoptive father had quarreled with his own father who would not believe in his innocence. Yes, that would sure be a blow to Dad and his integrity, the ever-upright Madison Overton. I could see how it would estrange Dad from his family. Bad, bad family feelings. Stirring up the past. Miss Emma knew what she was talking about.

I placed the packet of letters back in their corner, knowing I would return to read the rest at some point.

There was only one more item in the trunk I had not checked out, a cool, red-leather diary. This time I did not hesitate. I opened it, surprised to find only one entry, dated July 1st.

What a scum-bag my father-in-law is! He couldn't prevent us from getting married, and he cannot make us stay under his roof. "I thought you might want to keep a diary," he tells me. "My wife keeps one, and all the Overton women before her did, too." I know very well why Thomas Overton, who rarely gives anyone anything, has presented me this diary as a "gift." He wants me to write all our secrets, mine and Washington's plans and hopes, so that he can sneak my diary away and read it and plot how to screw us. He's so afraid my "family of lesser means" will try to get their hands on some of his precious money. He even insinuates that I am carrying someone else's baby in my belly! What a bastard! A meddling, conniving, controlling fool who'll die friendless and loveless. He's even worse than Wash and Madison have described. Read THAT, you old SOB! Wash and I will be out of here as fast as we can get our wits together.

Nothing wishy-washy about these two. I'd evidently inherited my streak of determination from both parents. But another, equally interesting thought intruded. If Grandmother Lenore kept a diary, she surely must have written something about Rosabelle in her life. If Miss Emma and Abe were unable or unwilling to help me find out what I wanted to know about the strange and scary episodes I'd encountered, perhaps I could get the down-low from the horse's mouth, so to speak. Sorry about the mixed metaphor. All the Overton women had kept diaries, according to Marian. So, where are they? A family as fixated on history as the Overtons would keep such treasured heirlooms in a safe place. I began another search of the cluttered attic. Likely-looking bureau drawers and cedar chests held only disintegrating ball gowns, rusting swords, and pieces of cracked china, pottery, and glass. Old wooden toys, a mildewed, leather-covered Bible, dozens of yellowed *National Geographic*. No diaries.

At last, I discovered a closet I had not before noticed. Paneled like the walls, it was virtually hidden from view. The door gave way reluctantly, spewing dust and woody splinters at my face. Phew! Stepping in, I waited for my eyes to adjust to the dusty gloom. Pushed back against the closet wall was a large, old-fashioned wooden desk; on top was a long, rusting footlocker that looked like a metal coffin. It was locked tight. Could I force the lock? Maybe a screw driver. Or a hammer. I bent to peer into the keyhole. Maybe a strong piece of wire or a crochet hook could work like a key. After all, if the diaries were here, a virtual library of Overton history, I was entitled to read them, wasn't I? Snoop that I was, I'd lost all shame.

Shutting the door, I ran over some plans in my head. Like a homing pigeon, I returned to Marian and Washington's trunk one more time, rummaging until I found, again, the packet of letters. If I could not find the diaries, I'd read more of the letters. Fair enough, right? Stuffing the packet under my T-shirt, which was sticky from sweat, I found my way out of the attic. I would hide the letters in my room and read them at my leisure. In the meantime, I'd think hard about how to get into that enticing footlocker. My instincts told me the family diaries must be locked inside. I had a fleeting, pleasing thought—all the Overton women kept diaries. How naturally I am following the tradition with my own diary. Someday, in the way distant future, would some curious young Overton get a kick out of reading my personal memoirs?

In a funk, I left the attic. Seeing photos of my biological parents, reading their thoughts, touching their possessions. Okay, I'd felt a connection like never before. But I was left with such a cold, empty sensation, a numbness, a dead feeling. I knew I should look for Jeff, but I only wanted to be alone with my misery and tears, free to feel sorry for myself.

Chapter Thirteen

Absorbed in my thoughts, I puttered aimlessly around the grounds. The way the creek snakes between the trees reminded me of a paint-by-numbers picture I had worked on as a child, a bright mix of greens and blues meandering between vine-shadowed banks, highlighted now and then by golden shafts of light. Jeff and I liked to sit beside the water here and watch the eddies suck in leaves and sticks as we tossed them into the water. After a good rain, the currents could run surprisingly swift and deep for such a merry little stream. I stood, feeling the pleasant warmth of the fading sun on my arms. Had Marian and Washington sat on this bank and watched these very same whirlpools? Had Lenore? Does time stand still as people move in and out of its dimensions, or do people stand still as time moves them on a continuum?

The clatter of approaching hooves broke into my musings. Uncle Hunter and Jeff were well into a late afternoon ride, judging from the color in Jeff's cheeks and the sweat beading over his nose freckles.

"Whoa!" Uncle Hunter called from the saddle. "Whoa, Goblin." He reigned in the spirited chestnut, a big gelding of seventeen hands. Four white stockings and a white blaze set off the shining auburn coat. Impatient to get on with his run, Goblin snorted and stamped.

Mounted on Sunshine, Jeff called to me. "Hey, Ashby. Come ride with us." He looked at his father.

"Yes, do." My uncle nodded.

"Thanks, Jeff. Maybe I will. A brisk ride might be just what I need."

"You look sad," Jeff said. "Are you sad, Ashby?"

I managed a feeble smile. "Oh, I've just been thinking, that's all. Sitting here beside the creek and thinking."

"Is everything all right?" my uncle asked.

I knew those eyes of his could see into my soul. "I'm okay. It's just that today I went through the trunk, you know, my...Marian's trunk. It's left me kinda blue." I knew I would break down crying if I had to say much more.

"I came within an inch of not telling you about that trunk, Ashby. I was afraid your digging into the past would be more hurtful than beneficial."

I stood up very straight. "Thanks, Uncle Hunter. But it's all good. I'm glad you told me about the trunk. I guess you could say I found both comfort and grief in it."

"All right, then. I'm glad it worked out for you. Will you join us?"

"Wait! Wait a minute, please. I wanted to ask you about something I discovered today."

My uncle raised his brows. "Oh? What would that be?"

"My mother's maiden name was Mills. Luke said it was Eddie Mills' dog that attacked me. Are...were they related? Eddie and Marian?"

His pupils contracted until they almost disappeared and a little vein pulsed in his forehead. His voice was perfectly even, however, when he replied. "Unfortunately, yes. Eddie would be Marian's cousin. Her first cousin, that is. A large, clannish family." He hesitated. "Marian was nothing like Eddie, though."

"Luke says Eddie—" Jeff began, but his father cut him off.

"Not now, Jefferson."

I gave Jeff a look that asked him to be patient. "I found a letter in the trunk my father wrote to my mother. It sounded like their parents opposed their romance."

"Oh, there was a great deal of opposition, Ashby. My father considered the Mills family to be beneath the Overtons. Socially inferior, that is. The Mills people had always worked as tenant farmers, but until some slightly more prosperous relative left Marian's father a piece of worthless red clay, they never owned so much as a blade of grass." My uncle shook his head. "Owning property, rising up the economic ladder, would have elevated the Mills family, and Marian, to an 'acceptable' position so that she and Washington could marry well enough, without a lot of nasty gossip about social climbing." When he caught my incredulous look, he added. "It was a generation ago. Things have changed, but we are in the South, you understand, my dear."

My uncle was silent for several moments. "Though I'm not sure exactly when the feud started, my thought is the whole thing climaxed over the claim by Otis Mills, Marian's father, that our father, Thomas Overton, stole his acreage through some legal shenanigans."

Abe's unflattering description of Thomas Overton flickered though my mind. "Thomas Overton got what he went after in these parts." Something to that effect. And Marian's diary was even more graphic.

"In the end, it was all about the money. Worthless as Mills' supposed property was, when the dam was built and the farms flooded to create the lake, my father received a tidy sum of money for selling off those acres that Mills claimed were his. And ever after, condemned to poverty, Otis Mills and the rest of his clan have had it in for us Overtons."

"Then it all started a long time ago," I said.

"Yes. But when you were born, the families declared a sort of truce. Babies can effect such a change, you know."

"Then—they both died." My voice was as flat as my feelings.

The vein in my uncle's forehead jumped to life again. "I—"

He was interrupted by the sound of his cell phone ringing in his pocket. "Excuse me, Ashby. I'm expecting an important call," he said, removing the cell and putting it to his ear. He spoke only a few words, then closed the phone and slipped it into his pocket. "I'm off. I must attend to business."

Jeff's face fell. "Awww, Dad. Can we ride a little longer? Please?"

"Sorry, Jefferson. Duty calls. Come along now and be quick about it."

I watched my cousin's expression change from hope to…to what? Was that a flicker of resentment in those Overton eyes? Jeff did not move.

"Jefferson! I will not accept disobedience," Uncle Hunter barked. Hunter shifted gears. "But I'll tell you what, son. We'll go back to the barn and you can help

Ashby saddle up Sasha."

"An' me and Ashby can ride? On the trail?"

My uncle threw me his piercing look. "I'll let Ashby decide."

All thoughts of my gloomy discoveries left me, to be replaced with a sense of responsibility that I found both welcome and worrisome. "We'll be careful, Uncle Hunter," I told him. "I can't think of anything I'd like to do better right now than ride with Jeff."

"You rock, Ashby!" Jeff cried. "Bye, Dad," he remembered to say at the last minute.

An odd expression rose on my uncle's face—almost a look of disappointment. Did he regret his decision to allow me to take over as Jeff's riding companion? Other than driving his boat, his rides with his son seemed to be his only source of real pleasure. The thought unsettled me. Why would my uncle encourage me to do something he'd end up resenting?

All the way to the stables, Jeff prattled about our anticipated ride. As we went through the motions of saddling Sasha, he remembered something he'd wanted to say about Eddie Mills. "Ashby, Luke says Eddie has an axe to grind. What does that mean, anyway?"

"An axe to grind means he's got a problem with someone or something."

"So, if Eddie's got a problem with Dad…" He trailed off. "Then Dad's the axe?"

"Something like that, Jeff. Sounds like it goes back a long, long way. Maybe it's best to forget it, huh?"

"Let's ask Luke! He hates Eddie. Then maybe you won't be sad anymore, Ashby."

My young cousin had picked up on a lot of my conflicting emotions, I realized. With his mention of

Luke, I realized how much I wanted to see him. Wanted to get back that brief moment of camaraderie we'd achieved in Luke's tidy kitchen.

As I saddled Sasha, Jeff poked around looking for Luke, calling his name. Just then, I heard the sound of tires spinning out of the stable parking area, and I looked up in time to catch sight of Luke leaving in his pickup. "I wonder where he's off to," I said in a half-voice. Wherever it was, it had nothing to do with work, judging from the neatly combed hair and fresh shirt I had observed in the seconds before he pulled away. The mystery date. The phantom girlfriend. Bummer.

****

Dear Diary,

My first "solo flight" with Jeff ended almost before it began due to a sudden thunderstorm that drove us back to the stables. The cool news is I now have the Good Housekeeping Seal of Approval from my uncle. He actually entrusted his son to ride with me and only me. The thought of some sort of accident for Jeff while under my supervision gave me the jitters, though. As Monica said, Hunter can be rather intense when it comes to their son.

Well, I'm an emotional mess. Going through my parents' trunk has taken me up and down so many times, I am beyond dizzy. Beyond nausea. All I want to do is fold myself into the ancient arms of my room and let my favorite lullaby sing me to sleep. Is the melody in my head, or is it in the chemistry of the air breathed only in this room?

Of course, I'm consumed with curiosity over the love letters I stole. But I haven't the heart for dealing with all that was lost when Washington and Marian died. I have hidden the packet in a place where no one would ever think to look. On a better day, I'll find the guts to read them and scour them for anything that can clue me in as to what my birth parents were like and, consequently, who I am.

For now, I have to move on, think about something else. Call me a regular Nancy Drew, but there are lots of other clues I'm itching to investigate, clues about someone or something that has been waiting a long time for me. What a pity I can't count on Luke to share in my quest. Luke, the skeptic. Luke who does not believe in ghosts. Luke who is not interested in the past. Luke who has a ravishingly beautiful girlfriend he gets all gussied up for. Sigh.

So, now I'll take time to smell the roses, so to speak, and let Sweet Afton lull me to repose.

Chapter Fourteen

I awoke in the dark to find myself fully clothed and curled against the old headboard. My computer lay open in my lap. A storm lashed its fury outside my doors. Everything is larger than life here, was my first thought. The grass is greener. The trees taller. The storms fiercer. Feeling a chill in spite of my layer of clothing, I pulled the covers up under my chin. The room was more than dark and I knew the electricity had failed again. Ever thoughtful, Miss Emma had placed a fresh candle in the holder. I planned with the next flash of lightning to run to the dresser and light it, for comfort, if nothing else. Just then, the sky exploded and I leaped from bed, half out of fright, to grope for the matches and light the candle.

So, so quiet. Dark and quiet. Another whiplash of thunder shattered the silence, so startling that I almost dropped the lighted candle. At that moment, the music started. There were no lyrics, but the gentle, mournfully flowing rhythm was tangible enough to reach out and grasp in my fingers. Lilting tones filled the space around me until I was dizzy with the swirling notes.

As suddenly as it began, the music stopped. Bewildered, I held out the candle as though it might illuminate the melody I had heard so clearly only moments ago. Except for the dying sputter of the storm, all was quiet again. My ears strained, listening. Faintly, yet distinctly, I heard the tune again, this time in the hall outside my closed bedroom door. Barefoot, holding the candlestick in front of me, I moved slowly to the door, drew the latch, and, without thinking, only feeling the music, I followed the mellow strains, like a child of Hamlin behind the Pied Piper. Descending the steep steps, on the first floor, now, I continued to follow the path of the music, through the dining room, to the keeping room and out a door I had never used or even noticed before,

I halted, shook my head, trying to clear out the hypnotic tones that crowded out all thought and plugged my senses. Once again, the music abated. It was like a game of musical chairs. Where was I? No longer in the house, I felt the damp night air on my bare arms, and rough floorboards beneath my bare feet. Holding the candle at arm's length, I crept forward, a step at a time, my other hand grasping at the air in front. I felt like a blind person without a guide dog.

My reaching fingers brushed across a grainy surface, and crumbling powder dusted my fingertips. Instantly, I recognized the metallic smell of rusting screens. I knew then I must be on the ancient screened porch tucked between the wings of the house, the crumbling porch with the antique rocking chairs. The ancient part of the house, reached only by the door in the keeping room. The music had led me here. Again the strains wafted over and around me, holding me captive as I stood, shivering, gazing at the dim light of my flickering candle.

The music stopped as abruptly as it had begun. Struggling to clear the cobwebs of sound spinning in my brain, I took a deep breath and looked around. I sensed, rather than saw a movement in my periphery. When I turned, I became aware of one of the rocking chairs. Gently, so as to be barely perceptible, the chair rocked itself back and forth as though someone invisible sat in it, enjoying the languorous, rhythmic motion. Rocking, rocking, rocking, without any sound at all.

Not conscious of moving, I found myself standing beside the ancient rocker, now motionless, dusty, the seat sagging within inches of the floor, as though it had not moved in a hundred years. I had not dreamed it. The chair had rocked itself, and someone or something had led me here to witness it. Led me with the music. I had the evidence. On the decaying cane seat lay a single fresh rose just out of the bud.

****

My feet were like blocks of ice. How long had I stood on the moldering porch with the rose in my hand? Though it must have been well after midnight, a light burned in the office adjacent to the stables. Was someone up at this time of night? Or had the light been accidentally left on? Retracing my steps through the keeping room, I let myself out the back door to the stables. Though the storm was over, the skies were heavy and dark and the stone path stabbed at my bare feet, but I pressed on.

Nearing my destination, I became more wary. All the talk about Night Riders and my encounter with, well, with what? A ghost in a rocking chair? What did I think I was doing running around outside in the middle of the night? Fear prickled at the nape of my neck, but I stumbled on. Arriving at the opened door of the office, I saw Luke bent over a book. My gentle tapping on the door frame caused him to jump and whirl around, standing up so swiftly that he knocked his book from the desk. It thudded to the floor.

"It's just me," I whispered. "Ashby." I don't know why I was whispering. It seemed somehow appropriate in the depths of night.

"You scared the... With the Night Riders on the loose! What the hell are *you* doin' out here anyway," Luke growled and shouted all at the same time. I'm sure I'd scared him, but he did his best to hide it. He leaned over to scoop the book from the floor and place it on the desk.

"I told your uncle I'd watch out for the Night Riders." Calming down, he shrugged. "Guess I wasn't doin' a very good job of it."

I craned my neck to see what he'd been reading, but Luke had placed the book face down.

"What're ya lookin' at?" His voice was testy.

"Just wondering what you were so absorbed in."

"Mighty nosy."

"I'm a big reader. I'm always curious about what people are reading. I like historical romances myself, and gothics," I said, realizing I was on the defensive with Luke once again and babbling like an idiot.

"Well, y'caught me." Luke moved out of my way and allowed me to turn the book over. "But there's nothin' romantic about calculus."

"Calculus? You're reading a calculus book out here in the middle of the night?"

"You might say I'm fallin' asleep over a calculus book." His tone was rueful.

"What? You have a secret yen for higher math?"

He gave a short laugh. "The secret is that I've been

goin' to college th' last three years. Community college. I had class tonight, in fact. If I can get through this calculus course, I'll have my associate's degree by th' end of summer."

I stood there, blinking. "So, that's where you drive off to? To college?"

"Don't tell anybody, okay? My Aunt Emma is th' only one who knows. In fact, she's th' one who encouraged me t' try. T' keep at it. If Abe finds out, he'll get all upset and worry that I'll leave and never come back t' work 'our land,' as he calls it." He drummed his fingers on the desk. "I've already applied t' Virginia Tech." He looked at me a little quizzically. "An' I've been accepted. I plan t' begin as a junior this comin' fall semester. Pre-med. I'd like t' get into th' veterinary medicine program there. Maybe practice as a farm vet."

"Well, *duh*!" I smacked my forehead. "You're a natural, Luke. I mean, you're absolutely fantastic with horses, and you know so much about them."

"There's a lot more t' learn, b'lieve me. I've taken every math an' science course offered at community college. Problem is, Tech's too far away t' commute, so I'd have t' live on campus, maybe come home an' help out on weekends. But I haven't figgered out how t' tell Abe, yet. He's kinda frail. I don't wanna upset him."

It was then that Luke noticed the rose in my hand. "What's that?"

I hesitated, trying to set the right tone. "Luke, I need to talk to Abe again. To find out more about the ghost. My grandmother had a ghost friend. Rosabelle." I watched his jaw tighten. "I have to know. Can't you understand?"

He began that maddening tapping on his desk again. "Look, Abe's got a weak heart. He's already had one attack that almost killed him. And after y'left our house that day we found the dead wolf dog? He spent the rest of the day lost in the past, goin' over and over that damn scrapbook. Totally tuned out. I jes' hate seein' him like that."

"But things have happened. Unexplainable things. I'm scared, Luke."

Luke exhaled loudly. "Maybe it's only your imagination. Imaginations can run wild in a place like this. Crazy, romantic notions an' all."

"Imagination? Romantic? Well, what do you say to a vase of rosebuds on my balcony thirty feet in the air and rose petals left beside a murdered wolf-dog. Then there's a song, 'Flow gently, sweet Afton, amang thy green braes.' It wakes me up in the middle of the night and leads me places." I waved the rose in his face. "Why do you think I'm here now? I was led out of my room to the old porch, where I saw a rocking chair. And I do mean rocking chair. Rocking itself. That's where I found this," I waved the rose again. "It was just lying there in the chair."

"So?"

"Is that all you can say—so?"

"So, have y'been hurt? Robbed? Is someone out t' get you?"

Tossing the rose onto his desk, I looked at him, temporarily at a loss for words. When I spoke again, I tried to be rational. "When I'm in the middle of an episode, I'm not afraid. I mean, I don't feel any sense of danger. It's more like being in a trance, or hypnotized, or something. I feel like I'm in savasana."

Luke looked blank.

"Sorry. Savasana is the final pose for a yoga session. You lie so still and relaxed that you almost float off the mat, but you're still aware of your surroundings."

Luke tilted his head. "Okay. I'm listening."

"But when it's over—I mean the Rosabelle thing, not yoga, that's when I realize how creepy it all is. How do I know if someone is out to get me, as you put it? For all I know, somebody might want to kill me."

"I can't expect you t' understand. You're an outsider. You're new here. You have no idea what it's like t' live with these ridiculous old memories day in an' day out."

"So, does that make me a Yankee? Or a damn Yankee?" I asked without trying to hide the hurt in my voice.

"Hey, look, I'm sorry about callin' you an outsider. Hell, you're a member of th' family. I'm th' outsider here from that point of view, I s'pose. Believe whatever y'want. Just leave Abe out of it. Promise, Ashby? Can y'promise t' leave Abe be? No more talk about the past?" He reached for my hand.

I knew he was railroading me, but there was no stifling my automatic response. His deliberate reaching out, the gentle pleading of his voice. And, I realized with a jolt, it was the first time he had ever called me by name. I felt myself melting.

"C'mon. I'll walk y'home." He still held my hand.

"Uh…" I looked down at my bare feet. "Got an extra pair of shoes I could use? Size seven, narrow?"

"No problem." He swept me off the floor. "Put yer arms aroun' my neck." And that was how he carried me all the way to the back door, as if I weighed no more than a doll. Lowering my feet to the ground, without releasing his hold, he pulled me into a close embrace. I could feel his heart beating hard against my chest as he held me to him. Then, he bent his head, and his lips, warm and full, met mine, pressing, firm and sweet, to my own ready response. We stood there in the summer night, held in a kiss that neither of us wanted to end.

After a long time, we pulled apart only enough to lock gazes. "You're beautiful, Ashby. Do y'know that? I've been wantin' t' kiss you for a long time."

"Oh, Luke. I was beginning to think I would forever have to adore you from afar." I had to smile and add, "I read that line in one of my romance books."

We both laughed, but gently, so as not to destroy the beauty of the moment. Then he leaned in for another long, long kiss.

"I'd better go in," I said, when I could catch my breath. In my heart I knew, had he suggested it, I would have stayed there with Luke until the sun came up.

"This was a nice break from calc," he laughed. "Let's do this again."

As I turned to go, I couldn't resist a playful question. "Does this mean there is no phantom girlfriend?"

Though he appeared to consider my question seriously, when he answered, the lightness of his tone matched mine. "Any phantom girlfriend would have t' be a phantom of your romantic mind. Ashby."

Only later, back in my room and reliving the moment, did I realize I could take his comment more than one way. At least, he had not said "*another* phantom of your romantic mind."

Chapter Fifteen

"What's that? Did you see that, Ashby?" Jeff reined in Sunshine and listened.

I brought Sasha alongside. "What's what?"

Sasha's ears flickered and he stamped, impatient to get on with his run.

"Dunno. Nothing, maybe. I thought I saw something moving in those trees over there." He pointed. "Let's walk the horses over."

We had gone only about twenty feet off the trail when there was a sudden crackling of underbrush and a man emerged from behind a big oak not six feet in front of us. Startled, I drew back on Sasha's bridle.

"Well, hey," the man said in a deep drawl. "What's this?"

He was not much older than me, with light hair and rough skin. He wore a faded red work shirt and jeans. His teeth looked like a broken zipper.

"What're you doing here, Eddie?" Jeff asked, with an edge I had never before heard in his young voice. He urged Sunshine closer to the guy. Without notice, the fellow reached for Sunshine's bridle, pulling horse and boy within inches of his pitted face.

"Stop it, Eddie. What d'ya think you're doing?" Jeff struggled to pull Sunshine away.

"Th' question is, what're *you* doin' here? Yer on Mills' prop'ty, Tadpole."

"Who says?" Jeff demanded with surprising pluck. "This is our woods, Eddie. You better get lost before Luke finds out you're trespassing again."

The man scoffed at Jeff and leered at me. "Who's yer purty friend, Tadpole?" The twist of tobacco that bulged in his cheek muddled his already slurred syllables, and I had to practically read his lips to understand him. He moved to block my way.

My heart rapped a wild rhythm in my chest. I should be the one to stand up to this bully, not my little cousin. "Look," I said, with all the force I could muster. "Look, Eddie. We aren't bothering you. Let my cousin alone, okay? Just let him go."

"Oh, so yer the Tadpole's cousin, eh?" His lips sneered into an ugly line. "Well, well. If yer who I think y'are, that makes me and you cousins, too. Did y'know that? Marian's father an' mine was brothers. We're kissin' cousins, I'd say." He flashed his gruesome teeth.

Evidently pleased with himself, Eddie momentarily relaxed his grip on Sunshine's bridle, prompting me to call out, "Go, Jeff! Quick! Get Luke!" With a hard tug on the reins, Jeff turned and bolted back down the trail. Oh, God, I thought in distraction. One of the house rules—never ride the trail alone—what if he hurts himself? Uncle Hunter will never forgive me.

But I turned again to the intruder, this time with fierce purpose. "Do you get your kicks bullying little kids, Eddie Mills? Is that your idea of fun?"

"Aw-w, y'didn't have t' send th' tadpole off," Eddie groused. "I wasn't gonna hurt 'im. An' I ain't aimin' t' hurt you, neither." His bravado gone, Eddie was all sulk and whine.

He kept turning to look nervously back at the trail

Jeff had taken, watching out for Luke's arrival.

He returned his attention to me, holding Sasha at bay. "I seen y'before, and I knowed who you was. Yer the one Wolf scared." Eddie's colorless eyes squinted. "It was a accident. He got loose is all. He wouldn't hurt ya'. I was right on his heels. I saw y'faint, jest before I grabbed Wolf an' hauled him off home." He looked down at the ground and scuffed his boot in the underbrush. "They won't no need to kill Wolf." A look of real pain twisted his features. "Don't talk about bullyin' when your own uncle went an' killed my Wolf."

I was completely nonplussed. "My uncle did not kill your dog," I said with heat. "When he found him on the dock, the animal was already dead."

"You say. I heared that story, too. But I know a thing or two 'bout Hunter Overton." Eddie Mills locked eyes with me. "Killin's nothin' new t' him. He killed yer mother and father, y'know."

I was blown away. What was he saying? It was outrageous.

"I figgered y'wouldn't know nothin' about it. Th' Overtons is good about hidin' all th' skeletons in they closets. There won't never no charges or nothin', a' course, since they's rich an' got th' money to pay off all th' cops an' lawyers an' judges an' sech." He spat. "Jes' like they done when they stole our prop'ty."

"Listen, Eddie. What you're saying is impossible. My parents died in a car accident."

"It was a icy night an' it was Hunter put in a call to Marian and Wash to come quick becuz Ol' Man Thomas was a dyin'.' Hunter, he knowed how fast his brother liked t' drive and he reckoned on them crashin' on the curvy, icy road." Eddie paused before his punch line. "With his brother out the way, Hunter would stand t' inherit the whole shebang. House, grounds, horses, an' th' money." Crossing his arms, he glared at me, defying me to deny his story.

"No way could my uncle possibly predict such a wreck. It was an accident. That's all. A terrible accident."

"Don't y'see? That's the point. Old Thomas Overton wasn't dyin' that night. Why, he lived on near a year afterwards. I'm tellin' ya', ma'am. Yer uncle was makin' damn sure to inherit everything."

"How do you know Hunter was the one who called my parents that night, Eddie?"

Eddie's smirk creased his pocked cheeks. "Well, y'see, Marian and Wash was goin' to a party that night. They left you with a baby sitter."

"So what?"

"It jest so happens, my mother was the baby sitter. She took th' call from Hunter that night. The minute Marian an' Wash come in from the party, why, she sent 'em on their way to Overhome. Said to hurry becuz Wash's father was a dyin.' Hunter said so." He leaned against a tree and spit a stream of brown tobacco juice into the brush. "Wash was speedin', and he'd had a drink or two at the party. His car never made the curve before the driveway. They was both killed instantly. Jest like Hunter planned it."

In the distance I heard the sound of horses, and I knew Jeff was returning with Luke. Eddie heard it, too, for he turned tail to run back into the woods. But, he could not resist a parting shot. "Jest don't fergit. Yer only half Overton. Other half's Mills." He took off at a trot, disappearing between the trees.

I went to meet Jeff and Luke. One look at Luke was enough to make me laugh. He was riding Donnie, the gaited pinto pony who was up in years and ornery as Lucifer himself. Donnie's favorite trick was to run his rider under low-slung branches in hopes of knocking him off. Luke rode bareback, his long legs trailing the ground.

"Donnie was the closest horse at the time," he explained. "Y'don't mess around with Eddie Mills. I'm goin' after him."

I put a hand on Luke's arm. "No, Luke. Don't. He tried to bully Jeff and he told me a whacked-out story I refuse to believe. Leave it alone. It's done and he's gone."

"He didn't hurt anybody," Jeff piped up. "If you go after him, Dad might find out you sent me riding back alone. Then we wouldn't be allowed to ride any more…" Jeff blinked nervously. "Don't tell Dad, Luke. Okay?"

Jeff turned his big blues on me. "You, too, Ashby. Promise you won't tell Dad? He'll never let me and you ride together again!"

Luke was first to give in. "Oh, I guess we can keep it b'tween the three of us. It's just that I don't like Eddie thinkin' he can bully you an' trespass on Overton property actin' like it's his."

"Ashby?" Jeff looked at me pleadingly. "You won't tell Dad?"

"I don't know, Jeff. Your dad entrusted you to me. If I don't tell him and he finds out…"

"We'll tell him later, then," Jeff exploded. "Just don't tell him now. Okay, Ashby? Pul-eeze?" Tears gathered at the corners of his eyes.

This was about more than Jeff's longing to ride with me. He looked truly frightened at the prospect of his father's finding out we'd broken the rules—allowed Jeff to ride alone—even if for an emergency. This realization and Jeff's persistence wore me down. "All right, already. For now."

We had reached the bridge, where Jeff moved ahead to allow Luke and me to follow single-file. Letting my cousin ride ahead a bit, Luke moved astride Sasha and took the opportunity to ask guardedly, "Eddie didn't try to hit on ya', did he Ashby?"

"He spent the whole time telling me about…about the axe he has to grind with my uncle. Know what I mean?"

"'Fraid so." He reached for my hand and gave it a squeeze.

At the stables, Luke left us and Jeff and I led the horses to the ring. It was then I noticed a strange car at the crest of the drive, a sleek green Jaguar and a smartly-dressed, distinguished-looking man who stepped from the driver's side. Waving, he approached the riding ring. "Hello! Fine day for riding."

I looked to Jeff to supply an identity. "It's Dad's lawyer. I forget his name." He shrugged.

"Hello," the man said again as he approached. "I'm Fred Taylor." He hung over the fence. "You're making me wish I wore my jodhpurs. I used to do quite a lot of riding myself, right here at Overhome. Hunter and I spent hours trailing these woods when we were not much older than young Jeff, there. You must be Ashby, down from Jersey." His smile was dazzling.

Leading Sasha, I moved toward the fence. "Nice to

meet you, Mr. Taylor."

"On my way back from town, I decided to stop and save Hunter a trip to my office."

I must have looked blank, for he smiled again and said, "Matters of estate, my dear." He looked fondly at the horses. "Now, much as my heart is here, I'd best get on with my work. Is your uncle home?"

"I have no idea, Mr. Taylor," I said. "If you'll go up to the house, I'm sure Miss Coleville can tell you."

Just then Abe appeared at the stable door. "Who's that?" he rasped. "Who's here?" His eyebrows knitted a line over his nose.

"It's Dad's lawyer, Abe," Jeff told him.

Abe looked ready to blow the man's head off. "Hrrumph. Whatta y'want?"

The lawyer tried to calm the old man. "Just looking for Hunter, Abe."

"I'll take you to the house, Mr. Taylor," Jeff offered unexpectedly. "Ashby, will you stable Sunshine for me?" When I nodded, Jeff scrambled over the fence, leading the way to the house.

Abe watched them disappear. "Hrrumph!" he snorted again. "Never could abide that struttin' turkey."

"Why? Mr. Taylor seems nice enough to me."

"Becuz. It's Fred Taylor that's give Hunter Overton a bad name around here. If y'ask me."

"My uncle has a bad name?"

"Him and Taylor, haulin' all over the countryside buyin' up distress land, makin' surveys and subdividin' property, and foreclosin' on mortgages. Folks don't like that, y'know? Land's what it's all about. Don't nobody take kindly to sellin' out under stress." He shook his head. "I know it's none a' my bizness, but people talk.

'Young Hunter is turnin' out jest like his ol' man,' they says. 'Jest like old Thomas Overton, robbin' the poor to serve the rich.'" With a look of disgust, he continued. "Why, Luke told me 'bout Lawyer Taylor always wantin' to check the account books. Luke says the guy has a lotta nerve pokin' his head in where it's not needed." He frowned. "Fred's a lot like his father, Bill. Bill Taylor was Thomas's lawyer. I didn't care fer him, neither." He snorted again. "Like father, like son, so they says."

He wandered off, muttering under his breath, but, as I wiped down the horses, I was left with new impressions of my uncle. First Eddie Mills, then Abe. Two totally different people coming from completely different angles, and both arrived at a singular conclusion—Hunter Overton, Villain. It seemed Uncle Hunter had a dual personality. He had been nothing but kind and polite to me, helpful, nice as could be. Should I trust my own impressions, or should I believe what I had heard today? I would have to think about it. It was definitely a matter for my diary.

****

Dear Diary,

This is the most unpredictable place imaginable. Just when I think I know someone, my whole perspective changes. Monica, Hunter, and Luke. My first impressions were so totally false about each and every one. And I always prided myself on being an excellent judge of character! My aunt seems so poised, so perfectly in control, interested only in the social and the superficial, yet she's filled with insecurity, with fears and desires for her husband and son, and thinks I am a savior and a role model. My uncle appears to be the quintessential country gentleman, but he has a "Robbing Hood" reputation among the locals. And Eddie Mills calls him a murderer. Ah, then there is Luke. Luke, the redneck hick with the charismatic smile, is, in actuality, a pre-veterinary-med college student champing at the bit to move on with his life and get away from Overhome. Jeez! Where does this all leave me? Here, I've been dreaming up the settings and themes for my first book, and it's all based on totally false characters. Reminds me of a play we studied in a college lit course. I'd have to call my romance "Three Quirky Characters in Search of a Novel."

Sigh. In spite of my best intentions and efforts, I still know next to nothing about my roots. And, at the end of every day, I have to ask myself, do I really believe in ghosts? Who, or what, is Rosabelle? Will I ever find the answers?

For the record, Diary, though I've been kissed many times in my life, never have I encountered the likes of Luke Murley. The warmth, the passion, the desire he stirs up is downright scary. I like to think of myself as a woman who knows her own mind and body and who maintains absolute control of both. Now, I am not so sure. Maybe it has something to do with those damn roses.

Not a bit sleepy, and still enveloped in a cloud of romance, I decided to pull out my parents' love letters, which I had hidden inside a small box deep between the bed springs and mattress. So well hidden were they that it took me a good five minutes to locate and extricate them, reaching blindly within the guts of the old bed. With a decisive yank, I finally retrieved the packet. Changing my radio station from country to my favorite light rock, I sat on my bed, poring over page after page of Washington's letters to Marian, wondering all the while how she might have answered them.

I paused over one dated in May, then went back to re-read a paragraph. "I'm going to be a father! What perfect timing for us! I graduate in two weeks and then we can have the lovely wedding we've been planning for so long. So what if the baby is a tad 'premature?' I tip my glass to Spring Break. It was as productive as it was refreshing, huh? Growing up with two brothers makes me hope for a sweet little girl, but anything we team up on is bound to be the greatest! Our baby! I am proud and excited and happy all at once and I love you more than ever, if that's possible."

So I was 'premature' as they referred to it in the Victorian era. Marian in her one-entry diary had mentioned Thomas Overton's insinuation that the child she carried might not be Washington's. I suppose my surly old grandfather wanted to believe the worst, that Marian, or the Mills family, had manipulated the Overtons into a "shotgun wedding." Certainly, I had never considered such a possibility, but for some reason, the fact that I was conceived before my parents married didn't matter at all. Perhaps because it was clear my father's own reaction was completely positive. Carefully, I replaced the letters in their envelopes, tied the pink ribbon in place, and returned the packet to its hiding place. I slipped into bed, thinking about the love my mother and father so obviously felt, for one another, and for me. I drifted off, wondering if love and hate exist side by side in every family, as they seem to in mine.

****

The dream was very real. "Rosabelle," I spoke into the oval mirror above the old dresser. "Rosabelle, if you're here, give me a sign. Please. A sign, Rosabelle." I barely breathed, looking, listening, for what I did not know. I was not surprised when the notes of the song began, falling like pebbles into a brook. "Flow gently, sweet Afton, amang thy green braes."

My eyes fixed on the reflection shifting in the pitted glass of the mirror. It was not a face, but a form—white, gray, black. It swirled and mixed, steadying at last so that I recognized a woman's features. She wore an old-fashioned white cap. A high, white collar encircled her throat. Where her eyes would have been, two black hollows looked out blindly from a gray face.

"Rosabelle." I was whispering now. "Whatever you want from me, whatever you have for me, I'm ready. I'm here. It's me, Ashby. I feel your presence. I know you're here."

Slowly, the impression faded from the mirror until I saw only my own wide-eyed face, pale as death, looking back at me. I strained my ears, listening for the music, but it had disappeared along with the ghostly image. I felt no fear, not of roses or songs or signs. Here, in this room, I knew I was safe. Protected. Watched over by someone who had returned from a long-ago time.

The visions and images, the feelings, were still fresh in my mind when I awoke next morning. As the sun glanced through the French doors, I took a few moments to relive the dream and what it might mean, if anything. Stretching wide, my fingers touched something tucked under my pillow, something crisp and light. It was a single sheet of paper, parchment paper, almost transparent with age.

Hand-lettered in fading ink and written in a graceful, old-fashioned script was a poem.

MY LUVE IS LIKE A RED, RED ROSE
By Robert Burns

My Luve is like a red, red rose,
That's newly sprung in June;
My Luve is like the melodie,
That's sweetly play'd in tune.

~~~

As fair art thou, my bonnie lass,
So deep in luve am I;
And I will luve thee still, my Dear
Til a' the seas gang dry.

~~~

Til a' the seas gang dry, my Dear,
And the rocks melt wi' the sun;
And I will luve thee still, my Dear,
While the sands o' life shall run.

~~~

And fare-thee-weel, my only Luve!
And fare-thee-weel a while!
And I will come again, my Luve,
Though 'twere ten thousand mile!

A simple poem, but I read it over and over. Robert Burns, a famous Scottish poet from the distant past. If I remembered my Brit Lit, he had lived in the eighteenth century. Robert Burns who also wrote the song "Flow Gently, Sweet Afton." Burns, a poet from the Romantic Era, his theme—love. Love is red roses, melodies, and that which endures forever. It was hyperbole for sure. Love lasts until all the seas go dry and the rocks melt with the sun and the sands of life itself run out. But it was the last two lines that held me… "And I will come again, my Luve, Though 'twere ten thousand mile."

For a long time I sat, propped on my pillows, reading and re-reading the page, until I had memorized the entire poem. The message was crystal clear—love does not die with death, and the one who loves enough will come back, no matter the distance. I knew then what I had suspected all along without being able to put my finger on it—the warmth, the protective feelings, the flow of the music—they were evidence of a deep and abiding love. But why had I been chosen for this devotion?

Dreamily, I lay back against the headboard, knowing without question that the two were connected, the dream and the poem. When, at last, I reached to turn on my radio, I was not surprised to hear the twang of a country hoedown.

Chapter Sixteen

"Bonus! An afternoon off, Luke!" I was shouting into the wind. Luke maneuvered the wheel of my uncle's ski boat as we skimmed the shining surface of Moore Mountain Lake. Luke had been teaching me how to drive the boat and we had just switched places. Piloting a boat, I decided, is much like driving a muscle car equipped with power steering and a quick throttle, but no brake. Also, there were no lines on the water way for direction—just channel markers to follow. Oh, and it's important to learn who has the right-of-way. Jeff sprawled over the bow seats, his hair slicked back with the breeze, his face tilted to the sun.

"Your uncle insisted I deserved some time off. Must've thought it was important, 'cuz he himself helped me all morning. Said he wanted us t' take Jeff out in th' boat while he an' your aunt play in some golf tournament. Or was it tennis?" He slung an arm over my shoulder. "Whatever. I'm just happy t' be here knowin' we can ski as long as we like."

"Oh my God. Now you'll see how klutzy I am. But learning to drive the boat, how sweet is that?" Closing my eyes, I threw back my head, enjoying the massage of sun and wind and water. John Denver's old song ran through my mind. "You fill up my senses…" Luke, muscular and fit in his swim suit, the earthy fragrance of soap and sweat radiating from his skin, the sun-streaks in his flying hair—it was a regular banquet for my senses.

"Here we are! Best ski cove on th' lake," Luke slowed, then cut the motor. Not another boat or PWC in sight. "Flat 'n shiny as a mirror. Get out th' ski rope 'n gloves, Jeff." Luke moved toward the stern to retrieve the skis from the locker. He looked back at us. "You wanna go first?"

Jeff hopped to his tasks, easily looping the rope over a chrome pylon that stuck up from the mid-section of the craft. "Can I wakeboard?"

"Sure." Luke slid the board over the side as Jeff stepped from the stern to the teak swim platform and then leaped into the water. "Okay! Throw me the rope!"

Winding the multi-colored rope like a lasso, Luke sent it sailing toward Jeff, who grasped the handle and held it high for Luke to see. "Got it!" He maneuvered the rope until it was taut and then yelled, "Hit it!"

From my position in the spotter's seat, I watched, awed, as my young cousin glided from side to side, skimming the wake and landing with a light plop, only to switch directions and fly over the water again in the opposite direction.

"Was he born on a wakeboard?" I asked Luke, who was also keeping an eye on Jeff in his rear-view mirror.

"Looks like it!" Luke laughed. "Actually, th' kids start out on a knee board or a bob-sked or somethin' more stable 'til they get used t' bein' behind a big boat. From there they move up to skis and wakeboard. I'd say Jeff's been doin' both since he was about five."

His ride ended, Jeff waited for Luke to circle back to get him. I helped him bring in the board, then handed him a towel. "Amazing run, Jeff," I said. We high-fived each other.

Jeff shook his hair dry. "Luke taught me. I'm the only one at camp who can do tricks on the board. You should see Luke do a 360."

Luke shrugged like it was no big deal, then looked at me. "You next, Ashby?"

I felt a flutter of butterflies. "Umm…how about you go first, Luke? Trust me to drive for you?"

"There's nothin' to pullin' a skier. Jeff's your spotter. I'll let him know when I'm ready t' get up and when I wanna drop, an' he'll tell you. Jeff knows all th' signals, but y'can also watch me in your mirror. Thumb up means go faster, down means slower. Cut th' throat," he demonstrated, "means I'm droppin'." Pulling on his gloves and tightening his life vest, Luke grabbed a long slalom ski from the locker. "Just remember what y'learned in our drivin' lesson. We'll do fine."

I nodded, hoping not to show how nervous I really was. The cove offered a long straight-away and, being mid-week, there were no other boats to maneuver around. It was as good a time as any for me to pull a skier. Besides, I wanted to see Luke in action.

"Once I'm up, run me at about 4000 RPMs. Jeff'll let y'know if y'need to adjust th' speed." I watched Luke ready himself, pulling on gloves, adjusting his life jacket before he tossed his ski overboard and jumped in.

"Hit it!" Luke yelled. Taking a deep breath, I pushed as smoothly as I could on the throttle, accelerating gradually and feeling the weight of his body pull against the boat as he muscled his way to the surface.

Jeff turned to me from his spotter position. "A little

bit faster."

"Okay. Here goes." Nudging the throttle up a notch, I took a quick glance in the mirror, catching Luke's nod that meant the speed was right for him. I am sure I bit my tongue as I concentrated on the speedometer, trying to keep the RPMs steady, while steering as straight a line as possible. As we neared the curve of the cove, I signaled a left turn, remembering to maintain the throttle through the natural slow-down of the turning boat. Once settled on the back-swing straight-away, I relaxed enough to get a good look at Luke in the mirror.

I had never been up-close-and-personal to such powerful slalom skiing. Luke swept in an enormous arc across the wake and out into the smooth water on either side of the boat—back and forth—with hardly a ripple—leaning into the angle of the turn until his extended body stretched out only inches from the surface.

"Awesome!" Jeff exclaimed, with such animation, I swear his freckles jiggled all over his nose. Carved up by Luke's ski, an enormous spout of lake water sparkled in the sun. It looked like a waterfall of a thousand prisms. "Look at that rooster tail!" Jeff crowed.

I maneuvered another left-hand turn and straight-away and another before Luke gave the drop sign. Circling back, I could only grin and wag my head. "Wow!"

"I'm outta practice," Luke said, shaking droplets from his hair.

"Oh, get real," I replied. "You were amazing."

"An' I'm outta breath." Then he grinned. "Great

pull, Ashby. Now it's your turn. A slalom ski?"

"Hey, I only just learned to ski on a pair, you know." I sputtered, hemming and hawing, but Luke paid no attention to me.

He rummaged in the locker, eventually extricating a smaller ski for me. "This should do. How tall are y', anyway?"

"Five feet six inches." My voice of reason said I ought to tell Luke to forget it, but my racing pulse drowned it out.

Luke saw my hesitation. Giving me a quick hug, he said, "Hey, don't worry, you're gonna do great. Just keep your arms straight. Butt down. Skis up. Th' boat'll do the rest."

I guess he knew what he was talking about, because, after a half dozen tries, when my arms felt ready to fall off, I miraculously found myself standing on top of the ski, skimming the surface of the wake, unsteady, but upright, nonetheless. It was like latching onto a jet-propelled balance beam, an electrifying experience. I took a couple of long runs and made a few turns before I lost it and crashed into the water.

As I climbed back into the boat, Jeff gave me a high five and Luke said, "Ha! Told y'so. Way t'go!"

I felt like a conquering hero and had to admit the slalom ski is much more fun than a pair.

Hours later, as we drifted into the slip, with Jeff on the dock maneuvering the lift switches, Luke took the opportunity to pull me close and whisper in my ear. "Meet me here, on th' dock, t'night. Aroun' eleven. I'll be home from class by then. We'll take a night swim, sit on th' dock, an' look for shootin' stars."

"Shooting stars." I looked into his eyes. "All right."

****

With Luke off to his calculus class, Aunt Monica and Uncle Hunter at their club and Jeff attending a birthday party somewhere, I figured I'd have a good three hours to get back to the attic. I was determined to get into that footlocker where I was betting I'd find the Overton diaries.

Miss Emma was working in the kitchen. Grabbing a dish towel and drying some pots and pans on the counter, I ventured, "Uh, Miss Emma, could you unlock the attic for me one more time?"

She shot me a critical look from under her brows. "Curiosity got hold of you?" She reached for her clutch of keys hanging at her waist.

"While you've got those keys out, Miss Emma, uh, I don't suppose you could locate one to an old footlocker up there? In the closet in the attic?"

She didn't miss a beat. "You mean the footlocker full of family diaries?"

"I really would like to read whatever all those Overton women wrote. Living history, you know?"

"Unfortunately, Ashby, there is no key."

I blinked. "What do you mean, no key? If there's a lock, there has to be a key, right?"

"Once upon a time, I suppose there was a key, yes. Lenore and I used to pore over those diaries when we were young girls looking for adventure and romance in the attic. Somewhere along the line, the footlocker got locked up tight. I don't think I've ever seen the key."

"Then…how did you and my grandmother get into them in the first place? I mean, if they were locked and there was no key."

Miss Emma gave me one of her closed-in looks.

"Let's just say somebody unlocked them for us. Can we leave it at that?" She finished her task and then led me to the attic door, which she opened for me.

"Umm...Miss Emma, you wouldn't happen to have a dust mask, would you? It's really sneezy in the attic."

"I believe there's one in the mud room. Shall I get it for you?"

"Oh, yes. Please. That would be great." She disappeared from sight.

With the kitchen to myself, I rummaged through drawers, locating a couple of different sized screw drivers, a sharp steak knife, and a small meat hammer. These I bundled up in a plastic grocery bag, which I stuffed under my shirt.

Miss Emma returned and handed me the requested mask, watching me pull it over my mouth and nose. "Thanks, Miss Emma! Wish me luck!"

I sprinted up the attic stairs two at a time, jerking off the mask along the way. So, there is no key. Okay. Then, I'll just try to pick the lock, I thought, retracing my steps to the camouflaged closet, my bag of burglar's tools in hand. Slipping the smallest screw driver from the bag, I tried inserting the tool like a key, into the lock of the footlocker. No luck. It was too big to fit in the lock. "Maybe a hammer to break it open." I was talking out loud now. Tentatively I tapped at the lock with the hammer, not hard, more of a love tap. To my surprise, the lid cracked open a few inches, creaking on old hinges. Hello! What happened? That was easy.

Raising the metal lid wide, I took in volume after volume of leather-bound books, more than a dozen, overlapping one another like shingles on a roof. It was much as I had expected, the stored and preserved memoirs of a family prominent enough, or arrogant enough, to consider its own history a valuable archive.

What caused me to catch my breath in astonishment was something else entirely. Scattered over the proliferation of diaries was a handful of fresh red rose petals. I almost dropped the lid. Opening the footlocker had been easy all right. Way too easy. Someone else had already unlocked it for me, just like Miss Emma had said. Cupping the petals in my hand, I couldn't resist a sniff.

Gently laying the petals aside, I opened the covers of the books, one by one, to glance over the title pages and dates. Judging by the condition of the covers, it was evident that some were much older than others and there seemed to be no particular order to them. Had they lain scattered here since Miss Emma's childhood days? Had she and my Grandmother Lenore read them and then flung them back willy-nilly? Susan Hunt Overton - 1900 to 1920, read one. Margaret Overton Blair - 1821 to 1825, another. Carefully, I piled the volumes in chronological order. Where to begin? I checked my watch. I would have to get a move on. I set to my task.

Chapter Seventeen

I quickly discovered that, owing to the faded ink and cramped, flowery penmanship, anything predating the 1850's was all but illegible. Putting those diaries aside for when I had more time, I moved on to Susan Hunt Overton's early 1900's memoir.

The ice was cut from the millpond today and packed with straw in the icehouse. The children, Lenore and Frederick, particularly, relished jumping onto the straw pile. The thrill increases, it seems, as the level falls with use. I have warned them of the dangers of this activity, and they promise to cease, yet they always laugh when little wisps of straw turn up in the iced tea. "But, Mother," Lenore says, "you know that finding straw in the tea is good luck." Lenore is high-spirited and clever, both a delight and a challenge to her parents.

Lenore, my grandmother as a child. Fascinating. Flipping pages and scanning, I read on until something caught my eye.

The dining room candles were all ablaze tonight for our dinner party of a dozen. Roast venison and potatoes and fresh watercress from the stream pickt earlier in the day. Afterwards, some of the young people paired off and strolled to the gazebo. I could not help but notice that young Thomas Overton and our Lenore exchanged serious looks. Thomas is quite a distant cousin on my husband, Harry's side. I believe he and Lenore to be as far removed as fifth or sixth cousins, so there's no natural hindrance to a romance. However, I have my own reservations about his being a beau for our Lenore. He seems quite taken with himself and perhaps too willful for his own good. I must say our feisty Lenore stands up to him, but still, 'tis a worry.

The same long table in the dining room. The same candelabra. I could easily place myself at turn-of-the century Overhome, engaging in family gatherings, climbing the stairs to the catwalks in the oldest part of the house, strolling through the garden maze, carrying out love affairs at the gazebo. It was a romance novel just waiting to be written. Reluctantly putting Susan's diary aside, I reached further down into the pile and selected one diary after another, speed-reading and gathering historical moments in my mind without finding any mention of what I sought most, some mention, any mention, of Rosabelle.

With growing despair, I picked up a heavy diary whose title page read, "Written by Angelina Elisabeth Overton." The beginning date of December, 1861 revealed the young adult Angelina living through the turbulence of the Civil War.

All the men of the family, Father, three uncles on the Overton side and two of Mother's brothers, and others hereabouts have enlisted in the Confederate Army. Both of my brothers, Robert and Johbe, have joined Early's Brigade of the Virginia Infantry. They drill on the flat commons behind Henderson Store under command of Captain Board. Soon they will join up with Early himself. Only the women and the old men are left at Overhome to tend to crops and horses and property, along with the slaves, of course. We quilt and sew and preserve fruits and vegetables and pray constantly for our brave men to return home to us uninjured in body, mind, and spirit.

Our Christmas this year is a mix of joy and apprehension. Joy that our Confederate Nation proved victorious at Manassas and that President Jefferson Davis presides over our capital in Richmond. Joy that so far none of our own family have been killt or injured, but apprehensive that this war we thought we would win so quickly may persevere. President Lincoln seems determined to reverse secession and pull the Confederate states back into the Union. Too, a new Yankee general, Ulysses Grant, looks to be building strength to the west. I hear so often that our Cause will stand firm against the North because of our brilliant generals, Lee and Jackson, especially, but I also can sort fact from hope.

One year and many pages later, Angelina wrote,

Shall we ever again see the easy calm of life at Overhome? Though no one will admit it, we all know our brave Rebel stalwarts grow weary. Our reduced forces encourage invading Yankee soldiers to have their way with us. None of us could believe week before last with what braggadocio the Union troops mounted the steps to the porch and forced us to provide them meals while the Negro kitchen help looked on. And when they had glutted themselves with our precious rations, they invited the slaves to occupy our own seats at table while we served them! Both we and our slaves were mortified. The next time we saw the approach of the enemy, we fled to the slaves' cottages where they willingly hid us til 'twas safe to come out. We were gratified that not a single one of our slaves betrayed our sanctuary, though Lincoln's troops had arrived at our door with shouts of freedom for all of them.

As discomforting as the incident was, I shan't dismiss entirely the motives of those Yankee soldiers. It is common knowledge, the cruelty some of the plantation masters lay upon their slaves. Lulu, my personal slave, has related horrible stories of how she was treated before coming to Overhome. She was fed subsistence provisions, whipt and beaten, traded wantonly and separated from her own family. Why, she and the other slaves at her former master's manor were fed scarce more than scraps left over from the big house table.

I thank God that at Overhome, our slaves have freedom to gather what they need from the gardens. There is always milk for their children, and we would not conscience physically abusing a one of them. How unfortunate, I believe, that slavery has become so important to our economic survival. Even with the best of masters with the best of intentions, in my heart and mind I know slavery to be a cruel and inhumane practice. A growing number of us here in Virginia feel this. Indeed, it is rumored that General Lee himself strongly opposes slavery, yet, we are helpless to remedy the situation.

This Christmas our elders pretend good cheer, but underneath they harbor many fears for our future. Western Virginia is now solidly commanded by the North and we have only just heard news of less than a victory in Dranesville to our north. For Christmas dinner we managed a festive table bedecked with silver, crystal and linens which we have been able to hide from the marauders. And traditional foods—from stuffi goose to plum pudding—graced our table. But the absence of so many still at war cast a pall upon the season. Oh, that this war were over.

A Civil War Christmas recorded by an eye-witness. Talk about bringing history alive. The reality of slavery hit me full force. Slaves working for their masters— right here on the land, in the house. I flipped some pages and read on,

My faithful servant, Lulu, has finally succumbed to "the misery," as she called it. Without being able to pinpoint her age, I would surmise she lived into her sixties, a ripe old age for the kind of abuse she endured as a young slave, before Father purchased her and sent her up to the manor to be a house slave for the rest of her life. Here at Overhome our slaves are like family to us, though I doubt they would feel the same way about us.

For Lulu's funeral, her people carried out their own curious burial rituals; I know Lulu would have been pleased at how they sent her on her way back to Africa for a better life. Lulu explained it all to me. Burials are a time for celebration, a chance to return to the homeland, with the promise of freedom and the hope of achieving nobility there in afterlife. Death for our slaves is not just the end of life, but a gateway into another world. They take much pride in their burial traditions. So many fellow slaves from surrounding plantations, with singing and dancing and such vast quantities of food that we cannot fathom where it all comes from. Though not all plantation owners are so inclined, we at Overhome are more than willing to grant our darkies their grieving rituals. God knows they have little else in their bleak lives to celebrate. Is it not sad that the only way to freedom is through death?

And so, my dear Lulu was buried with her most prized possessions; a tiny ivory figurine brought over from Africa by her ancestors on a slave ship; a silver medallion stolen from a former master and sneaked away, hidden in a place so secret, she refused ever to reveal it; a lace doily passed down by her grandmother. How she managed to hold on to these treasures is a mystery to me. She rests now in the cemetery on our grounds, situated on an east-west axis, in the flower-bedecked pine coffin so lovingly placed in the earth by her friends.

Because of the expense, most of the slave graves lack named headstones. We Overtons have always provided headstones for our own slaves, though they are but rough stones compared to Overton family markers. Many plantation owners consider their slaves to be merely property; we know they are people. Yes! Flesh-and-blood people just like us. Legend has it that periwinkle will find its way to a slave's grave. I will check for it from time to time, perhaps coax it to grow strong on Lulu's grave, as thick as the Virginia creeper we deliberately plant to hide our own graves from Yankee marauders who will actually dig them up, looking for valuables.

How sorely I shall miss Lulu, not as a servant, but as a friend and confidante. In these perilous times, she was ever the first soul I sought out for comfortable conversation. I shall miss her soulful songs, her nimble seamstress fingers, her sage advice, her always pleasant temperament, and her undying faith in God.

May she find her way in the next life to the nobility she deserves.

What a terrible time my ancestors and their household lived through here at Overhome. It was fascinating to read about, but, it was not what I was looking for, so I read on, Volume II, Angeline Elisabeth Overton.

Christmas, 1863. The war is interminable. We won two Virginia battles, Fredericksburg and Chancellorsville, very impressive victories, both. However, my Uncle Chandler on Mother's side was killed, and Father has returned from the battle at Gettysburg with a disfiguring wound, a musket ball through his cheek bone. He plans to cover the scar with his still-thick beard, and to spend his time fashioning an oak spindle bed for him and Mother. He says he will never leave this bed for another as long as he lives.

Alas, our invasion of the North failed. Then, July 4th, Vicksburg fell. It is impossible to keep up a brave front here at home. Still, I managed to wear my finest dress, purchased from Paris before the war, as we went to Christmas dinner with the Chestnut family, or what is left of it, for they have suffered sore casualties among their kinfolk. We enjoyed the oyster soup, mutton and ham and wild partridges, and wines. I suspect they have been scrimping and hoarding for weeks in preparation for this holiday dinner. For one day, at least, we were able to pretend our lives would forever be blessed with the plenty and camaraderie of the past.

Remembering that the Civil War ended in the spring of 1865 and, by now completely engrossed in the saga, I continued turning pages of Angelina's diary, wondering how that last Christmas could have been celebrated.

December, 1864. All is lost. Sherman's march through Georgia delivered the state to Lincoln as a Christmas present and sounded the death knell of the Confederacy. We hadn't the heart, nor the resources, to celebrate our own holiday in any way, due to news that both of my brothers, Robert and Johbe, have perished and that at least one Overton uncle is sorely wounded and may never recover. How can we go on living, knowing that we will never again see Johbe and Robert, my dear, dear brothers, joking and roughhousing, and enjoying life amongst our beautiful mountains? It is too sad to dwell on.

All the younger slaves have bolted for the North where they hope to work as freemen. I wish them Godspeed. Only white-haired Micah and his wife Mary remain as hired help now. Father is helping them enlarge one of the outbuildings where they are welcome to live out their natural lives at Overhome. I cannot say I am sad to see the death of slavery. I only wish we had seen fit to take the moral stand and free our slaves long before Lincoln's Emancipation Proclamation. I shall go to my grave with that burden of guilt.

That was all Angelina wrote about the saddest Christmas of all. There were no more entries until several years had passed.

December, 1868 - I know now I shan't ever marry. So many of our loyal soldiers perished in the war that it has left precious few available men to choose from. And so I stay at Overhome, a spinster, as life passes. We had been looking for Father's silver cup since he returned, wounded. We had buried all the silver when the Yankees came and were able to dig up most of it afterwards, except for the silver cup, which eluded us. Today the cook found a dirty object which the hogs had rooted up in the field behind the smokehouse. When we cleaned it up, to our surprise, it was Father's cup! We sent it off to a silversmith in Williamsburg to be refurbished. That cup has been in the family since the Revolution, originally owned by George Washington and passed on to our family by his descendants.

I wanted to read every word, but I had to stay focused on my goal. I was about to put down Angelina's memoir, when something near the closing caught my eye.

So you see, I have my own guardian angel, Rosabelle, my friendly spirit. Mother told me about her shortly before she died. "Rosabelle, the nanny," Mother said. "She has been with Overton women for over half a century. She will care for you, watch out for your safety and be a protector for you as she was for me and those before us." How true! A lullaby. A perfect rose. A basket of ripe berries with a pitcher of cream when I awaken. How nice. How pleasant. I can forget I am a lonely spinster when Rosabelle is with me.

I read and re-read the short entry, hardly breathing at my discovery. The date was 1875. Such a long time ago, yet Rosabelle had appeared to Angelina and to other Overton women for almost a hundred years prior to that! There had to be more. Eagerly, I moved my eyes over the rest of the diary until they burned, looking for the elusive Rosabelle to be named—the same Rosabelle who hovered over my grandmother Lenore. The same Rosabelle I'd sensed from day one at Overhome. I was glad I'd developed the skill of scanning pages when I worked on the lit mag at school.

But no luck. I could find no more mention of Rosabelle.

Laying the diaries back in the locker, I wondered where Grandmother Lenore's diary could be. Lenore was so comfortable with her knowledge of Rosabelle that she freely talked about her with Miss Emma and Abe. Surely, then, Lenore would write about our ghost in her diaries. Either Lenore's writings had been lost, or they had been deliberately removed from the rest of the family diaries in the footlocker. I was betting on the latter.

I would need more time to rake over the other diaries for information about Rosabelle. Checking my watch, I was shocked to see the time. Though I had learned so much about life at old Overhome, my appetite for tidbits about Rosabelle had only been teased. I felt like Tantalus in Greek mythology, reaching to satisfy his hunger, only to find food and drink forever beyond his grasp. It was frustrating, to say the least. I replaced the diaries and closed the lid of the locker. I scooped up the wilting rose petals, planning to take them back to my room. Then I brightened, remembering my pledge to meet Luke at the dock, to watch the stars. I shut the closet door with a promise. "I'll be back."

****

"The Milky Way!" I exclaimed. "We don't see the Milky Way at home. There's too much air pollution, too many city lights." The sky was as bright as a diamond display in a jewelry store. Luke and I lay side-by-side, propped on the dock lounge chairs, which we had dragged from under the roof to the open sky of the gently rocking floater dock. Except for the plop of an occasional fish breaking the surface, the smooth, dark quiet of the lake at midnight went undisturbed.

"There's Venus," Luke pointed, "an' th' Big Dipper. See th' North Star?"

"Hmmm," I murmured. "This is awesome. Even without shooting stars."

"Y'don't actually see many shooters 'til August," Luke said. "But it was a good excuse t' get y'out here." He folded me in his arms then, burying his face in my hair.

"Like you needed an excuse." I turned my face up for his kiss.

Deftly maneuvering me onto his lounge chair, Luke pressed his body to mine until we lay together, our lips hungrily meeting, tasting, teasing, long into the star-point night. After many minutes, on impulse, I leaped up, doffing my clothes right down to my bikini and took a running dive off the dock. Laughing and flinging off his T-shirt, Luke followed. The night waters bathed us in a silky languor. We floated on our backs, our arms entwined, like the vines of water lotus, our eyes full of stars and our hearts full of love.

****

Dear Diary,

Oh, the thrill of star-gazing, the allure of night swimming! The wash of warm water, the tingle of cool air, the secrecy of starlight. My romance story is writing itself!

I admit, the swim was my idea. It was getting a little too hot and heavy there on the dock. Hey, I'm no Virgin Mary and I'm no stranger to hook-ups. It's just that, dammit! I want this to be right. Real. Special. Not just a summer fling. The way I feel about Luke is totally different from anything I've ever experienced before and I want to savor it, go at my own pace. My brain registers this, but logic tends to melt with passion. I know I am in love and I think Luke feels the same way about me. For sure, I have stars in my eyes.

Chapter Eighteen

It was probably inexperience. No way could I blame Sasha. We were trotting along the trail just fine, thank you, and next I thing I know I'm in an embarrassing heap on the ground. A branch caused my horse to shy, catching me in La-la Land, daydreaming about Luke's touch instead of paying attention to my riding. Off I went, grabbing for the saddle horn before I remembered I was riding English now.

Jeff looked like he didn't know whether to laugh or to offer sympathy. "Are you okay, Ashby? Should I get Luke?"

"I don't think I need Luke to rescue me this time, Jeff. Nothing is hurt except for my dignity." I gathered myself up, brushing leaves and sticks from my clothes.

"Luke likes to rescue people," Jeff said. "Especially you, Ashby."

"Oh yeah? Who says?"

"I saw you holding hands. I know what that means." He made a face that left me guessing whether he approved or disapproved of what he thought it meant.

As I stepped into the stirrup, and reached to steady myself, a sharp pain circled my left wrist with the bite of a handcuff, so penetrating that tears sprang into my eyes. "Dammit! What was that?"

Jeff looked disappointed. "Uh-oh."

"Sorry, Jeff. My bad. I shouldn't have said that in front of you."

"Dammit?" he scoffed. "That's nothing. My friends use worser words than that, like—"

"Okay, okay. I get it. Now I guess we'll have to go back."

"Like I said, 'uh-oh,'" Jeff sighed. "I guess we have to go home. The ride's over."

Nursing my wrist, biting my lip, and cursing silently, I led Sasha back to the stables. If I could make it to the house, put some ice on my wrist and avoid any hoopla over my injury, I might escape my aunt and uncle's scrutiny. No sense in making a big deal about a stupid fall. But no such luck. Wouldn't you know my uncle would be in the stables checking on one of the horses.

"Ashby fell off Sasha!" Jeff squealed before I could shush him. "She hurt her hand."

"Oh. Let me take a look," my uncle said. Gently, he examined my wrist. "Hmmm. Looks to be swelling." He moved searching fingers around my wrist, applying pressure. "Any pain here? How about here?"

"Ouch!" An electric shock ran up my arm all the way to my funny bone. Only there was nothing funny about it. "That hurt!"

"I'll give Dr. Ross a call."

"It's just a bump." I sniffed back tears.

"It could be broken. We'll let the doctor do the diagnosis." His look stopped me before I could protest. "I promised your mother and father we'd take care of you, Ashby, and that is that. No argument. Now, I'll give the doctor a call. Jefferson, you go with Ashby up to the house, and give Miss Emma the details, please.

She'll know what to do." With that, he reached for his cell phone, watching to make sure Jeff and I followed his orders.

"Dammit," Jeff said as soon as we were out of earshot of his father. "How're you gonna ride with a bum wrist?"

"I'm tougher than you think," I said. "Now, promise me you won't say that word again, please."

Miss Emma stretched me out on a chaise on the sun porch, applying a baggie of ice to the sore wrist and telling me over and over that everything was going to be all right. I was beginning to look at the porch as my personal infirmary, since I'd recuperated in this same spot after Eddie's wolf dog scared me senseless. Jeff danced all over the porch, literally bouncing off the walls, hopping first on one foot and then on another, until Miss Emma spoke to him in an exasperated voice, "Heavens, child. Settle down!"

"I'm bored!" Jeff said.

"Really, Jefferson," Aunt Monica's voice wafted her onto the porch. "Ashby cannot be expected to entertain you every minute. Now, go to your room and play."

Subdued, Jeff left, but I was sure I heard him mutter "dammit" under his breath.

I was pleasantly surprised when Dr. Ross informed me that I had suffered no more than a deep-bone bruise and a strained wrist. "It's going to turn black and then green and it will be quite tender to the touch. If it still pains you after a week, we'll take an x-ray to check for a hairline fracture, but I'm ninety-nine percent sure it's just a big, deep bruise." He wrapped it in an Ace bandage and told me to keep up the ice packs and take

Extra Strength Tylenol. "No using the wrist for a week."

Hearing the doctor's diagnosis, Monica gave a sigh of relief. "Hunter will be happy to hear this. He and I both feel you have bonded with Jeff so well this summer, and you have been such a marvelous addition to our little family here."

My cheeks heated at my aunt's praise, knowing in my heart it was undeserved. I wondered what she would think about how I'd bonded with Luke.

"Sorry. I seem to be accident prone," I said.

"Ashby, Independence Day is almost on us. We have the most wonderful way to celebrate July 4th here at the lake. We watch the fireworks off Marker's Point by boat. It is really quite spectacular. You will join us, won't you? Hunter and I insist." Her eyelashes flickered ever so briefly. "Of course, we will invite Luke, too."

So, my aunt, who spent precious little time at Overhome, had it all figured out just like Jeff. It was hard to keep a secret here. Hard, but not impossible. When it came to secrets, there was one biggie, Rosabelle. I made up my mind I wasn't leaving Overhome until I'd discovered everything there was to know, everything about Lenore and her three sons, the Overton brothers, and Rosabelle. Only then would I begin to know my own secret self. Who is Ashby Overton? Really?

****

My uncle occupied the captain's seat while my aunt perched daintily across from him, all decked out in white Capri pants, topped with a designer big shirt embossed with Old Glory. Her dangle earrings glinted ruby and sapphire. Luke and I made ourselves comfortable on the long stern cushion with Jeff between us. White-bright anchor lights from hundreds of bobbing boats illuminated the darkening skies. It was like a scene from Star Wars—a flotilla of spaceships hovering over the onyx surface of the lake. Patriotic music exploded in surround-sound from the CD players of boats and boom boxes everywhere. Bars of "God Bless America," mingled with "Dixie," and "The Battle Hymn of the Republic." Beside us a boat full of tanked-up frat-boy types belted out Lee Greenwood's "I'm Proud to be an American" with more gusto than tune.

We sipped icy drinks and snacked on chips and dip and fruit from a cooler. "Want to sing "Yankee Doodle" with me?" I asked. Jeff, preoccupied with all the festivities, ignored my comment, but Luke snorted.

"Long as 1 c'n wave my rebel flag at th' same time."

As the skies darkened, the fireworks display began, puncturing the sky with golden spikes of star-burst, which ricocheted off the lake in dazzling reflection, before dissolving to gold glitter-dust. "O-o-o-h! A-h-h-a!" from the crowd. Each display grew more colorful, more intricate, more engaging, as red, blue, and green whirly-gigs burst against the black velvet backdrop of night. Silver daggers stabbed from sky to water, purple fingerprints whorled, while whizzing, booming cannon shots played back-up loud enough to shake the mountain in hollow echoes. Monica was right. It was the most spectacular fireworks display I'd ever seen, with mirror-images and ricochet-sounds.

Caught between us, Jeff gazed, mesmerized, until his mother called him to come share her seat up front.

At first, I figured she was trying to give Luke and me some alone-time, but as I watched him snuggle into her arms, I had the warming thought that she was just being a loving mother. Wasn't that what she'd always wanted?

Taking care to avoid my bandaged wrist, Luke took the opportunity to pull me close, and we did some of our own snuggling, and even managed to exchange a few quick kisses when we thought the front row was zeroed in on the finger-painted sky.

After a colorful and chaotic finale, we puttered back to Overhome, along with hundreds of other boats, careful to observe the NO WAKE requirement. By the time we approached the dock, Jeff was so sleepy he could hardly stand up.

"Ashby, do you mind getting Jefferson tucked in?" Monica asked. "Miss Emma will be waiting up for him."

"Your aunt and I want to boat over to a friend's house near the club. They're having a dock party," Uncle Hunter added.

That explained my aunt's elaborate outfit, I thought. "Sure. No problem."

"Do be careful about your wrist," my aunt called from the retreating boat. "Miss Emma can get him into his pajamas. Just give him a good night hug and kiss for me. Thanks, dear." And they were gone.

Luke lifted Jeff in his arms, carrying him up the long, steep steps from the dock. As I trailed behind, watching the child's sun-streaked head resting on Luke's shoulder, I decided Luke was the most tenderhearted hunk I've ever met. He stuck around long enough to deliver his own hug and kiss to the warm and dozy little form before steering me outside. No sooner had we moved beyond the back stoop than we fell into one another's arms. Luke's scent and touch and taste drew me in with a powerful, dizzying sweep. "Now it's our turn for a hug and a kiss," Luke said, as his lips overtook mine.

"I never want t' let you go," Luke whispered after we had stood linked tightly for many minutes. "But I have t' lock up th' stable office." He cupped my face in his hands. "An' it's gettin' late. They'll be cruisin' in from their dock party soon."

"I'll come with you, Luke," I said. "I'm not ready to let you go, either."

Holding hands, we walked along the rocky path to the stable, when we both noticed at the same time something unusual, something wrong. The stable door was wide open.

"Uh-oh." Luke raced ahead. By the time I arrived, he stood scratching his head and looking baffled. "Man, this is weird. Makes no sense. They were all shut in their stalls when I left for the fireworks. How…how did Sasha…"

"Sasha?"

"Sasha's gone. His stall's empty. All th' others are there, but Sasha's gate is down; he's nowhere t' be found."

"Night Riders? Eddie Mills?" I could barely articulate through numb lips.

"My first thought, too." Again the bewildered look. "Th' Riders like to leave their sign, y'know, th' rebel flag. But not this time." He opened his hand then, to show me the rose bud. "I found this on th' floor of Sasha's stall."

It took me a while to find my voice. "The Night Riders have their sign, Luke. Well, Rosabelle has her sign, too. She's done something to…with Sasha. My Sasha! Do you see now why I'm upset, why I have to find out what's going on here? Just when I come to the conclusion she's my loving protector, she goes and snatches my horse?" Covering my face with my hands, I burst into tears.

With one step, Luke's arms were around me, holding me until my sobbing stopped. Leaning back, he wiped my tears with his fingers.

"Can't we look for Sasha? Can't we look now? I mean, he has to be in the woods somewhere."

"I'm sure we'll find 'im," Luke said. "It's not like Sasha t' stray too far from his food trough. There's nothin' we can do tonight. The woods 'r too thick an' dark; trust me. But first thing tomorrow. I promise, we'll find Sasha. We'll get t' th' bottom of this."

I could not let it go. Sasha's disappearance was too real, too awful. "Luke, Luke, listen to me, please." I fixed my eyes on his. "I know you're skeptical about Rosabelle. I mean, I can understand why you want me to leave Abe out of this, and I respect that. I've tried and tried to pry information out of Miss Emma. But she drops little hints, and teases me with just enough history and hearsay to confuse me, and then she drifts off, sometimes in mid-sentence." I looked deep into his eyes, pleading for him to feel my urgency. "If you can't believe me, could you at least help me look for the truth, for some answers?"

Luke moved the rose from one hand to the other, a distracted look on his face. The silence got to me. I broke in, "I don't know why, but, I've never, you know, talked…really talked to Uncle Hunter about the spooky stuff. But I'm so totally freaked out now. Maybe he can explain…"

"Don't," Luke said so suddenly that I jumped.

"Don't tell my uncle? Don't talk to him about…about the rose you just found? About Rosabelle? Why not?"

"Did y'ever notice th' only folks workin' here full time are old codgers who've been aroun' forever? Know why? Becuz nobody else'll work for Hunter Overton. Locals despise th' guy, and th' old folks've only stayed on 'cuz of your Grandma Lenore. Abe was in love with her, and Aunt Emma was her best friend. Me? I got no choice."

"Why is my uncle so despised, as you say? What's he done that nobody wants to even work for him?"

"I don't know all th' details. Never wanted t' know, t' tell y'th' truth. I'm not even sure I believe half of it. But it started with your grandfather, Thomas Overton. A lot of folks felt he was a real bad-ass. Cheatin' people out of their property an' then flippin' it. Y'know, sellin' it for a huge profit. I figger maybe Hunter took some lessons from his old man. Hunter an' his buddy Fred Taylor, the family lawyer. People say they're in cahoots. Payin' officials under the table to rezone bought-up farmland so they can build resorts an' condos an' stuff."

"Okay, I see your point. But what's Hunter's reputation got to do with me? With Rosabelle? Why not talk to him about what's happening to me here?"

Luke took me in his arms again. "I don't know if y'can trust your uncle. About anything."

I pulled away. "Got any bright ideas then? All I

know is I read about Rosabelle in a diary from Civil War times, which I found in the attic. It was Angelina Elisabeth Overton's diary." I let the syllables run together with an exaggerated, fake-Southern accent. "Rosabelle was there for Angelina. She called Rosabelle 'my guardian angel' and 'my friendly spirit.' Don't you see? Rosabelle died years and years ago, but she appeared among the living in the 1860's and for who-knows-how-long before that. And she's here now, like, for me. Or maybe against me. If I can't get some answers pretty soon…"

"So, y'been nosin' aroun' in th' ol' fam'ly records, huh?"

"If I could only find Grandmother Lenore's diary. I'm positive she kept one. My mother alluded to it in her own diary." I caught Luke's look. "Okay, okay. So, yeah. Like, I have been nosing around, but it's all good. It's not so much snooping as sleuthing."

"Well, I may be able to help y'out." Luke held the rose to his face. "I can't say I'm a believer, but I have t' admit there's been weird stuff goin' on, especially since you got here." He handed me the flower. "Tell y'what. I have an idea. I'll work on it an' let y'know. I promise. In th' meantime, please hold up. Don't take your uncle into your confidence…about anything."

When I tried to ask what he had in mind, he put his finger to my lips before he silenced me with a kiss. "See y'early tomorrow. Stop worryin'. We'll find your horse. Now get some sleep."

****

Dear Diary,
Luke says we'll find my horse, but I'm worried sick about Sasha. I can come up with only one scenario—I

162

fall off Sasha and hurt my wrist. Rosabelle intends to shield me from all harm. The way she sees it, Sasha has caused me pain, so Sasha must pay the piper. I remember Abe telling me what happened to Lenore's horse after the accident killed her, how the barn burned a week later, how the only horse to die was Lenore's. This terrifies me, Dear Diary, to think Sasha might suffer a similar fate, all because I am such a klutz. Then there was the wolf dog—so quick—so brutal—so dead. I always come back to my gut feelings, that if Rosabelle loves me as poignantly as it appears, she would do nothing to upset me, certainly nothing to hurt my beloved Sasha.

So, Diary. I've gotta say this sucks. I'm wide awake. I won't sleep until I have Sasha back safe and well.

Pausing over my laptop to lean back against the headboard, I listened for the familiar lullaby. Nothing disturbed the silence of the night except the occasional sighing of the wind around the eaves, or the creak of the old timbers supporting the balcony. Once the distant pop-pop-pop-of a late night firecracker echoed over the lake. But nothing more.

"Rosabelle, if you hear me, please don't desert me now, not when I need you most," I pleaded. "Rosabelle? Are you here?" Nothing stirred in the deathly quiet. No whiffs of rose perfume in the air. No rose buds to be found. I tried one final plea. "Please, Rosabelle. Don't hurt Sasha. He means so much to me." Perhaps it was my imagination, but I did sense a presence, then. A puff of cool air against my cheek, as light as a kiss, and in my side-vision, a movement. A wisp, which disappeared in a blink. I waited and waited, but the room itself seemed asleep in the deep, still silence.

I must have dozed off, for I felt my laptop slide. I jerked awake, then moved the mouse to log off. My hand froze in mid-air as I saw the words staring up at me from the screen. Among lines of a random scattering of letters and numbers, a single word leaped from the screen, blood. That was all, blood.

My hand flew to my mouth to stifle my gasp. Blood. The word looked alive, writhing and oozing red, scaring me and churning up questions simultaneously. Whose blood? Mine? Sasha's?

Blood. Was it a warning? A threat? A sign? If the terse message was designed to scare me, it had succeeded beyond the writer's wildest dreams. The writer—Rosabelle? What could it possibly mean?

Closing the computer, I slumped wearily onto the mattress and gave in to sleep. In my dream I labored over an old-fashioned loom I'd discovered in the attic. I tried to weave different-colored cords of silk, but the finished cloth emerged only as a tangled, muddled tapestry, blurred and flawed, with no evident theme. When I attempted to pick apart the strands of matted cloth, my fingers began to bleed. Feeling no pain, I watched my fingers morph into vermillion rose petals, as I heard in my dream-mind a ghostly whisper— "Promise. Promise. Promise."

Chapter Nineteen

I awoke to a mix of dread and hope. The chilling message on my laptop, the surreal dream, the unmistakable message of promise. Must find Sasha. It's the only thing that matters. I was distracted by those blessed birds dive-bombing the panes of the French door in feathered frenzy, more vigorous than usual. It was like a Shakespearean play, where all of nature turned and churned on an unnatural event. Abducted horse, disturbing dreams, storming birds. I made a note to do some research on Southern bluebirds. After all, there was an extensive library right here at Overhome. In a daze, I dressed and descended to the dining room where I encountered Uncle Hunter alone at the long table, up earlier than usual.

"A bit of excitement last night, eh?" He sipped his tea. "You look exhausted, Ashby. Did your injury keep you up? Why not go back to bed. I'll have Miss Emma bring you a tray."

"Oh, no! I have to hunt for Sasha."

He paused, his cup half way to his lips. "But, of course, you couldn't have heard…"

"Heard? Has Sasha been found?"

"We haven't had a chance to look for your horse yet. It's Abe. In the middle of the night. They think it was a heart attack."

I rose hastily, my own heart in my throat. "Sit

down, Ashby. There's absolutely nothing you can do. Luke drove him to the hospital—it was faster than waiting for the ambulance. Luke's with him there now. I'm sure he'll call if there's any change."

I exhaled slowly. "Then—he's not dead?"

"His condition is critical. What with his age, well, we have to be prepared for the possibility of…a lengthy recovery."

"Luke's been worried about Abe, about his heart. His mind, too."

Hunter tilted his head to one side and seemed to study me before he spoke again. "We all have our concerns, certainly." He patted his pocket. "Luke has my cell number. Now, let's collect Jefferson before he gets off to camp. You'll need your hiking boots and some long pants. If your wrist is not bothering you too much, the three of us will go in search of a wayward horse."

I pointed down at my jeans and boots. "I'm already dressed for the search." I moved my wrist in circles for his appreciation. "The bruise is surfacing, just like Dr. Ross said it would. It's ugly but it doesn't hurt. I'm good to go."

He smiled. "I'm quite sure Sasha is loose on the grounds; we'll find him. Now, I'm going to rouse Jefferson. I don't think he'll mind missing his day camp just this once."

My mind returned immediately to Abe. Well, my world was upset, for sure, but even Shakespeare wouldn't go so far as to strike down an innocent old man over a missing horse. Thank goodness I'd followed Luke's advice to leave Abe out of my quandary. I didn't need that guilt trip on top of feeling responsible for Sasha's disappearance. Poor Abe. Poor Luke. I felt helpless to make things better for either of them.

Luke and I had exchanged cell numbers, but I'd never called due to the dead zone in my room, Rosabelle's room. Oddly, though, the signal seemed strong enough elsewhere on the estate.

"Can I meet you outside?" I asked my uncle. I had to try to get hold of Luke. Hurrying to the porch, I considered trying to call but abandoned the thought, knowing Luke would be involved at the hospital. I'd try a text message instead. I got busy with my thumbs. PRAYING 4 U & ABE. CB IF U CAN. I L U. Okay, so the I L U was a bit brash. Well, what better time to get the idea out there? Now I would have to be patient and wait to hear about Abe's condition.

Uncle Hunter and Jeff met me in the yard. We started on the trail because we figured my horse would most likely seek out familiar territory from wherever he had wandered. Had I not been so worried and preoccupied, I would have totally enjoyed the sounds and smells of the cool morning woods seeping into every pore of my skin. Sticky pine needles lent the forest floor a holiday scent, and skittering squirrels practiced gymnastics in the jungle gym branches above. Lost for a while in my thoughts of Abe and Luke and Sasha, I realized the others had moved so far ahead that I could no longer hear their thrashing through the brush and tangle of the woods. There was only the swish-swish-snap of the squirrels in their overhead playground.

Stopping to listen for my uncle and cousin, I almost collapsed in terror when two rough hands reached out from behind and clamped themselves over my eyes. I jumped and shrieked.

"Ha! Caught ya!" It was Eddie Mills. He whirled me around to face his huge, gnarly smile.

"Jeez, Eddie! You freaking scared me half to death."

"Jes' wanted to s'prise you is all. I can track jes' about anything through th' woods quiet as a Injun. Even sneak up on deer. Done it many a time."

"Well, I'd appreciate it if you never sneak up on me again." I didn't like the look on his face—like he wanted to put a move on me. I edged backwards as he inched closer and closer.

"They ain't nothin' t' be afeared of," he said in a wheedling tone. "I ain't a-gonna hurt ya."

I backed over the roots of a tree as he closed in. When he saw I could retreat no farther with my back solidly trapped against the rough bark of a giant oak, he grabbed me in a vice-like hug. Adrenalin kicked in and I pushed against him with my fists, screaming at the top of my lungs, "Stop! Stop it, Eddie!"

To my surprise, he backed off. "Aw…I jes' wanted a li'l kiss is all."

I cradled my throbbing wrist. "Leave me alone, Eddie. In fact, you'd better get the hell out of here. You know they heard me scream. They'll be on you like a sweat."

A cagey look came over him. "Hey, what if I tol' ya I done foun' somethin' on Mills' prop'ty. Somethin' y'been lookin' fer. Would ya give me a kiss? Don't ya wanna know what I foun'?"

"Sasha? You found Sasha, Eddie? Where is he? Take me to him. Now!" Much as I disliked being close to him, I grabbed him by the shoulders of his T-shirt and shook him until his head rattled.

"Jes one li'l kiss?" he pleaded.

Without further thought, I smacked a peck onto his cheek, then pulled him by the arm. "Okay. You got your kiss. Now, do you have my horse, or not?"

He looked defensive. "Hey, I didn't take him. I jes' found him, all caught up in some ol' rusty fence wire in th' woods. On old Mills' prop'ty, like I said." He looked pleased with himself. "Now, any other time, I'd a let a stray horse from Overhome jes' keep on strayin',' if you know what I mean. But, when I rec'nized it wuz yer horse, well, I figgered I'd do a good deed fer my kissin' cousin. So, I tied him up tight an' come lookin' fer ya."

Just then, the underbrush crackled and Hunter, followed by Jeff, hove into view. As Eddie, the Indian scout, melted back into the forest, my eyes lit on the rope lead my uncle trailed behind him with Sasha safely in tow.

"Sasha! Oh, Sasha!"

He whinnied as though he were delighted to see me. I couldn't resist throwing my arms around his warm, furry horse-neck for a hug. "Ugh. He's full of burrs and sticks. He must've tromped all over these woods."

"Actually, we found Sasha tethered to a tree. Over there." My uncle pointed in the direction where Eddie had disappeared. "It's as if someone found him wandering in the woods and tied him up to keep him safe. I can't imagine who…"

"It was Eddie Mills, Uncle Hunter. He was here a minute ago but you and Jeff scared him off. He said he'd found Sasha—found him on Mills' property."

"Mills' property. Well, yes. What was once Mills property, at any rate." He stroked his chin and appeared to be deep in thought. "Why would Eddie, or the Night Riders, steal Sasha and then make sure we'd find him safely tied?"

"I'm not so sure Eddie had anything to do with Sasha's little adventure," I said. "Eddie told me he found Sasha in the woods and tied him to a tree, and I believe him."

My uncle appeared to digest my comment before shaking his head in dismissal. "Well, at any rate, Sasha is none the worse for wear. Let's lead him back to the stable, get him cleaned up and fed. I'll work this out later."

I deliberately left out Eddie's revolting advances on me. But I did learn one thing while he was in my face. He had a tattoo on his right bicep. A tattoo of a Confederate flag.

My cell phone buzzed in my jean's pocket, beeping out the signal for an incoming text message. I flipped open my cell, to discover a line of message, ABE OK CAN U COME 2 HOSP?

I gave a soft cry of excitement. "Abe is okay," I told my uncle and cousin. "Luke wants me—us to come to the hospital."

I think Uncle Hunter was surprised that Luke had contacted me instead of him.

"I'd thought we'd wait to see the prognosis for Abe before visiting him, but if Luke is asking…"

"Can I go, too?" Jeff cried.

"The hospital may have regulations about young children and visiting hours, Jefferson. Since we've already missed your van pool, what say I drive you to day camp. I'm sorry, Jefferson, but I'd hate for you to get to the hospital and be disappointed at being turned away." My uncle looked at me. "And, from Jefferson's camp, Ashby, I can take you to the hospital. We can be there within an hour. Will that work for you, my dear?"

"Absolutely." I squeezed Jeff's hand and gave him a "trust-me-to-fill-you-in" look. I beamed my biggest smile on him. "Thank you. I've been so worried about Abe." I tapped quickly, SASHA OK. C U 1 HR.

****

Uncle Hunter let me off at the main entrance to the hospital while he looked for a parking space. Luke sat on the brick wall not far from the door, waiting, his head in his hands. He stood when he saw me, and I fell into his arms, alarmed at his weary look. I could feel choked sobs rising in his chest. "Luke, Luke. What is it? What's wrong? You said Abe is okay."

"They just rushed him to Intensive Care. He was doin' great, talkin' an' jokin' with the nurses, an' then...then he kinda fell limp onto the pillows." Luke wiped his eyes. "They don't know if he's gonna make it. What'll I do without him?"

We held on to each other, crying like babies. Luke was first to gain control. "This is no good. I have t' be strong for Abe." He sniffed and brushed his tears from his cheeks and then from mine. "Thanks for comin', Ashby. It's hard facin' this alone."

Just then my uncle strode into view. "I spoke with the doctor," he said. "Abe is going to be under sedation and in isolation for the rest of the day. Why don't you go home, Luke. Get some rest. You know the hospital will call if there's...when there's a change."

Luke answered him in a shaking voice. "I can't

leave him all alone like that."

"Look," Hunter said. "Go home, take a nap, grab a shower, and you can be back at the hospital by early evening. Spend the night on a cot in his room, if that will make you feel better. That way, you'll be there when they move him out of isolation and back into his room."

Luke looked skeptical.

"I'll arrange for help to take over the chores at Overhome for as long as necessary. Now, go on. You won't do Abe any good if you're exhausted."

I could see Luke giving in. "I agree," I said, looking Luke in the eyes.

Luke gave a look of resignation. "Okay. I guess you're right."

"I'd like to ride back with Luke. If you don't mind," I said.

"Excellent idea. I have some business to attend to in town, anyway." He gave Luke a stern look. "I mean it. Take as much time as you need." Turning, he left us.

"Hunter acts like he has a poker up his ass most times. For now, well, he seems like a reg'lar guy," Luke mused.

"He thinks a lot of you."

"Humph. He knows I'm keepin' things runnin' for him. An', believe me, he can be paranoid about those accountin' ledgers."

"Well, if my uncle likes you, he's okay in my book," I said.

"Let me run back an' tell th' desk how they can reach me," Luke turned toward the entrance. "My truck's in th' parking tower behind th' hospital. A-26 or 27. Here's th' keys," he passed them to me. "I'll be right back." He disappeared through the automatic doors.

As I walked to the parking tower, I wondered if Luke had noticed the constant winter that lay behind Hunter's eyes, a frigidity that pushed out all possible warmth. Locating the truck, I let myself in. While I waited, I flipped through a "Tourists' Map of Southwest Virginia" I found in a side pocket. I was surprised at the number of attractions.

Sliding into the driver's seat, Luke pulled me in for a kiss. "God, I'm glad you're here, Babe," he breathed. As we idled out of the parking ramp, he patted my knee and said, "C'n we pledge not t' talk about Abe...or about things that go bump in th' night. Okay with you?"

"Did you just call me Babe?"

"I believe th' correct local term'd be Sugar Babe."

"Okay, but I only remember Babe as a pig in a movie."

"Would you prefer Sugar?" Luke asked.

"In that case, Babe. I think I can get used to that. And now, what do you say we take it one step further and have nothing but positive thoughts. Like, put ourselves in a happy place."

"All right by me, Babe," he agreed.

"Hey, let's plan some outings." With a flourish, I shook the folds out of the Tourist's Map and waved it in front of him.

"Okay. But first tell me about Sasha. Where'd y'find him?"

"Believe it or not, Eddie Mills found him and tied him to a tree. He couldn't wait to tell me about it. Sasha was dirty and hungry, and as happy to see me as I was to see him."

"Mills didn't give y'any crap, did he?"

"Let's just say his bark is worse than his bite. As long as we're thinking positive thoughts, you know, let's not mention Eddie Mills."

"Th' big jerk," Luke growled. "Okay, okay. I'm ready. Let's go to that, what'd y'call it? Happy place?"

And so, we played the child's game of "When You Wish Upon a Star," talking non-stop about our wishes all the way back. We decided to drive someday along the Blue Ridge Parkway and admire the mountain views with a picnic at a scenic overlook. Another day we would visit the D-Day Memorial in Bedford. Some time we'd be sure to check out the birthplace of Booker T. Washington, and we'd make a pilgrimage to Poplar Forest, Thomas Jefferson's second home. We'd hike up the Peaks of Otter, then have lunch at the Lodge. Ever mindful of history, we'd tour Appomattox Court House, where Lee surrendered. Together, we planned to explore all the wonderful worlds within a short distance of Overhome, knowing full well we would run out of summer way before we could begin to do all these things. But that was hardly the point. We were both acutely aware of sadness and fear below our light-hearted surface, and the very real possibility of the death of a loved one.

It seemed like in no time we were turning into the driveway to Overhome. "You know, Luke, I can't help but remember my maiden voyage in your truck, when you picked me up at the bus station that first day. I swear, the roads seemed like something out of one of Jeff's board games, all loops and curves."

"You were sorta pea-green as I recall," he chuckled. "An' I thought you were probably a real…something better left unsaid."

"I didn't have such a flattering impression of you, either! So, how did we ever come to this?" I stroked his stubbly cheek.

Stopping the truck and idling under the leafy privacy of the green tunnel, Luke released his seatbelt and then mine. "Must a' been fate." He moved close for a long, deep kiss.

After a while, I slid back to my side of the seat. "You're wiped out. You should go home and sleep. And listen, I have a gut feeling Abe is going to snap back. We just have to keep the faith."

"I hear you, an' I'm doin' my best with th' positive energy thing. But I'm afraid you're right, Babe. I'm ready to crash." Shifting into low, Luke gentled his truck slowly up the driveway. He stopped at the house and I reached for the door to let myself out. "I haven't forgotten my promise t' help."

"Help me…"

"With ol' Ring-Around-the-Rosie." For a moment, his tired eyes danced. "I gotta couple ideas an' I plan t' speak to my Aunt Emma. I'm sure she knows a whole lot more'n she's lettin' on. I'll pry it outta her. I mean, she's always had a soft spot for me in her heart an' she finds it hard to turn me down when I really need somethin'. I'll just turn on my charm."

"Okay. I hope you're right. And now that you've opened the topic, there's another weird wrinkle to the saga—something I haven't told you about. Rosabelle left me a message. On my laptop."

Luke snorted. "So now we're dealin' with a techno-ghost?"

"I know it sounds incredible. I mean, I can barely

believe it myself. First, the radio station and now the computer, but this time it's not all fun, like the bluegrass music. I am totally freaked, by what she left for me on the screen."

"So are y'gonna tell me, or not?"

"Blood. She wrote the word blood."

"That's it? One word? Blood?"

"You got it. I have no clue as to what it means."

Luke looked totally baffled. "Blood. What th'… Blood?"

I left him muttering under his breath, but I felt a warm surge as I zeroed in on what he'd said, "We are dealing with a techno-ghost." We. I loved the sound of that plural pronoun.

****

It had been a draining day. Late in the afternoon Luke emerged from his house claiming he was rested, but still looking haggard. He'd had no word about Abe's condition, and the tension was wearing on him. He planned to attend his calculus class and then drive directly to the hospital, no matter what. While we both wished I could go along, it just wasn't practical, since Luke was planning to stay overnight in Abe's hospital room.

Ready to crash myself, I cracked the lid of my lap top and took a moment to record some thoughts in my diary.

****

Dear Diary,

I am a whirling blender of emotions—happy that Sasha is safely home, though no closer to understanding how he got out. Happy that Luke and I are, at last, on the same wave-length about my favorite ghost. Sad about Abe, but hopeful he will recover. Hopeful, too, that Luke will follow through with whatever his plan is to help me find some answers. Who is Rosabelle? What is she trying to tell me? And why? While I'm on the hopeful motif, dare I mention how hopeful I am that Luke loves me as much as I love him? Okay, so I'm no Jane Eyre and Luke's, for sure, nothing like Mr. Rochester, but why does the pace of our relationship seem as slow as a Charlotte Bronte novel? I'm ready for some plain old modern action, with, like, a touch of Victorian commitment. Yeah, yeah, I know. That makes me for sure a romantic fool. Just call me Jane Babe Eyre.

I was too weary to write more. I'd just have to wait to see what tomorrow would bring.

Chapter Twenty

I sat up, wide awake, my heart pounding against my ribs. *Ashby. Ashby.* Paralyzed, I waited for the haunting sound of those syllables to whisper again through the night air. *Ashby. Ashby.* I had not dreamed it. Someone was calling my name, someone outside my balcony. Scrambling from the covers, I flew to the French doors, where slanting streaks of moonlight filtered through the old-fashioned panes. I moved onto the balcony, feeling the damp roughness of the floor on my bare feet, following the sound. *Ashby. Ashby.* Leaning over the railing, I looked to the lawn below. Bleached in the silvery light of a full moon stood a figure clad in a pastel robe, long, flowing draperies cascading from the shoulders to the ground. I gasped, clutching the railing to steady myself, my eyes fixed on the ashen figure.

Slowly the head moved, tilting all the way backward, revealing a face whose features blurred into the moonlight. *Ashby. Ashby.* The voice was eerie and hollow.

My mouth opened but no sound emerged. Fright had frozen my vocal cords.

Ashby, don't be afraid. There's nothing to fear.

"W-who are you? What do you want?" I finally managed to articulate through numb lips.

"I didn't mean to frighten you. It's only me. Emma

Coleville."

I slumped against the railing, closing my eyes on the vertigo, and trying to catch my breath. I did not know whether to laugh or cry as I looked down at the old housekeeper basking in the moonlight, dressed in her long, pale bathrobe. "My God, Miss Emma. What are you doing out there in the middle of the night? You scared me to death." Gradually, my senses awoke to the damp chill on my bare arms, the smells of dew on grass, the distant rippling of the lake.

"I couldn't sleep," she said, her voice hoarse from projecting in the night air. "You see, Luke talked to me before he left for his class tonight, urged me to tell you what I know. He made me realize I've waited long enough, that I need to let you in on…on things I know. Things that concern you."

"Don't move. I'm coming down to talk to you. Please don't leave."

I shot back into my room, grabbed a short robe and some flip-flops and dashed through the hall, down the stairs, and out the back door to the lawn. Miss Emma eyed my night clothes. "Oh, maybe I shouldn't have awakened you, Ashby. Perhaps I should have waited…"

"No, no. It's all right. But let's find a place to sit. Do you want to go inside?"

"Oh no. I never feel right talking about Lenore, about Rosabelle, about the past when I'm inside the house. Call it superstition, but it creeps me out, as Jeff would say." She shivered slightly.

"Let's go down to the dock, then, Miss Emma."

"I'd feel more comfortable in the gazebo. It's where Lenore and I spent so many hours together. Do you mind a little ramble over the fields? I'll hitch up my robe so it doesn't drag in the wet grass." She reached for the rope-ties at her waist.

And so we followed the old stone wall, not talking, just breathing in the fragrance of night, our path guided by the lantern of the moon, until we approached the fence and lampposts surrounding the gazebo. Down the stone stairs, through the maze of boxwoods, we moved to the wooden benches under the arch of the ancient structure.

"There." Miss Emma settled her slight frame onto the seat. "Just let me catch my breath."

"This is really beautiful at night. The moonlight hides all the imperfections, you know, the weeds, the peeling paint, the crumbling wood. This must be the way the garden looked long ago."

Miss Emma took her time and I worried that all of her energy had been spent. For a long while, she sat with eyes closed, leaning against the back of the gazebo bench, until I began to fear she would go to sleep.

At long last, she opened her eyes, took a deep breath and began. "I think I'll start with the attic. Or, perhaps I should say it all started in the attic."

I nodded, encouraging her to go on, afraid to break her momentum with my voice.

"Lenore and I spent hours and hours in the attic, the same attic you explored, Ashby. Why, even to this day, one whiff of the dusty, musty air up there takes me back immediately to those girlhood forays. We felt so clever sneaking into the diaries in the locker. Little girls up to devilish deeds, deliciously vowed to secrecy. We knew the diaries were supposed to be hidden away from prying eyes, but, with a little help from Rosabelle, we always got to them when we wanted to, and what we read was, well, it was simply irresistible! Love and lust and envy and pride. Family feuds, war, retribution. It was all there, all human, all real, and more fascinating than any romance novel or movie could ever hope to be."

"I felt the same way, Miss Emma. About the attic and about the diaries. I know exactly what you're saying. But some of the older diaries were so faint and faded. Were you and Lenore able to read all of them?"

"Oh yes. But, of course, we had the luxury of days and days and weeks, years really, to do so. Sometimes we would sneak one out and bring it here to the gazebo to decipher the flowery old script, using a magnifying glass." Her eyes glowed with the memory. "What a thrill it was, to be conspirators like that. And what we learned was amazing. Unbelievable, and yet we had to believe. Can you understand how it was, Ashby? With Lenore and me?"

"Absolutely, Miss Emma. But, please, go on. Tell me everything."

"All in good time, child. All in good time." She was quiet for a moment. "I've thought and thought about how I would do this, and I aim to do it right, if it's the last thing I do. You see, I believe I may understand something you've found puzzling." She raised an eyebrow. Pausing for effect. "That word that appeared on your laptop?" She paused again when she saw my surprised look.

"Oh, yes. Luke told me about it. Blood. Is that right? Blood?"

"Yep. That was the word. Of course, I was puzzled. Puzzled and scared."

"Well, Lenore and I discovered several entries in the earliest of the diaries, one written by Emilie Overton herself. Remember, Emilie and her husband, Francis, were the original owners of the Overhome property. The date was in the 1780s. Emilie wrote fondly of a Scottish servant who had come to work for her under the oddest of circumstances. A young lady with a most extraordinary background and experience. Her name was Rosabelle O'Connor."

I caught my breath. "Did you say the 1780s?"

She ignored my interruption. "Born in Scotland around 1740, Rosabelle O'Connor, some twenty years later, boarded a ship bound for America. But Spanish pirates shanghaied the vessel, and she spent several years imprisoned on an island off the west coast of Africa, forced into slavery. Rescued, she again set sail for America, arriving in Virginia about 1765, and working for several years as an indentured servant. Living through the Revolutionary War, she settled in Staunton, where she got wind of the Overton family's need for a nanny, or nursemaid, as the position was called in those days. The name Overton rang a bell. Evidently, there was some family connection in Scotland with the O'Connor family. Using that slim tie, Rosabelle requested an interview and Emilie Overton granted her a trial period as nanny.

"Emilie was quickly impressed with Rosabelle's skill with children, the wee babbies, as Rosebelle called them. Since she was possibly a remote relative anyway, the Overtons moved Rosabelle into the great house, giving her a room in the wing newly constructed from the barn. Your room, Ashby. As I told you that first night, it was Rosabelle's room."

"What an amazing story, Miss Emma! And it's all in Emily Overton's diary?"

"Oh, there's more. Much more, Ashby. By the turn of the century, Emilie and Francis ran a grand estate with some 2,000 acres of land and dozens of slaves. The Overtons had a large brood of children, all under the loving care of Rosabelle, but the youngest, evidently, was the apple of Emilie's eye. Mary Frances was just a toddler when the nanny took her on a picnic in the north field one spring day. Rosabelle had taken along her sewing basket, since her Scottish work ethic did not allow for any idle time. As Mary Francis toddled about the field picking dandelions, a bull broke through the fence and headed straight for the child. Rosabelle stabbed the bull in the nose with her sewing scissors, then swooped up the child and ran to place her safely over a secure part of the fence. Sadly, the bull recovered in time to gore poor Rosabelle from back to front and through the heart. The nanny died instantly, though Mary Frances lived to a ripe, old age."

"So, Rosabelle died over two hundred years ago," I breathed. "The same Rosabelle who—"

"The same. The diaries confirm it. Rosabelle died a violent death in the line of duty. Who knows? Maybe she felt her work was left undone. Maybe she was too shocked or too angry about her death to cross over to the other side. But she stayed on at Overhome. I don't pretend to know how such a thing happens, though I have some ideas as to why. But I do know that her spirit has arrived regularly as a protector for Overton women." Miss Emma caught my eyes. "She is here with us now."

I could not stop myself from looking over my

shoulder. Though Miss Emma's words were a shock to the rational mind, hearing her voice what I had already sensed, that some kind of spirit resided at Overhome, was, if anything, reassuring. I knew there was more. "But what about the word? You know, the word blood. You said you understand what it means."

"I'm getting to that. Please bear with me. You see, Rosabelle has appeared over the last two hundred years only to bloodline Overton women, not to women who marry into the family and simply carry the Overton name. By reading the diaries and sorting out the branches of the Overton family tree, Lenore and I figured out why Rosabelle turned up in some of the diaries, but not all of them. Over the years it became accepted that an ancestral ghost appeared, at random, or so folks thought. Lenore and I knew better and we were convinced we were the only ones alive who knew. Before she died, Lenore asked me to watch for you, to tell you the truth."

"So, with the word blood Rosabelle was telling me I am a bloodline Overton? That Washington was my father and not simply an excuse by the Mills family for a shotgun wedding with Marian? Is that what you believe?"

"Yes it is. She's telling you, and, inadvertently, she's telling me."

"But, why, Miss Emma? I'm afraid I still don't get it."

"There's more, of course. But as dawn's almost upon us, I'll try to make it short. I told you earlier that Lenore implored me to keep two wishes just prior to her death. Actually, she laid a third request on me that night."

"I remember clearly, Miss Emma. My Grandmother Lenore asked you to see that Uncle Hunter grew up to be a gentleman and she wanted you to watch for me to come to Overhome. But...what was the third wish?"

"You must understand, child. Lenore came to fear and hate her husband, Thomas. She laid it all out in her own diary—his violent temper, his intolerance, his verbal abuse of her and physical abuse of their sons, his fraudulant land deals and other crimes, his ill-got riches. Her diary and I were the only ones privy to all the details. She was afraid Thomas would destroy such an inflammatory record as her diary, and that the record itself might be important one day, so she entrusted it to me for safety, made me promise to keep it to show the next Overton woman, so that she would understand. Believe." Miss Emma's face fell, her voice dropped to a whisper. "But I failed Lenore. My dearest friend. I failed to keep my promise to her on her deathbed."

Moved, I reached for her hand, keeping my silence. At last, she recovered.

"Sorry," she said. "I can't get over the fact that I lost Lenore's diary."

"Lost it?"

"Rather, it was stolen from my personal belongings. Oh, from time to time things disappeared, you know. Stolen by a new cook or borrowed by a day worker and never returned, I assumed. Then, one day when I went looking for it, perhaps two years ago, Lenore's diary had simply disappeared. I've known since then that I would have to somehow make a believer of you without the evidence. Without the diary. And I've waited...oh I hope I haven't waited too long. I hope I'm not too late."

"Too late for what?" I pressed her hand.

"Don't you see? Whoever stole Lenore's diary—he or she knows everything Lenore meant to keep secret. In the wrong hands, it might be, it could mean danger."

"Danger? For me? I don't understand."

"There are other reasons why I can't... Let me just caution you to be careful about revealing what you've learned. Careful about where you go and what you do. I realize I should have told you this long before now." She frowned and shook her head. "Luke made that clear when he spoke to me yesterday." She gave me a knowing look. "The dear boy is in love with you, you know." She stood stiffly. "I only hope there's still time... Now, we need to get ourselves in before the sun hits the lake and the household arises."

As we made our halting way back to the house, I could see that Miss Emma was worn out. She had been up for much of the night, had walked a fair distance over dew-wet terrain, and had poured out her soul in emotional memories. I remained silent as we worked our way along the stone wall, but when we reached a flat stretch of land, I could no longer resist asking something that had been gnawing at the edges of my consciousness. "Miss Emma, if Rosabelle was Lenore's protector, how come she didn't take it out on her dirtball husband, my Grandfather Thomas?"

"Oh, but she did, Ashby. She bedeviled that man in every way possible." The house keeper shook her head.

"Bedeviled? What do you mean?"

She drew a breath before answering. "Well, Rosabelle caused Thomas never-ending trouble by wreaking havoc on the property, upending the heavy watering troughs for the horses, breaking boards in the bridge, opening the barn doors at night, and such."

"You mean, like the Night Riders?" I gasped.

Miss Emma appeared not to hear my comment. "It was almost comic, at times," she went on. "Almost like annoying, practical jokes. But, after Lenore died, Rosabelle outdid herself abusing Thomas." Again, she wagged her head slowly from side to side. "And when they were damming up the lake, and it was up to Thomas to move Rosabelle's grave and the slave graves, why her fury was unleashed, for sure. She began ripping up trees by the roots, denting his truck, pouring sand into the gas tank of his tractor, actually threatening bodily harm by luring him into danger with a candle. She deliberately killed his prize-winning cow. It won a blue ribbon at the county fair one day. The next it lay stretched out, stiff and bloated, with flies swarming all over it."

"So, you're sure it was Rosabelle doing all these terrible things? Not just some horrible string of bad luck or something?"

"No doubt about it. She always left her sign, you see." The old woman yawned and wearily rolled back her shoulders one at a time. "For the cow she left a whole bouquet resting beside the corpse."

"God. No wonder you're reluctant to dredge up the past." I put a sympathetic arm around her stooping shoulders. "You must be exhausted, Miss Emma. Thank you for telling me all of this. I know what an effort it's been, but you've given me a lot to think about."

"I'm afraid I'm all done in, Ashby. My voice is raw and my bones ache. I plan to take to my bed and stay there all day, if possible."

As I watched her let herself into her quarters on the lower level of Overhome and made my own way to the back entrance, I pondered the surreal events of the past few hours.

****

Dawn painted the horizon as I let myself into my room. Faint pink streaks bleeding into the sky cast a rosy glow onto my stucco walls. But it was my sense of smell that drew me, the odor of strong, black coffee. Coffee was something I had missed at tea-drinking Overhome. Now, there was no mistaking the rich smell wafting me to the bedside table where I was surprised to find a daintily-set tray. Beside a folded linen napkin sat an exquisite cup and saucer of pale, delicate bone china. A scalloped pink flower designed the edges with graceful, hand-painted roses. It was identical to the china stored in my parents' trunk in the attic. Next to the cup and saucer was a tall, slim china pot. Creamy white, with tiny cracks spreading like veins over its patina, it looked ancient. Fragrant steam curled from the spout.

Throwing off my robe and kicking out of my flip flops, I propped myself against the headboard, staring for a long time at the graciously-laid tray. Any other day I might have considered the tray a pleasantry provided by Miss Emma. Unusual, but not completely unlikely. But this morning, of course, that would have been impossible. As I reached for the napkin to spread on my lap, from under the soft folds, something dropped to the floor. I retrieved it, knowing already what it must be. Lifting the delicately fragrant flower, I held it to my cheek, inhaling the freshness. Placing it on the night table, I leaned forward and poured myself a cup of coffee, then turned on my radio to reflect against a background of Garth Brooks.

In reflective solitude, in the blushing light of sunrise, I sat drinking the strong, hot coffee from the antique cup. Coffee with Rosabelle. In my room—our room. I was warmed from the inside out as I consumed the entire pot, cup by cup.

Morning was well on its way when I reached for my laptop. For once, the bluebirds had taken a break from pecking at my door. The silence was most welcome. Where to begin? So, so much had happened in a few short hours.

****

Dear Diary,

Since when does two and two not equal four? How many books have I read where spirits are to be feared? A Christmas Carol. The Exorcist. Beloved. Wuthering Heights. *Speaking of that, Miss Emma's soulful cries of "Ashby, Ashby" were chillingly like Catherine's "Heathcliff, Heathcliff."*

And I've seen horror movies like Poltergeist *and* The Amityville Horror. *Cold, scary, blood-curdling stories about spirits. When Miss Emma describes Rosabelle's fury and her violence when she's pissed off, okay, so then my ghost fits the stereotype.*

Yet, here I lie in Rosabelle's presence. Warm. Contented. Grateful! My ghost puts me into a trance, where I can feel and hear her and smell her perfume, where I can sense her in every way, even see her in my mirror or in my dreams, but where I seem to have no control over myself, my actions, or my feelings. Today I tasted her strong-brewed coffee. Took it for a love offering and enjoyed every drop.

189

Miss Emma says to beware the danger. Does she mean danger from Rosabelle? I simply cannot equate danger with my loving, watchful Rosabelle all around me. And Miss Emma says my spirit is a protector and a champion for Overton women. For sure, I am a legitimate Overton woman. Where, then, is the danger? Who, then, should I be wary of? My own kinfolk? Eddie Mills? Someone lurking in the woods? Someone who knows more than he or she should? How should I conduct myself any differently? What is this old family retainer holding out on me? And, why?

Also, how very odd it is that Rosabelle's vendetta against Grandfather Thomas parallels what Luke and Abe call pranks of the Night Riders. If it is, indeed, Rosabelle who is now vandalizing the property, the question that looms large is why? Surely she doesn't have a bone to pick with poor old Abe. Or does she take revenge on men, in general?

I've learned a lot from Miss Emma, my "ghost" on the lawn, but I have the feeling it is only the tip of the iceberg. I am as confused as ever.

Oh, Diary,

I need Luke. Need to let him know that he was successful—that he convinced Miss Emma to let go of some secrets, if not all she knows. Need to confide in him that there may be danger for me here. Need him to put his strong arms around me and tell me everything will be all right. Then, I think, how can I be so selfish, knowing that Luke is rightly centered on Abe's critical condition. I never imagined that the home of my ancestors would dredge up so many conflicting emotions and events as to change my life forever.

Well, on with my day. I'll catch some Z's, and then

I can look forward to an afternoon playing mindless games with Jeff, riding my beautiful Sasha, paddling away my worries in the lake. I vow to put the night's revelations behind me for as long as the sun shines on this day and place all my thoughts and hopes, instead, on Abe's recovery.

The antique cup can hold my little pile of saved rose petals.

Chapter Twenty-One

"Oh, boy! Did I get in trouble today!" Jeff announced with a grimace as he skipped from left to right, serpentine-fashion, through the green tunnel.

I had never seen a kid tell on himself like my cousin. "What happened, Jeff?"

"Oh, Tina made me sit in the timeout chair for fifteen minutes during recess."

"Tina?"

"Tina's my counselor at day camp. Sometimes she's mean."

"What did you do? I mean, why'd you have to sit in the timeout chair?"

"I was bumping the seesaw is all. Stupid Jennifer told on me." He frowned. "Girls don't like it when you bump the seesaw. They only want you to tap it on the ground. Sheesh. Girls are such sissies." He looked at me quickly. "'Cept for you, Ashby. You're way cool."

He stopped to watch a salamander crawl over a rock. "Can you ride? Is your hurt hand okay now?" Before I could answer, his quick mind had jumped ahead. "Let's ask Miss Emma if she can pack a picnic for us to take on the trail. We can eat under a tree."

I laughed. "My wrist is A-OK. And the picnic would be a fine idea, except that I understand Miss Emma is taking the day off. How about you and I make up some PBJs and a thermos of lemonade?"

"Hey! Maybe Luke can come, too... Oh, I forgot. Luke's still at the hospital with Abe, isn't he?" Jeff's face clouded. "When is Abe coming home, Ashby?"

"I wish I knew, Jeff."

We entered the house with Jeff headed for the kitchen at a sprint. "Come on, Ashby," he hollered at the top of his lungs.

"Jefferson, Jefferson! Where is your indoor voice?" Aunt Monica held her hands to her ears as she emerged from a side room. "Now, I want you to go back to the front door and come in again, this time like a civilized young man who has learned some manners."

Jeff rolled his eyes at me when he was sure his mother could not see. "Sorry, Mom. I've had a rough day."

I suppressed a laugh, gratified to see that my aunt was also amused. "He had to sit in the timeout chair," I said in an aside to her. "Bumping the seesaw." She chuckled.

"Oh, that is much better," she said as Jeff entered the house in slow-motion and practically on tiptoe. "Now, I have some very good news for you and Ashby. I have just come up from Miss Emma's room. She is feeling too tired to work today, but she wanted to be sure you both know. Luke called to say Abe is out of ICU and that he is on the mend."

"Oh," I squeaked. "That's wonderful. Jeff and I were just wondering when Abe would get back home."

"That has not yet been determined," Monica said. "But Luke sounded very relieved. I believe he plans to come home himself sometime today."

"Abe's getting well? He's coming home? We'll have to celebrate, right, Ashby?" His gaze turned from me to his mother. "Can me and Ashby pack a lunch, Mom? We want to take the horses for a picnic in the woods."

"Ashby and I, Jefferson," Monica corrected. I watched her hold out her arms for a hug from Jeff before she bent to kiss his flying hair. "I love you, sweet boy, you know that?"

Jeff took off like a runner from the racing blocks, squealing his sneakers on the tile floor. "Thanks, Mom!" he called back over his shoulder. "Oops. Sorry about that." He slowed to a walk but still managed to slam the door behind him.

"Thank you, Ashby," my aunt said with a smile, leaving me wondering what she meant as she moved to go. "Oh, by the way, Hunter said to ask you to join us for family night at the Club this evening. It is a seafood buffet, I believe. Music, games, I suppose. I am afraid we have not attended very many family nights, but I hope that is going to change."

"Thanks, Aunt Monica. Thanks for including me, but I'd like to be here if Luke comes home from the hospital tonight. We've…we've become…good friends. I think he may need someone to talk to after the scare with Abe and all…"

"I understand completely, my dear. So thoughtful of you to want to be there for Luke. I shall tell Hunter it will be just the three of us for tonight." With a warm smile, a little wave, and what I thought might be the barest hint of a wink, she turned and wafted down the hall.

I heard a signal from my cell phone. Quickly stepping outside, I flipped it open to read the text, MEET ME AT STABLE, 6:30 2NITE. L.

My thumbs flew as I typed my reply. C U THEN. LUV U.

I took a deep breath, exhaling slowly to calm myself. Jeff and I would take our horseback ride, enjoy our picnic, and I'd still have plenty of time to freshen up before meeting Luke. I had so much to tell him. So much to ask. And, then, there were those strong arms of his. My heart flipped at the thought. "Luv U," I whispered to the phone.

****

A crack of thunder startled me from a deep sleep. The last thing I remembered was propping my laptop for a quick diary entry as I settled back against the headboard. I awoke with my hands still resting on the keyboard. Shaking my head, I tried to clear the sleep-fog from my mind.

Jeff and I had had a long, hard, exhilarating ride, a race and a canter and a trot and another race after our peanut-butter picnic. My slumber party with Miss Emma at the gazebo the night before had drained me, and the heavy Virginia humidity before the thunderstorm had sapped every atom of my remaining energy. I'd returned to my room, sweaty and exhausted, taking what I thought would be a few minutes to refresh my mind at the keyboard before showering. I planned on ample time for dressing, primping, even a little makeup, which I rarely bothered with.

So, I'd slept for two hours, according to my digital clock. It glowered its neon-green numbers. Seven o'clock p.m. Bloody hell! Luke would be waiting for me at the stable, wondering what was keeping me. If he'd tried to text me, my dead zone of a room would've prohibited communication.

As I scrambled to log off my computer, the screen held my attention. What was this? A whole page of gibberish. Numbers, letters, capitals, symbols, even some italics scattered at random, all splattered on the screen as if a two-year-old had played the keyboard like a piano. Did I write this? Hey, I knew I was pooped when I went to type a diary entry. I mean, I fell asleep over the keyboard, but no way could I have written this gobble-de-gook. I tried to pull up my pre-sleep mind. I remembered writing *Dear Diary*. Yes. Those two words were clear. They were the only two real words to be found. Except…wait a minute! From the alphabet soup before me, I sorted out one word, all caps, FREE. Actually, it was 3u*c-!FREE!P9&fft. My eyes scanned the page again and again until I was convinced that was all there was to be read, FREE.

"Rosabelle's left me another message." I sighed. "Rosabelle!" I shook my fist at the ceiling. "Your timing is terrible! I'm a mess and I'm late and I so wanted my meeting tonight with Luke to be perfect." I looked all around for the telltale rose but came up blank. I could not shake the notion that I, myself, had actually written the script before me.

With no time to clean up, I threw on a fresh T-shirt and ran a brush through my frowsy hair, looking with alarm at myself in the oval mirror. There was nothing romantic about the way I looked.

My eyes fell on the china cup in which I'd been collecting my rose petal mementos. What? Out of nowhere a round crystal container had appeared beside it. Invitingly feminine, the container looked every bit as old and fragile as the ancient coffee cup. Lifting the lid, I smelled the faint fragrance of roses emanating from under a yellowing powder puff. Wondering how long the dusting powder had resided in its container, I powdered a liberal sprinkling under my arms and down my bra. "Okay, Rosabelle," I whispered. "I get it." Then, smoothing my spotty cut-off jeans as best I could, I jammed my feet into my flips. "Hang on, Luke! I'm on my way."

Outside, I was showered with a curtain of rain. I needed a shower, but not this kind. I tried to jump over the puddles along the path to the barn, which did nothing but splash muddy water clear up to the cuffs of my shorts. My rubber flip-flops slipped and slid on the wet stones, causing me to slow down, lest I pitch head-first into the muck. By the time I reached the stable, I was a total disaster, soaked, muddy sweaty, and panting with frustration. Sasha greeted me with liquid eyes and a nickering for treats, but Luke was nowhere to be found.

"Luke? Luke?" The door to the office was open, but the tiny room was empty. Did he give up, think I wasn't going to show? I wondered with a sinking feeling in my gut. Then I saw the hand printed sign on the desk, "ASHBY: Follow my shoes."

Completely baffled, I looked around for Luke's shoes. Running shoes? Boots? Sandals? What the heck did he want me to do? Leaving the office and returning to the stable, I finally spied a decrepit pair of flips butting flat up against the wall. "Am I supposed to follow his shoes through the wall?" I grumbled. "Good grief, Luke. What are you thinking?" Only then, as my eyes traveled directly up from the flips, did I realize there were wooden slats nailed into the stable wall, straight up like a tree house ladder and the same weathered gray as the siding. "Of course. The hayloft." Sloughing off my own slippers, I dug in my toes and began the climb to the trap door in the ceiling, which I had never before even noticed.

Reaching the top, I knocked on the small hinged door with one fist, gripping the rustic ladder with my other hand, afraid I might plunge straight to the floor of the stable. The trap door opened only a few inches on its rusty hinges.

"What's the password?" Luke poked his head through the crack to ask.

"Sorry I'm late," I said.

"Nope. Sorry I'm late is not the password. Try again." He shut the trap door, then flung it wide and reached for my hands and pulled me up into the loft.

We both laughed before he took me in his arms. When I could catch my breath, I looked around. The small area was set off by a cliff of hay bales on one wall. The warm smell of dry hay permeated the loft and made me sneeze. Occasional puffs of damp outdoor air from the one window freshened the atmosphere. Rain tapped percussion on the tin roof. Luke had spread a blanket over a couple of bales to fashion a makeshift table where he had arranged plates and napkins and forks, a platter of cold fried chicken, potato salad, and a pile of brownies. A battery-operated light that looked like a Coleman lantern cast a soft glow over the repast.

"I checked in with Aunt Emma. She claimed she'd been resting all day and was full of energy. She insisted on sending me away with all this food," Luke said. "Y'shoulda seen me tryin' to haul it up here. She threw in an old quilt for good measure. D'ya think she knew there'd be two of us for dinner?"

"Wouldn't surprise me one bit," I plopped on the floor that was slick with years of hay storage. "Miss Emma is omniscient."

Luke handed me a bottle of cold soda, then opened one of his own. "The soda is my contribution. Dig in. If you're as hungry as I am, we can finish this off in no time."

"Come to think of it, I'm starving." I held out my plate for chicken and salad. "Now, tell me all about Abe. Everybody is so worried."

"Abe's a tough old bird. Th' doctors were actually surprised, I think, when he rallied like he did."

"When will they release him from the hospital?"

"Don't know. It's one-day-at-a-time."

"Luke, Miss Emma took me out to the gazebo in the middle of the night to tell me all kinds of things about Grandmother Lenore and Rosabelle and…"

"I know all about it." He pointed to the picnic dinner. "While she whipped up this dinner, she filled me in." Luke pulled me up from the floor. "I thought we'd never be alone."

I swiped my hand over my hair, suddenly self-conscious about my disheveled look. "I wanted to look nice for you tonight. But I fell asleep, and when I woke up, I couldn't believe what I'd written on my laptop…and I don't understand how…"

He put his finger on my lips. "Shush. You're even more beautiful than ever. And you smell like roses!"

They say love is blind, I thought. I made an impatient gesture. "But I have to tell you about my computer screen. There was all this crazy writing, and…"

"Remember when we were stargazing?" Taking

my hand, Luke led me to a low stack of hay bales, tossing Miss Emma's quilt on top. The natural light was growing dimmer by the minute. "There's no stars tonight, so let's just lie here and listen to th' rain on th' roof." Pushing one of the hay bales against the wall to make room, he folded his arms around me and bent his face to mine.

Luke jumped up with a yelp. "Crap! What was that?" He began swatting the air around his face and shoulders. "Wasps! I must've jostled a nest when I moved that hay bale. Damn! They're all over me!"

Grabbing Luke's hat from the floor, I flailed like a windmill, batting the manic insects right and left, trying to avoid stepping on them with my bare feet when they fell to the floor.

We were two whirling dervishes as the wasps drove us to the other side of the loft. "Whew! They're gone," Luke sighed, after several stressful minutes of combat. He rubbed the front of his shirt. "They got me good."

"Here, take your shirt off. I'll pour some of the cold soda on it and swab the bites." I helped him pull the shirt over his head, gingerly stroking several swollen, red welts on his torso with my fingertips.

"No need for swabs," Luke said. "Can't y'just kiss the ouchies and make 'em well?" He pulled me against his bare chest.

His skin smelled like summer, earthy and fresh. I could hear the drumming of his heart, louder than the rain above us. Against my cheek his chest hair felt silky and soft as a baby's downy head. I pressed my lips to his warm, berry-sweet skin.

"Did the wasps bite you?" His voice was low. "Can

I kiss your ouchies for you?"

Together we pulled off my T-shirt and unhooked my bra.

Lightly, he stroked me with gentle fingertips. His lips were more insistent. With every touch, I felt liquid fire radiating beneath my skin, coursing through my body in peaks and valleys. "Th' quilt," I heard Luke say through the rush of feelings sweeping me from coherent thought.

In one motion, we slipped to the floor.

****

We sat cross-legged on a bale of hay, devouring fudgy brownies, still moist and soft from Miss Emma's oven. The glow from the lantern cast funnels of light on the grainy walls of our little nest and the rain pattered a light rhythm on the roof as the storm tapered off. "Well, Luke, my favorite romance writers would certainly approve." I licked my fingers.

"Ya mean…about our roll in th' hay?" He chuckled.

"Don't tell me! You've been reading English romances."

"Ha! No, I'm hooked on calculus." He snagged the last chocolate morsel from the plate, holding it aloft like a prize. "Wanna share?"

"Chocolate and love." I smiled. "I'm full."

We sat quietly contented for several minutes before Luke spoke. "Now, what was it you were sayin' before… Somethin' about your computer screen?"

"Oh, yeah. It was crazy. Words and letters and symbols all jumbled up and covering a whole screen page, not just a few lines like the BLOOD message. It made no sense until I made out the word FREE. I'm positive it wasn't just a random spelling or something. FREE. What do you think it means?"

"Rosabelle again?"

"Funny, there was no rose. No song. No burned-down candle." I thought for a moment. "Well, but there was this rose-scented powder." I looked down my shirt and sniffed. "But when I woke up, I still had my hands on the keyboard. It was like I wrote it in my sleep. Like I was in a…"

With an expression that clearly showed he questioned my sanity, Luke finished my sentence, "In a stupor?"

"Uh, not exactly. Oh, I don't know. I've read about such a thing. It's called automatic writing—or something like that, when you write out words physically, but somebody else's thoughts are guiding your hand." I shivered. "Like Rosabelle is using my computer screen as her own electronic Ouija board."

"Well, it's got me stumped. Aunt Emma gave me her take on th' BLOOD message, y'know, about th' bloodlines, but what's this Free? Free what? Free who? Why would a ghost, even a techno-ghost, write FREE on your screen?"

"Maybe Rosabelle wants to free me of something."

"Hmmm. She could be referrin' to herself, I suppose. Guess we'll have t' run this one by Aunt Emma, too."

"Oh, I haven't told you about the coffee, either. When I came in from my gazebo gabfest with Miss Emma, I found a tray with coffee and a rose waiting for me on my bedside table. What do you think of that?"

"I think you need a shoulder to lean on," Luke put his arms around me.

"While I'm leaning on your taut and muscular shoulder, maybe you can tell me why Miss Emma thinks I may be in danger. She has her suspicions, but she won't tell me why or how or whom I should watch out for."

Luke pulled back to give me a skeptical look. "Taut an' muscular? Ha! I like that. More from your romance writers?"

"Nope. Straight out of my own book."

"Well, I don't know what info my aunt could be hidin', but if I had to guess, I'd say messin' aroun' with a violent ghost would have t' be way up there on a list of dangers." There was not a hint of sarcasm in his voice.

"Maybe you're right. Know any ghost busters around here?"

Luke appeared to consider the question seriously. "Th' way I understand it, kissin' is the best way t' ward off evil spirits. It sure worked for th' bee stings."

He leaned in for a kiss, but I stopped him. "Wait. Remember the Wizard of Oz? There was a wicked witch who caused all the trouble and then there was Glinda, the Good Witch of the East. Well, I know deep in my soul that Rosabelle is the Glinda of Overhome, at least for me. Why else the roses, the lullaby, the coffee? There's an old love poem and she tunes the radio to serenade me with her favorite country music and writes me all-important messages on my lap top. Rosabelle is NOT wicked."

Luke frowned. "I wonder what ol' Rosie thinks about our makin' love. I'm not gonna end up dead on a dock like Eddie Mills' dog, am I?"

I grimaced. "God forbid! Although, Rosabelle does

seem to have it in for males, you know, the dog, Sasha, and maybe even Abe. You know, it seems like the Night Riders are getting blamed for the very same things Rosabelle did to aggravate my Grandfather Thomas, according to Miss Emma."

I turned my face up for the promised kiss. "Guess we'll have to wait and see, Luke. If Rosabelle's on my side, she's on yours. Still, unpredictable as she is, you might watch your step."

I scrambled to my feet, wiping brownie crumbs from my clothes. "Now, I'd better get in before our secret rendezvous is discovered."

"One last thing." He drew me to him.

"What? Another kiss? You're beginning to remind me of Romeo, like in the balcony scene with Juliet. I believe he says, 'Oh, wilt thou leave me so unsatisfied?'"

He tightened his grip. "Sorry. Shakespeare was never high on my reading list."

"Then, how about this. Juliet tells Romeo, 'Parting is such sweet sorrow.'"

"And he replies, 'I love you.'"

"Um…No, I don't remember that in the script."

"Forget the script. This is me talkin'. I love you, Ashby."

"You sure know how to get another kiss." I placed my hands on his cheeks, drawing him toward me.

We climbed down the loft stairs and retrieved our footwear. "I've gotta spend some quality time with my favorite calc book," Luke said, moving into his office. "Oh, I almost forgot." Reaching into a drawer, he drew out something I recognized instantly. Abe's scrapbook, crammed with my Grandmother Lenore's mementoes.

"I don't think Abe would mind if you looked over this, Ashby. You might find somethin' helpful in it."

I hugged the fragile book as if I might shield it from any harmful effects of night air. Another treasure from the past. My thoughts ran in rhythm with the soft plip-plop of my slippers on the damp stones. There was so much to think about.

****

Dear Diary,

Luke and I managed to escape for a few hours into a world of our own. A lofty world. A world free from ailment and uncertainty. "I love you." Luke said it! "I love you, Ashby." Yes, we're in love. We made love. It was as natural as the rain on a tin roof.

And now I have Abe's scrapbook full of newspaper clippings and all kinds of press info, with photographs and facts, dates and names and events covering a pretty good chunk of my Grandmother Lenore's life. I'm thinking I can find some clues here, thanks to Luke. He is keeping his word to help me solve the mystery of Rosabelle, the techno-ghost.

Chapter Twenty-Two

Feeling a little guilty about missing family night at my aunt and uncle's club, I agreed to go shopping with Aunt Monica in Bradford, the county seat. I'd rather have spent the morning climbing onto Sasha and riding like the wind. I'd become addicted to horseback riding. I think riding provides the same endorphin high runners crave. Missing just one morning's ride left me with withdrawal pains. Luke had gone to the hospital to see Abe, and Jeff would be hours at his piano lesson. I could have used the alone-time to commune with my beloved horse, but my aunt appeared so eager for my company, I didn't have the heart to turn her down.

We strolled through shops both quaint and trendy. Aunt Monica insisted on buying me some outrageously overpriced earrings and a silk scarf. The scarf I'd probably hand over to Mom someday, but I had to admit the dangly earrings were as fun as they were smart. I thanked her enthusiastically and, over a finger-food lunch at La Duchess Bakery, I modeled them for her.

Aunt Monica patted her mouth delicately with the lacy, linen napkin. "Those earrings are so you, Ashby. They bring out the highlights in your eyes." She placed her napkin beside her plate. "Now, I want to share a confidence."

I could not help remembering our last lunch date

when she'd told me about her stuttering trauma and about my uncle's "dark side," I believe she called it, generated by his mother's untimely death. Oh, Lord. What now? I thought. I never knew what to expect from my aunt, especially when we were away from the constraining mood and atmosphere of Overhome. Swallowing my inclination to protest, I smiled and tilted my head as a signal for her to begin.

"I have already told you, Ashby, how grateful I am for your bringing out the best in Jefferson. I was so afraid he would turn into the self-centered, spoiled, only-child with no sense of family love and values."

"I-I don't think…" I started to object, but she put up a hand to stop me.

"No, no. Let me go on. He has positively blossomed under your guidance this summer. He has become a happy, self-sufficient, normal little boy. You already know how I feel about that." She put her hand on my arm and gave it a squeeze. "But there has been a totally unexpected bonus from your stay at Overhome. I have only just begun to realize it myself." Shaking her head, as if with disbelief, she continued. "It's Hunter. He has become so much more attentive, so attuned to Jefferson, to me, to family in general. You know, though he willingly spends quality time with Jefferson, I always had the feeling Hunter was humoring me, condescending to spend any time on what he considers my whims. It was as if he and Jefferson and I were three separate entities with nothing to connect us. Now, why, it was his idea to attend family night at the club. He has been talking about all of us spending a day at the Salem Fair together, and he has begun plans for a real family vacation this fall. Ashby, we have never had a trip away from Overhome, as a family, for more than a few days. Having you here has stirred a latent need in Hunter, triggered, I believe, his realization that family is all we have to remember us when we are gone." She beamed with pleasure.

I tried to look like I shared Monica's enthusiasm, but I had the uncomfortable feeling she was making way too much of my uncle's so-called metamorphosis. She so wanted him to be warm and loving to her, to pay attention to her emotional needs, that she was eager to count any spark on his part as the kindling to a fire.

"Ashby, can you believe it? Hunter is now deep into researching an Overton genealogy. Oh, he has always been a history buff, but when it came to his own mother and father and brothers, he refused to talk about them, avoided any mention of the family's past, all a part of that childhood trauma over his mother's death, I suppose. Now, it seems he cannot get enough of poring over their papers and journals. Last night he got out a rubbing of the Overton gravestones he and Jefferson did some years ago. He is like a man possessed, determined to unearth every nuance about the family tree. He is spending hours in his study."

This revelation made me sit up and take notice. I gathered my wits about me before asking, as casually as possible, "Did you say Uncle Hunter has been poring over family journals?"

"Why, yes. A short while ago, I came upon his mother's memoirs quite by accident. I was looking for an old photo when I discovered Lenore's diary. It was tucked back in the corner of an ancient wardrobe in the keeping room, as though someone wanted to hide it. When I showed Hunter my find, he was quite excited.

Come to think of it, that was when he began to take interest in working on a genealogy."

The lost diary Miss Emma had been lamenting. Lenore's diary. I wondered what Miss Emma would have to say about it, and how it had come to rest, hidden in the keeping room. I couldn't wait to tell her.

Monica looked beyond me and waved at a smartly-dressed woman. "Oh, hi, Bitsy. How nice to see you here." My aunt beckoned her friend to our table.

"Ashby, this is Bitsy Coleman. She and her family belong to our club at the lake."

"Hello, Ashby." Bitsy shook my hand. "You're Monica's niece, I believe."

"Yes. Nice to meet you."

She looked at my aunt. "Oh, why don't you and Ashby come with me, Monica? There's a marvelous sale at the antique shop just a block away."

Aunt Monica cocked her head at me. "Ashby? Are you interested?"

"Thanks, Aunt Monica, Mrs. Coleman, but, actually, I would love to check out the County Historical Society. We walked past it before lunch."

"My family!" Monica looked at her friend with a toss of her head. "They're all obsessed with history." She turned to me. "Why don't you visit the Historical Society while Bitsy and I are antique shopping? We'll come collect you when we finish."

"That'd be great, Aunt Monica. Thanks." It was the moment I had been hoping for. Bitsy Coleman was a godsend.

Once I stepped inside the reference room, I didn't waste any time, but went straight for the files about the building of the dam. I'd been doing a lot of thinking about Rosabelle's FREE message, and something my aunt had just told me gave me an idea. I hoped I'd find something here to help me out.

I sorted through several files before I found what I wanted, the graves. An old newspaper clipping revealed that it took two years to find all of the graves located in the valleys to be flooded to create Moore Mountain Lake. Power company employees were given a map showing where the project would be built and were instructed to locate any and all graves. They talked with residents and churches for leads and spent a lot of time hacking through honeysuckle vines and other weeds to find headstones. The graves had to be found and the kinfolks located to see if they wanted their ancestors' remains to be dug up and re-buried. Otherwise, the graves would be forever submerged in very deep water.

The certified cemeteries were easy, according to one press release. It was the private graveyards and the slave graves that officials had to work to locate. In total, they pinpointed 78 individual cemeteries, with 1,371 graves. No grave could be moved without authorization. However, if the family wanted the graves left in place, they had to sign an agreement to that effect. Each re-location was documented with the name of the dead, the original burial site, and the re-interment site. The catalogue, the article noted, is available for genealogy research.

I closed the file. How very interesting. I approached the check-out desk and spoke to the attendant. "I'm, um, doing a genealogy. Can you tell me where I might find the catalogue of grave removals and re-interment done during the building of the dam at Moore Mountain Lake?"

The middle-aged man gave me a curious look. "Must be a run on genealogies." He smiled. "You're the second person to ask for that catalogue this week." He disappeared for a moment, then handed me a bound volume. "This is for reference only. It can't be checked out, I'm afraid."

"Oh, I'm just going to make a few notes here. If I can find what I'm looking for, that is."

"Good luck."

Checking my watch, I gave a silent plea for the antique shoppers to take their time, then I dived into the data. It did not take long to actualize what I'd begun to suspect. The listings for grave removals and re-burials from Overhome were quite lengthy and detailed; the power company had done a thorough job. I found many names I'd come to know—Emilie and Francis Overton, Johbe and Robert, and Angelina Elisabeth Overton. But, there was not a word about the slave graves. No Lulu. Nothing about Micah and Mary mentioned in Angelina's diary. When I turned to the documentation section in the back of the catalogue, there was a copy of the signed agreement authorizing the power company to leave all the slave graves on the Overhome property where they were, undisturbed. The agreement was signed by Thomas Overton. Those graves would all be at the bottom of the lake.

And one more thing—nowhere was there any mention of a gravesite for Rosabelle O'Connor.

****

As soon as my aunt and I returned, I went looking for Miss Emma, but she was nowhere to be found. She must have gone to town for groceries with one of the hired hands. I'd have to catch her later when we could

211

be alone. I watched Jeff burst through the door, charged with pent-up energy.

"Yuck! I hate piano theory!" he growled. "My teacher makes us listen to classical music. It sucks, Ashby. Long and boring and deary."

"Don't you mean dreary?" I laughed. "And watch your language."

"Even the girls were itchin' to leave."

"What say we saddle up the horses? I've been wanting a ride myself."

His face brightened immediately. "All right!" He bolted down the hall toward his room.

"Change into long pants and boots, Jefferson," his mother said as she came out from the library. "And remember to wear your riding helmet."

Unexpectedly, Hunter appeared in the hall. He was dressed in shorts and a polo shirt and a golf hat. "What say we go out on the boat, all of us. Make it a family outing. It's a beautiful lake day. Monica, my dear, we can shelter you under the Bimini top, if you're worried about sun damage."

My aunt melted under her husband's suggestion. "Oh, my, Hunter. What a wonderful idea. Give us time to lather up with sunscreen and collect some beach towels." She flashed me an I-told-you-so look. "Ashby? Jefferson? Are you game for an afternoon on the lake?"

Jeff stopped in mid-flight. "Sure, Mom." He looked at his father. "We can ski, right, Dad?"

"Of course," Uncle Hunter said. "Ashby?"

"Count me in," I said. To my horse I made a vow, "Sasha, I'll get to you later. I will get to you, I promise."

****

By the time we came off the lake, the sun had slipped below the mountain, streaking the sky with flamingo feathers of light. While my aunt and uncle whisked Jeff away to the house, I had to decide whether to hunt down Miss Emma to talk about Aunt Monica's discovery of Lenore's diary or to grab the last few daylight moments for a quick run on Sasha. It was not much of a contest, as emotion won out over logic, and I changed into jeans and bolted for the stable. Sasha greeted me with knickers and whinnies. "Yes, yes, I know dear Sasha," I crooned, stroking his muzzle. "You want a canter as much as I do, don't you?" He whinnied in what I was sure was complete understanding.

Saddling Sasha quickly in the growing dusk, I thrust my foot into the stirrup and flung my leg over my horse's back, giving him a nudge and a cluck. With a snort and a jerk of his head, Sasha took off. We rode without stopping, cutting a path through the soft, heavy Southern air, horse and rider as in tune with each other as the creek and the trees that whistled past, Sasha and I, rolling like the hills around us in a rhythm as mesmerizing as a poem. I lost track of time and place. My horse and I were united, breathing one breath, living one moment. When, at last, Sasha slowed to a trot, I realized the day had turned to night and that I did not have the slightest idea where we were.

Reining Sasha in, I peered in all directions, trying to form a sense of place. A darkening cloud cover blurred the line between trees and sky. I listened for the gurgle of the creek, but the night air was as still and thick as blackstrap molasses. Sasha snorted, asking me to lead the way, but I held the reins tight, looking for a signpost of some kind. I don't know how long we stood until I saw it, a spark of light. A flare? A flashlight? No bigger than a pinpoint, the light flickered, died, and reappeared.

Turning Sasha, I followed the bobbing light. On and off. On, off. Hypnotized, I pressed my horse forward. The glowing light shifted slowly, glancing off one shadowy branch after another in a random pattern. Sasha stumbled occasionally over the uneven incline of the path, but I urged him on, pressing my legs against his barrel, in pursuit of the elusive firefly light. Sensing only that we had strayed far from the beaten path, I found myself ducking under ever lower-hanging branches that seemed to grab at me with gnarled fingers as the light played its game, flaring to my left, then to the right. I felt myself go dizzy as I sensed we were going in circles.

I thought I heard a shuffling in the underbrush, but when Sasha stopped, so did the sound. On auto-pilot now, I pressed on, following the light that was like a laser pointing haphazard directions on a map. In the opaque velvet of the forest night, I had completely lost my way. At length, I realized I was shivering, whether with cold or fright or anticipation, I could not say. A damp chill had descended like a fog, bringing me, at last, to my senses.

"Ashby, you are a moron! You're so fixated on Rosabelle and her candles, you've lost your marbles," I said to my horse. Forget the Bronte sisters and their foggy moors. I mean, this setting was more like the one in 'The Hound of the Baskervilles' by Arthur Conan Doyle. And this guiding light was not Rosabelle's doing. There was no music, no sweet Afton, no warm, protective aura of her presence. Now I was lost in a black tangle. Sasha stumbled. I sensed a movement just ahead when, without warning, Sasha shied, then reared on his hind legs. Clutching at the reins and then the saddle, I couldn't stop my swift slide to the ground. I landed with such a thud it jarred my teeth. Rolling away from Sasha's flailing hooves, I sat up and came to my knees, reaching for Sasha's reins. Something hard and sharp struck me from behind. Everything went black.

Chapter Twenty-Three

Morning. What had happened last night? Moving my eyes slowly so as not to disturb my throbbing head, I saw that I was in a room I recognized only as a guest bedroom on the main floor of Overhome. Sunlight shone through gauze curtains at the window, making me squint and flinch in pain. I tried to sit up, but went dizzy with the effort.

Miss Emma bustled through the door, holding a water pitcher and glass. "Ashby! I've been so worried. We all have. When they brought you in last night, you looked, well, you seemed barely alive. All I could think of was Lenore when she fell from her horse." She held a straw to my lips. "Thank God you've come to." Her eyes held both anxiety and relief.

Again I struggled up from the pillow, but bright slivers of pain slashed through my head and I gave up the effort. "I'm kinda fuzzy, Miss Emma. I can't remember what happened."

"Hush, now. You need rest. You fell from your horse in the woods last night." She offered the water again, bending the straw so that I could drink without raising my head.

"Oh. Right. The light. Candle?" I struggled to focus—to remember. "I followed it, but we were lost. Sasha and I. Then he reared high, threw me off…" A wave of nausea washed over me. Spots danced before

216

my eyes, making my head feel so light I feared it would float off my neck. Then I knew I would throw up.

Miss Emma, evidently, had anticipated this occurrence, for she whipped out a basin and held it under my chin until I finished. I lay back, panting, too weak to wipe the drops of cold sweat coursing down my cheeks.

"Enough. Be quiet now. You can talk about it later, when you're stronger."

"Okay," I whispered. "Just tell me...how did I get home, Miss Emma?"

"Luke and I carried you." It was my uncle's deep voice in the doorway. "I've called Dr. Ross and he's on his way. You must rest now." He moved to my bedside.

"Don't try to talk, Ashby. Just listen. As he was closing up the stables, Luke noticed Sasha's empty stall. When he came up to the house to alert me, we both realized you were missing, also. We went looking immediately, of course. We found Sasha saddled and cropping grass in the meadow. So we headed for the woods, hoping to find you safe and unhurt." He patted my hand. "You were in the thickest part of the woods, but not so far from home as you might think. It was dark and treacherously slippery. My guess is Sasha stumbled, causing you to fall and hit your head on a rock."

Tears seeped slowly from the corners of my eyes. It was not the pain that made me cry so much as knowing how deeply people here felt about me. Evidently, my uncle had saved my life. And Luke. Dear Luke, always looking after me.

Miss Emma glided toward the door. "Don't leave," I begged her. "I have to tell you..."

"I am leaving, Ashby," she said firmly. "You've exerted yourself enough. Whatever it is you want to say, it can wait." She pulled the door softly, but decisively, closed.

Wearily I closed my eyes. "I'm not so sure it can wait, Miss Emma," I whispered before I drifted off. "I didn't fall and hit my head. I fell and hit my butt. Someone or something hit my head from behind. On purpose." I had completely forgotten I wanted to tell Miss Emma about Lenore's diary.

****

Dear Diary,

It's been three days since my accident. Dr. Ross said I sustained a fairly severe concussion and ordered complete bed rest. Miss Emma has guarded my threshold like a sentry at Buckingham Palace, keeping all visitors at bay, including Jeff and Luke, though both pleaded their cases eloquently as I listened to their voices in the hall outside my door. My head aches like hell, but otherwise I'm okay. I feel like such a klutz, falling off the horse yet again. I can't use the dark and stormy night for an excuse. But any way I look at it, I'm convinced someone deliberately spooked Sasha and then clobbered me for good measure. I suppose it could have been a freak accident, but unless a rock fell from the sky as I was getting up, how could my head injury have happened? I'm also sure it had something to do with the ghostly candlelight. The question, of course, is WHO would want to harm me or Sasha and me, and, more specifically, WHY?

Miss Emma says nobody's saying much, but I get the feeling Eddie Mills is the number one suspect on the part of my aunt and uncle. Poor, dumb Eddie. I know he enjoyed bullying Jeff, but I think he likes me and can't believe he'd play such a mean trick. On the other hand, I suppose it could've been the enigmatic Night Riders. When I try to talk about the accident, Miss Emma purses her thin lips and gazes at something invisible in the distance. She tells me she and Luke are comparing notes on the situation and that I am not to worry my "sweet little noggin" about it. Do they think I'm too fragile to handle the truth? I have to admit, thinking about it makes my head ache worse.

On a happier note, after some time in the downstairs guest suite, it's good to be back in my old room. I sense Rosabelle's presence in every inch of space, every breath of air. This morning I woke to find the antique coffeepot full of roses, not the usual solitary bud. It's as if she's saying, "I would never lead you astray, Ashby. It wasn't MY candle you followed, and here's my gift to prove it." Ha! Rosie is one visitor Miss Emma can't bar at the door. Her bouquet marks a Red Letter Day, as the doc says I can be up and about, as long as I take it easy.

In my absence, it seems there's been a bluebird population explosion. What a noisy crew they are, clamoring on my balcony like they're making up for lost time. At home bluebirds seemed so shy. This is nothing like the birdies chirping at Cinderella as she works. It's more like a choir of squawking, brawling kids.

Wonderful news! Luke is bringing Abe home from the hospital this afternoon. Miss Emma has found a nurse friend of hers to take care of him as long as necessary. Everyone hopes he'll be as good as new.

Oh, when I told Miss Emma about Lenore's diary, I

got a very curious reaction. Or, to be exact, I got no reaction at all. Just a stoic look and an "Interesting" from Miss E. Very curious, indeed.

****

Jeff threw his arms around me and hugged me until I was dizzy. "Gently now, Jeff, gently," Aunt Monica said, giving me her own careful embrace.

"Can we go ridin' today?" he asked, with a flicker of his eyes toward his mother.

My aunt laughed. "Let's let Ashby get used to walking again before she rides, Jefferson. All in good time," she added when his face fell in disappointment.

"I can't wait to hop up on Sasha, Jeff, but for now, I'd be delighted just to give him a hug and a kiss and brush out his mane." I reached for my cousin's hand. "Tell you what. After lunch we'll walk to the stable and have some quality horse-time, just you and me and the four-legged boys. Okay?"

Jeff flew at me with another hug. "Man, Ashby. I've missed you."

"I know somebody else who's missed you," my aunt said with a sly smile. "Luke's been up to the house every other hour checking on you."

"He couldn't get past the guard at the gate to my room," I said.

"Miss Emma held firm. 'Bed rest means complete rest. No visitors, and that's that,' was how she put it to everyone," Aunt Monica said.

"Nobody messes with Miss Emma." Jeff's earnest look made me smile.

"I just want to walk outside a bit. It's amazing how I've missed fresh air these past few days." I turned to Jeff. "Would you be my escort, kind sir?"

Jeff grabbed my hand. "I'm not sure what an 'escort' is, but I can walk real careful with you, Ashby." His eagerness to help left me weepy-eyed, but fortunately Jeff was too focused on his role to notice.

"You're sure you're strong enough?" My aunt had not missed my emotional response to Jeff's sweet expression.

I flashed her my biggest smile. "Jeff will take care of me. No need to worry."

We made a slow, steady tour of the estate, avoiding the dock because of the steep steps. It was a clear, bright morning. In the sun Overhome was picture book pretty, all white and green, solid and wise, old and important. Moore Mountain and the rolling hills that announced it encircled the lake like a jade necklace. I'd learned to love the look and feel of Overhome on a summer morning. Jeff burbled and babbled the whole way, causing my mood to lift with each passing minute, as I breathed the fresh, fragrant air, enjoying the feel of the sun on my arms. When he mentioned returning to "real school" in the fast-approaching fall, I realized with a sharp pang that I would, by then, have gone back to Jersey, separated from Jeff and Luke and Sasha, and all I'd come to love about Overhome. With effort, I pulled my mind away from the unpleasant reality, letting thoughts flow free with the up and down of Jeff's expressive voice as he chattered on.

After some time, we approached the gazebo garden. "Let's sit in the gazebo," I suggested. "I'm out of breath."

"This place is kinda creepy, huh, Ashby?" Jeff looked from side to side, pointing out the overgrown vines that shrouded the stone walls as we descended the stone steps. "Did somebody die here?"

I felt a chill at the suggestion, but tried to sound lighthearted. "It's only an old, old garden, Jeff. A garden where people enjoyed the flowers and played hide-'n-seek in a maze and sat in the gazebo."

"Amazed? What's that?" Jeff's freckles bunched over his wrinkled-up nose.

I laughed. "Not amazed. A maze. It's like a puzzle made with bushes or trees, with starts and stops and dead-ends so people get confused and sometimes lost."

"Oh! Like the treasure hunts in my Highlights magazine! Where you take a pencil and try to find your way to the reward at the end."

"Exactly."

"So…where's the reward?" he asked, puzzlement displacing the freckles once again.

Well, he had me there. "I suppose it could be the gazebo itself."

Jeff took my hand. "Come on, Ashby. Let's try the amazed!"

And so we made our way along the paths, once trimmed and landscaped, no doubt, but now studded with tussocks of grass and weeds and moss. It was sometimes necessary to assume single file to avoid the briary branches that crawled from the once trimmed sides of the hedges. Content at those times to let Jeff lead, I could sometimes anticipate a dead-end before he did, possibly because my height allowed me to see over some of the foliage. Eventually, we did, indeed, find ourselves in the clearing, facing the peeling skeleton structure of the old gazebo.

"Was I right? Have we found our reward, Jeff?"

Without appearing to hear me, he let go my hand

and headed straight to the periwinkle patch for the rose bushes I'd found my first time here. "I think somebody died in here." Grabbing a stick from the ground, my cousin poked at the bushes for a good while, before leaning down and brushing at the dirt with his hands. "Look, Ashby! I told you so!" Jeff exclaimed.

"W-what are you talking about?"

"Look!" He pointed triumphantly to a small raised rectangle in the earth. "It's a tombstone. Just like the ones Dad and I did the rubbings on over at the Baptist church where they moved the family graves."

"So…it's not a garden," I stammered. "It's…it's…"

"A cemetery." Jeff knelt again and scrubbed at the stone. "Ashby! There's words on it! A name!" He looked at me over his shoulder. "I wish I had some paper and charcoal. We could do a rubbing."

"Can you make out any of the letters, Jeff?"

"I need a rag. Something to wipe up the dirt."

I fished a tissue out of my pocket and handed it to him. He spit on it and rubbed. Spit and rubbed. "Okay," he said at last. "Here's what we've got, R-O-S…" he called out the letters.

"R-o-s-a-b-e-l-l-e? Could it be Rosabelle?"

"Yep. Those are the letters. And there's some numbers, too, but I can't quite read them."

"Probably dates."

"Oh yeah. The date they're born and the date they die. I remember how it goes."

"Who's Rosabelle?" he asked after a long moment.

How could I explain without scaring the bejesus out of my cousin? "Um, I think she was someone who lived here a long time ago."

"Is Rosabelle my ancestor?" Jeff wrinkled his nose. There went his freckles heaped in a pile again. "When we did the tombstone rubbings, Dad said they were our ancestors. Their names were on the stones. He said one was my great-great-great-great-great grandfather, or something like that." He frowned. " Rose...Rosabelle must be an ancestor, too, right? But what's she doing here?"

"Actually, I believe Rosabelle was a servant, someone who lived here and worked for your ancestors."

Jeff frowned. "I don't get it." He was deep in thought. "Dad said all the slaves were buried in a separate cemetery. He said when our land was flooded to make the lake, our ancestors were moved to the Baptist church and the slave graves were moved to a different graveyard, to a slave graveyard somewhere."

"Well, yes. I understand that when the lake was formed the slave graves were moved to an African-American church," I said, knowing full well Thomas Overton had left them all to be flooded over by the lake. I saw no sense relating what I'd discovered at the Historical Society. It was quite possible a sensitive kid like Jeff would be upset by that information.

Jeff turned back to Rosabelle's marker. "Maybe there's more graves here. Maybe this was the slave cemetery!" He began poking at the scabby ground with his stick.

"I follow your reasoning. But, you see, Rosabelle was not a slave. And she was not African. She came from Scotland as a free servant. She probably would not have been buried in a slave cemetery, or moved to a relocated slave cemetery, either."

It was too much for his seven-year-old mind to encompass, bright as that mind was. Letting the stick drop, he tilted his head and commented. "Well, I'd still like to do a rubbing. Let's come back here and do one, okay?"

I nodded agreement and pulled him gently to the gazebo seat beside me. But my mind was racing. I wondered if Miss Emma knew about Rosabelle's grave here at the gazebo. Did Abe know? Lenore? It was time I had another long talk with the housekeeper who knew everything.

Chapter Twenty-Four

After lunch Jeff and I visited the stables. Sasha tossed his head impatiently. He didn't understand why we were not saddling up. "Soon, dear Sasha." I stroked his thick mane. I always knew what Sasha was thinking. Could he read *my* mind? We offered our horses treats and promises, petted and talked to them, and reluctantly made our way back to the house where Aunt Monica whisked Jeff off for a play date. It was the opportunity I'd been looking for.

Entering the library, I went directly to the oldest-looking books on the shelves. There was a surprising collection of topics; agriculture, nature, animal husbandry, history, philosophy, religion. Several shelves were dedicated to novels and biographies and there was a whole shelf on the Civil War. I pulled out a volume entitled *Birds of Virginia*. Looking up bluebirds in the index, I read the brief description of appearance, behavior, call, and characteristics. I wasn't really surprised to find there was nothing about the tendency of bluebirds to hurl themselves at windows en masse, but it was worth the five minutes' review.

Then I saw it, surely a source that would be useful. *The Spirit World*, by J.J. Dickenson. The copyright indicated the book was not particularly old, but one look told me this was a well-read volume. In fact, it fell open to a section titled "*Exorcisms - Freeing Evil*

Spirits." Someone had highlighted line upon line of when to hire a priest exorcist, how the spirits are exorcised, and what to expect in the process. Thomas Overton, perhaps? Rosabelle had more than haunted him, she had persecuted him, according to Miss Emma. Flipping through the pages, I came to another highlighted section under the title "*Spirits Speak through Birds*." So maybe I was not the only one to be visited by dive-bombing, pecking, huddling, screeching birds. "Sometimes the restless spirit who has not passed over appears in birds. The fowl flock to the source of disquiet, clamoring for attention, willing to die in an effort to bring awareness to the minds of the living regarding the needs of the dead."

As I toyed with the idea of tucking the book under my arm and carrying it to my room for an in-depth read, Miss Emma appeared with her feather duster.

She seemed surprised to see me looking over the library shelves. "Doing a little research," I said with a laugh. "You know, Miss Emma, we haven't had any time to talk, what with my accident and all. Can you give your feather duster a rest and sit with me?"

"Of course, child. I've plenty of time. And dusting is my least favorite chore, so I don't mind putting it off. Have you been looking for some reading material to fill your free time?" She darted a look to the Dickenson book in my hands.

"Not really, Miss Emma. I just thought I might find some answers here. I feel like I'm always pestering you for information, and…"

"Don't be silly. Sit here," she indicated an overstuffed arm chair beside a reading lamp. Settling herself in a companion chair nearby, she looked at me with bright, expectant eyes. "I've come to relish our talks, Ashby."

I had to smile. What a dear old thing she is, I thought. So full of life, so caring. What would this family have done without her steady presence all these years?

"It's nice to see you up and about," she said.

"I had a good nurse," I told her. I settled into the soft leather chair. The mellow wood-paneled walls, the smell of old books, the quiet, comfy reading niches, put me immediately into a pensive mood. "It's going to be hard to leave Overhome," I mused. "Luke tells me there are quite a few colleges close by. Maybe I could stay here, apply to one or two. I've heard Hollins has a great writing program."

Miss Emma surprised me when she hesitated before responding, as if she disapproved of the idea of my staying, but did not know how to say so without hurting my feelings. "I know a lot of people who would be delighted if you were to make your home here." She smiled. "Including me."

Something in her tone belied the kind words, but I could not, for the life of me, put my finger on what it was. "Well, thanks. But, that's not what I wanted to talk to you about," I said.

She shifted in her chair and raised her eyebrows. "Go on, please."

I took a deep breath and launched into my question. "You know, while you were caring for me, I told you my aunt found Lenore's diary, which she gave to my uncle. She said Uncle Hunter was excited about the find and that he's working on a genealogy."

"Believe me, I've been thinking long and hard

about that nugget of information, Ashby. Lenore's diary, I mean. I believe I've sorted it out, or at least some of it."

"How about sharing?"

Miss Emma nodded. "I've kept some things from you—things between your grandmother and me. You know that. But I've had my reasons. Good reasons."

"I know how important your promises to Grandmother Lenore are. I have to respect that."

She was quiet for many minutes. When she began again, her face reflected both her devotion to her long-ago friend and the realization that the confidences she was about to reveal were important. "Let me begin with your uncle. It's hard growing up without a mother. For Hunter, it was more than that."

"My uncle was there that day when his mother fell from the horse, wasn't he, Miss Emma? Only five years old and he witnessed the tragic accident."

She looked startled.

"I read the fine print in one of the articles about my Grandmother Lenore's accident. In Abe's scrapbook."

"Oh yes, of course. Luke told me he'd given it to you. There's more," Miss Emma said. "For reasons I'm not entirely sure of, Hunter evidently thought that he had caused the horse to shy, to run Lenore under the tree branch. Something about waving a handkerchief, I believe."

"Oh, God. That makes it even worse."

"It was untrue, of course. But no manner of argument on my part could convince Hunter otherwise. He was haunted by that guilt. And I'm afraid his father did not help matters much. Thomas was a bully of the worst sort, the kind who takes out his frustrations on his own defenseless children. Lenore and her husband never saw eye-to-eye when it came to disciplining their children."

"Please, go on."

"Lenore put it all down in her diary, about Thomas's domineering and brooding temperament, how he was jealous of her devoted crowd of friends and admirers and of her skill and success as a horse woman." Miss Emma shook her head sadly. "That's why Lenore asked me to see that Hunter was brought up properly. She knew she could not count on his father to do the right things."

"She really laid a job on you."

"Hunter watched his mother fall, never saw her alive again, felt it was his fault. It affected him deeply. Well, after that he trusted no one. I tried my best to take Lenore's place, but he needed his mother. Oh, in many ways Hunter turned out well. He's a prominent, successful man, but there was just so much working against him in his formative years."

"I think I'm beginning to understand. Those steely eyes. The cold, unreadable exterior that makes him so different from Dad."

"Perhaps I should not be telling you this, but Hunter did spend some time in a mental hospital, right after Washington and Marian died. There's a lot of grief bottled up inside your uncle, Ashby." She looked sad enough to cry. "Since the day she died, I've been convinced Lenore is watching me try to carry out her wishes and has found me wanting."

I was at a loss for words and so sat quietly while Miss Emma gathered her thoughts, fidgeting, frowning, opening her mouth to speak and then shutting it again.

Finally she seemed to come to some kind of resolution, for she spoke. "You know I don't feel comfortable speaking of the past here, inside these walls, Ashby. I just *feel* Lenore's presence here so strongly. But we may not have another chance to talk." She paused, took a deep breath, and continued. "I want you to know that I have my own theory about what spooked Lenore's horse." She stood, then, and went to the window, pulling open the heavy draperies and throwing wide the window, as though to let out any spirits who might be hibernating in the wooden walls.

"You know, Miss Emma, I read something else in Abe's scrapbook. And I also have a theory about what spooked my Grandmother Lenore's horse."

"Well, let's have it. What's your theory, Ashby?" She turned from the window and sat down.

"One article on the accident said she was riding Capitola, you know, Cappy. Uncle Hunter said Cappy was my grandmother's favorite horse."

"Yes, that's correct. That's one reason no one could believe Lenore's horse could possibly be spooked. They were so…so *attuned* to one another." She looked at me and waited for me to go on.

"I remember Uncle Hunter told me once that my grandmother and her horse were so close that it seemed she could telepathize with Cappy. I didn't question it myself. I often feel Sasha and I understand each other's feelings. But…"

"But if Rosabelle was storming around persecuting Thomas, and hovering over Lenore, your grandmother could have been very upset. Emotionally distraught. Possibly, fearful," Miss Emma said.

"And Cappy, sensing Lenore's distress, might have

bolted unexpectedly…"

Miss Emma gave me an approving look. "It seems we've reached a similar conclusion, Ashby."

Deep in our thoughts, we sat in silence. I was the first to speak. "So, do you think that might explain why Rosabelle seems so angry? Why the bluebirds play Kamikaze on my balcony? Why she might set my fingers to the keyboard to write FREE? "To set the record straight, or something?"

"Rosabelle was always the friendly, helpful spirit. Then the worst possible thing happened to her 'mistress.' It very well could be like that."

"Free Rosabelle," I mused. "Free her from feeling responsible for Lenore's death? Are we talking a guilty ghost?"

"Free Rosabelle to cross over to the other side. She died a violent death saving her young charge centuries ago. If she *caused* a violent death—Lenore's death…I believe it's possible. Who knows? I told you, Ashby, Luke and I have put our heads together while you were convalescing. He explained the, what did he call it? The automatic writing on your computer screen, FREE. Like you, Luke and I both think it was another message from Rosabelle. As I said, I've done a lot of thinking about your situation."

"Miss Emma, did you know there's a grave marker for Rosabelle at the gazebo?" The thought surfaced unexpectedly.

"Rosabelle's grave and stone were moved from the family plot to the gazebo when the dam was built. Though he didn't consider Rosabelle worthy of relocation along with the family in the Baptist cemetery, your Grandfather Thomas was mortally afraid of her spirit and he did not want to incur any further wrath from her by allowing her to languish in a watery grave."

"But Rosabelle's name did *not* show up in the catalogue. Neither did the slaves'."

When Miss Emma looked blank, I explained my findings at the Historical Society.

"Well, you have been busy, haven't you?" Miss Emma patted my arm. "I expect Thomas figured with Rosabelle there'd be no next-of-kin around to contest his actions." She was quiet, thinking, for a few moments. "But the slave graves…now I understand what must have happened. And I never would've thought of going to the reference room at the Historical Society. You're a genius, Ashby!"

"Ha! It was an opportune moment, is all, Miss Emma."

"Well, you see, like the family cemetery, the slave graves were situated on a portion of the estate that was to be flooded for the lake. But, your Grandfather Thomas did not consider the slaves to be people, to be human. They were *property*, as far as he was concerned, nothing more. Lenore and he stormed about that issue more than once, as I remember. I can believe he couldn't be bothered to have them relocated."

"That makes sense to me. It was a pretty rotten thing to do but it seems to track with his character as I've come to know it."

She nodded. "There's no proof, of course. Most likely he simply removed the crude headstones, really not much more than large rocks, and tossed them away. Even though the power company was prepared to remove all graves without cost to land owners, your grandfather, no doubt, considered it frivolous, a non-issue. It sounds like the actual graves of those poor souls now rest under the lake."

"Didn't their descendants find out what my grandfather did? I would think they would be furious."

"Actually, most of the freed slaves were widely dispersed after the war, but I would not be at all surprised to see some local action. If I remember correctly, some of the descendants that are still hereabouts have launched inquiries as to the whereabouts of the Overton slave graves."

"What a low-life my grandfather was," I said. Then another thought surfaced. "So, where are the headstones? The slaves' headstones? Do you think he threw them in the lake? After the fact, I mean."

She shrugged. "I don't know. It's possible they were simply dumped somewhere on the property where they could not be easily discovered. We may never know."

She stood stiffly. "Well, I may have cooked my own goose with all this talk today, but I must say, for once, I'm feeling Lenore's approval."

"Why is that, Miss Emma?"

"Because I am nearly positive I know who stole her diary from me and I think I know why." She picked up her duster and began her task again. "It's not something Lenore could be happy about, which is why I must be sure before…before I do something…drastic. Lenore would expect nothing less. For the time being, all I can say is please be careful, dear Ashby. Watch your step. I realize there may be compelling reasons for you to remain here; however, Overhome could be a dangerous place for you to stay. You need to go back to your mother and father in New Jersey—and the sooner the better. Now, I'd best get to the kitchen," she said. "Have courage. I'm *this* close to full understanding." She held her fingers a fraction of an inch apart.

Unable to move, I sat and tried to digest it all. Any way I looked at it, there it was again, the danger card. A buzz from my cell phone brought me back to earth. It was always a surprise to realize that only my room, Rosabelle's room, was a dead zone for my cell. I flipped it open.

"Hi, Babe. It's Luke," a familiar voice said. "I'm still at th' hospital. How are y'feelin'?"

"Oh, Luke. I'm fine. Jeff and I meandered all over the estate today. I had a long, heart-to-heart talk with Sasha, and now I'm in the library where Miss Emma and I had a…a very interesting talk. I'll tell you all about it when you and Abe get in tonight."

"That's why I'm callin'." I could hear the disappointment in his voice. "We won't be comin' home today. They want t' keep Abe overnight. Somethin' about his blood pressure. They want it to come down to normal before they release 'im. I'm gonna stay with 'im. So we won't be home until tomorrow, probably late. I've already talked to Hunter about it."

"Oh. I miss you, Luke, but you're doing the right thing. Give my love to Abe, okay?"

"I love you, Babe."

"And I love you. See you soon, Luke."

A cloud of weariness, heavy and dark, descended upon my shoulders. With an effort to stand tall, I walked slowly to my room, my thoughts dulled. I opened the door to the soulful sound of Faith Hill wailing from my radio. "Ahh, Rosabelle. I'm home," I sighed, as I clicked the remote to "off" and flopped onto the bed. In the silence, I could hear the birds pecking and flapping at the windows.

To the lilting lullaby notes I had come to know so well, I drifted off humming, "Flow gently, sweet Afton."

Chapter Twenty-Five

"We need a change of pace," Uncle Hunter announced at the breakfast table next morning. "There's a big county fair at the auction center today. We're going. All of us. We'll pick Jefferson up at his camp on the way, make a day of it. What do you say?" He looked at Aunt Monica and me expectantly.

"Oh, Hunter. What a lovely idea! A real family outing," my aunt said.

He beamed. "Miss Emma!" he called into the kitchen. "Come here, please. How'd you like a well-earned day off?"

Miss Emma appeared in the doorway. "A day off?"

"The county fair. Crafts, quilts, baked goods. Paintings and lacework, jellies and jams and pies."

"Why, that would be nice," she brightened. "Just give me a chance to spritz up the kitchen and get out of this apron." She disappeared into the next room, looking pleased.

Aunt Monica pushed back her chair. "I'll have to get ready, Hunter. Oh, my hair's a fright. I'll need a little time to do something with it."

"Your hair is beautiful as always, my dear. We do want an early start, you know." Uncle Hunter winked at me. He was in a rare, jovial mood.

"The linen pants outfit," my aunt murmured as she left the room. "It makes just the right understatement."

"Well, Ashby." My uncle turned his smiling countenance on me. "It will do you good to get off the estate, have a little fun and a genuine experience with the country gentry."

I had been planning my answer for some minutes. "You know, the fair sounds wonderful, but I'm afraid I might be a real drag on everybody's fun. I still don't have my full energy back."

My uncle's face fell. "How thoughtless of me. I'm sure you know best. By all means, stay home. Enjoy the quiet and get your rest." He stood up. "Let me just check on the temporary stable hands we've hired to replace Luke and Abe and then we'll get everyone rounded up. You take it easy, now." He looked genuinely concerned.

"Thanks. Thanks for being so understanding."

I waited a good thirty minutes after they left before approaching my uncle's study. With trembling hands, I slowly opened the door, cringing when it creaked. *I'm doing the right thing,* I thought, every nerve on edge. *I may never have such an opportunity again.*

Okay, so I was trespassing, poking my nose into my uncle's private papers, but I had to find out what was in my grandmother's diary. If he was using it to work up his genealogy, it very likely lay in his office, in what I hoped would be an obvious place.

Never having been in the room before, I was curious enough to take in my surroundings. Very masculine in décor, the dark wood-paneled walls and deep red carpet contrasted with the bright sheen of the mahogany desk and its gleaming brass accessories, book ends shaped like world globes, a stand-up pen set, letter holders and trays. A handsome, well-ordered, spit-and-polish den with my uncle's imprint on every detail.

If I expected Grandmother Lenore's diary to be in evidence, I was sadly disappointed. The desktop held only papers, which appeared to be bills and invoices. The drawers were securely locked. I scrutinized the book shelves behind the desk, but no diary appeared among them. One look at my uncle's computer told me it was password blocked. Curious that there was no evidence of a working genealogy, I began sorting through a file folder of papers in the rack beside the printer. It appeared to contain legal documents, and I was about to replace it, when something caught my eye. It was a hand-written note at the bottom of an expense sheet with Fred Taylor, Attorney at Law printed on the letterhead. "You've had ample time, my friend. I don't care where you find the funds, but find them you must. I have my own debts to pay. There are plenty of people who'd benefit from knowing the truth about Overhome." It was signed, Fred.

Whoa. What was this? I re-read the note, then scanned the page above. It looked as if my uncle had been making payments to Fred Taylor in escalating amounts for a number of months. Could it be a case of extortion? I rifled through the rest of the file. There were multiple papers appearing to pertain to the estate, all couched in legal jargon I found incomprehensible.

Looking up from my reading, I turned and found myself staring into the dark blue eyes of my uncle, looking as poised and natural as if we were meeting at a garden party. "Is this any way for a convalescent to act?" His eyes glittered like polished glass. "May I congratulate you on your perseverance?"

In stunned silence, I stared at him.

"I'd say we have some things to discuss, beginning with your curiosity about my personal papers in my personal study while you thought I would be gone. Clever of me, eh?"

So it was a set-up. "I was looking for my grandmother's diary," I managed to croak, shaking from head to toe. "You stole it from Miss Emma, didn't you?" I surprised myself with my boldness.

"As a matter of fact, I did, my dear nosy niece. Not that it's any of your business."

"I beg to differ." I hoped my voice sounded strong and filled with confidence, but it was all fake. I was terrified. "I'll bet you wanted to know what your mother had to say about our ghost Rosabelle."

His face darkened and I backed away with an involuntary flinch.

He spoke through clinched teeth. "I long ago discovered the secret connection, the Overton bloodline. It was all in my mother's diary. But there was always the possibility you were Marian's bastard."

"So, you invited me here to see if Rosabelle would make herself known? To prove my legitimacy. Why would you care? And couldn't you just have a DNA test done on me, instead of going to all this trouble?"

"It was important to your uncle because of the change in Thomas Overton's will, Ashby," a clear voice intruded. Miss Emma's slim, upright figure glided into the room. "Don't look so shocked, Hunter. I found a ride back from the fair, practically followed you home. I suspected you wanted to find Ashby alone so that—"

"You meddling old fool," my uncle ground out between his teeth.

"I'm here to help you, Hunter." Miss Emma's voice was even and low and fearless.

My mind was awhirl. Whose side was she on, anyway? My uncle looked like he meant to do something drastic.

"You can still get out of this, you know, Hunter," she continued. "Tell the truth, the truth that your father changed his will the day before he died. Changed it for the sole purpose of keeping you miserable and under his control even after he was gone."

Rage radiated from every pore of my uncle's body. "My father had already disinherited Madison. Washington was dead. Overhome should be mine. All mine. And when I die, it must go to Jefferson, the rightful heir."

"Thomas Overton enjoyed hurting people, enjoyed the power he wielded with his wealth, didn't he, Hunter? He wanted to ruin your life." Miss Emma sounded like a psychologist reasoning with a patient.

"As I ruined his when I made my mother's horse run her under a tree. It was her handkerchief. I waved it at her, thinking she would want it for her riding habit, and it spooked her horse. I killed my own mother, the only person who ever loved me." He appeared to be talking to himself now.

I watched with bated breath while my pulse throbbed in my throat. A little at a time, I edged ever so slowly toward the doorway.

"No. It was an accident, as I have told you over and over ever since."

"Oh, I killed her all right. Just as I killed Washington and Marian. I made the call that sent them to their deaths. I called to tell them Father was dying.

They came, they died. But Father lived on and on. And then, at the very last moment, he changed the will."

"Washington and Marian's accident was a terrible coincidence, Hunter. That is all it was. Now is your chance to make it up to Lenore. She would want you to come clean, to tell the truth about the will—"

"My father was a monster. He left everything to the oldest living bloodline grandchild. That would be you, Ashby. Not me, not my son, but you. Of course, he doubted your legitimacy and so disregarded you as the inheritor." His eyes probed mine. "You are the one to legally inherit Overhome. And now that you approach the legal age…well, you see the problem."

"At the time, of course, Jefferson had not been born," Miss Emma said. "Hunter never imagined he'd have a son or grow to love him so much. But as Jeff grew, so did Hunter's concern as to the future of the estate."

My uncle's face took on a bewildered look.

"Oh, I understand you better than you do yourself, Hunter," she said. "Even that black-hearted father of yours was not able to eradicate *all* the goodness from your soul. You love your son as your father never dreamed of loving you."

Hunter stood, blinking, the vein in his forehead throbbing, as Miss Emma went on. "I had to find out for sure that it was you who'd stolen Lenore's diary and that you meant to harm Ashby. I wanted to be 100 percent sure. I promised your mother I would look after you, and I hoped, to the end, that I was wrong about your evil intentions. Now you have a chance to redeem yourself."

Anonymous as I wanted to remain, I had to ask a

question. "Fred Taylor, the lawyer. The payments and his demand for money." I indicated the balance sheet in the folder I'd read through. "What…?"

My uncle, apparently, regaining his composure, spoke in a monotone. "My father gave the will to Bill Taylor to hold in trust the day before he died. Bill kept the new will a secret, and, when he passed on some years later, his son Fred, my childhood playmate, took over the firm. Fred struggled to keep the firm going, but he's a spendthrift, a wastrel, and he needed money. He came to me when Jefferson turned six, showed me the will he'd unearthed from old files that left everything to you, and offered to destroy the revised will in exchange for property and money."

"Ahh. Fred Taylor got greedy," Miss Emma nodded. "He'd let it slip to me about the will, but I knew nothing about his ulterior motive. Now I understand. All those property foreclosures you two collaborated on, Fred's efforts to cook the books, which Luke discovered. If you didn't deliver more blackmail money, Fred threatened to expose the legitimate will. Yes. Now I understand."

My uncle turned to me. "Coincidentally, about the same time, your mother began pressing for a family reunion. It was only a matter of time until Madison would have returned to Overhome—the Prodigal Son, with the bloodline daughter discovered to be the true heir to the estate." He seemed almost apologetic.

"I had to take action to save Overhome for Jefferson. You do understand, don't you, Ashby? Of course, first I had to make sure you were really Washington's daughter. Rosabelle clinched that." He flashed a cold-eyed smile. "It is really quite regrettable, in a way. I must confess, aside from your resourcefulness, you've gained my admiration in other ways. You've turned out to be an excellent horsewoman, and, unfortunately, my son Jefferson is quite taken with you, as is my wife. Yes, Ashby, you've been full of surprises, a real challenge. I had to work hard to keep one step ahead of you."

Uncle Hunter's face morphed, melting like wax. The half-smiling lips turning downward, as he changed from Jekyl to Hyde before my eyes. As he talked, I had managed to move my way to Miss Emma's side, but no further. She touched my arm with her hand and cast her eyes toward the door. I knew she wanted me to make a break for it. I was sure she would try to shield me from my uncle to give me time to escape.

He was rambling now, the pupils of his eyes mere pin pricks, all but oblivious to the two quaking women in his presence. "I stole the diary because I wanted to reacquaint myself with her protective specter. One must be careful when dealing with the likes of Rosabelle." He made a noise that, in a happier setting, might have been a chuckle. "I certainly would not want old Rosie coming after *me*, now would I? But she's always had it in for wayward animals, so we'll just have to make sure the accident appears to be the animal's fault."

"Accident?" Miss Emma was unable to stifle the tremor in her voice. "What are you talking about? What accident?"

"Oh, but I have it all figured out, dear lady. It's taken me most of the summer to lay my plans and they are perfectly in place now. Fortunately, early on, Ashby managed to fall off her horse on her own. That was a bonus. Later, the night she followed my torch in the woods, I made Sasha rear and unseat her. I then attempted to finish her off with a good hard blow to the head. She survived, of course, but even that worked in my favor, helping to established a record of riding accidents that are well-documented by our family doctor." He looked pleased with himself.

"I thought you saved me that night, Uncle Hunter, saved me because you cared about me."

"Well, yes. That worked out rather well. Luke happened to come along and report you missing shortly after I returned to the house. He never suspected my part in it. It put me in the ironic position of being both your attacker and your savior." He laughed mirthlessly. "We'll just have to do it again. Only this time, we will succeed. The body count at my hands already stands at three, so what's to keep me from adding another one?" He glanced at Miss Emma. "Or two, to the account sheet?"

I was afraid to look at Miss Emma, afraid she was as immobilized by fear as I was.

My uncle went on. "Now that we all know Rosabelle is hovering about, all I have to do is make sure the accident looks like Sasha's fault. Rosabelle will appear to exact her revenge, will do away with your horse, and no one is the wiser." He gave a regretful glance at the old family retainer. "You, Miss Emma. You are, sadly, old and tired. I shall miss you."

"Don't be a fool, Hunter. You'll never get away with it." Behind her back she gently nudged me toward the door.

Horrified as I was, I had to keep my wits about me. She pushed forward and made a desperate grab at my uncle in an effort to give me a chance to run, but she only succeeded in delaying him temporarily. He swatted her away as though she were a fly. I watched in horror as she crumpled to the floor, where she lay as still as death. Knowing I could not waste a minute, I made a frantic lunge for the threshold.

"Not so fast." My uncle locked my wrists with a vice-grip of his hands. "We're going for a horseback ride, just the two of us. A nice ride on the trail."

Chapter Twenty-Six

He had thought of everything. Sasha was already saddled, along with his own horse, Goblin. My last thin threads of hope frayed. My uncle was an expert rider, the best in Virginia, Jeff had once told me. Goblin was powerful and fast. With the approach of his master, he snorted, ready for a ride that I knew would be fast and furious. How could I hope to escape?

"What are you going to do to me?" I asked, stalling for time, but unable to control my quavering voice. "How are you going to do it?"

"Curious to the end, are you? Well, where's the harm in telling you? You won't be around to report any tales." Still gripping me by the wrists, he thrust me toward Sasha with a rough shove.

"Go ahead. Climb on. I'll do the sporting thing and give you a head start. Then, a little chase to the bridge, a little tumble into the creek, an unfortunate drowning. All chalked up to an accident-prone, novice rider, out for a solitary trot."

In spite of my terror, I realized what a very sick man my uncle was. His attitude was so cavalier, so unfeeling, inhuman. He was a monster and he meant to kill me. I would not let myself dwell on how slim my chances of survival were. I focused on the idea that Miss Emma would revive, call for help, and that if I could prolong the chase until that happened, there was a chance for me, for Sasha. And my uncle could be carted off to the loony bin where he belonged.

Goblin whinnied and stamped his foot, impatient for a run. "Get on with it, Ashby. You see, Goblin is growing restless. The clock starts now."

Fastening my foot into the stirrup, I threw my leg over Sasha's back and urged him forward, my mind working feverishly all the while. Fear licked at my heart, burning into my dry throat. *Avoid the bridge. Avoid the bridge*, I droned over and over. With a clatter of hooves and a whoosh of dust, I bolted at full gallop across the fields and past the riding ring. To elude him, I would have to enter the woods, but in order to do that, I had to cross the creek without using the bridge where my uncle planned to stage the "accident." I held the slim hope I'd have enough of a head start to simply walk Sasha down the steep bank, across the creek, and up the opposite side. But if Uncle Hunter were hot on my tail, Sasha and I would have to make a huge jump across the creek, something we had never before attempted.

Behind me Goblin's hooves echoed; Hunter had made no attempt to catch up. "*The sporting thing*," my uncle had said. It was like a game to him, a fox hunt; I was the fox. He would enjoy the chase as much as the capture.

Sasha and I pounded our way to the line of trees at the north end of the field. My brain worked desperately, keeping pace with the rapid rhythm of Sasha's flying feet. *Avoid the bridge. Avoid the bridge, the bridge, the bridge*. My mantra struck a galloping cadence as I flew on the edge of the wind.

I sensed Goblin gaining on me from behind. Uncle

Hunter was eroding away my head start inch by inch, hoof beat by hoof beat. Harder, harder, I pushed Sasha, feeling the tension of his laboring muscles beneath my rigid legs. Sasha simply could not compete with the sinewy chestnut closing the gap from behind with each pounding moment.

I pulled tight on the left rein and turned Sasha directly back, head-on with Uncle Hunter. He passed in a flash of gleaming chestnut, Goblin's white blaze so close I could have reached out and touched it. The whack-whack of his crop on Goblin's flanks snapped close to my ears. My move surprised my uncle. I caught the glimpse of rage, but his joyless laugh was quick to follow. Catching his reins, he turned his horse, gaining on me once again. This time, he would surely reach me. The only escape was to leap the creek before we reached the bridge and plunge into the woods, head for the Mills' property and scream for help. Even Eddie would be a welcome sight at this point. I was quickly running out of options. *Avoid the bridge. Avoid the bridge.*

Sasha was holding his own, but he would not be able to keep up such a pace much longer. I leaned forward, willing my horse to reach the creek. Behind me, the hammering of Goblin's hooves grew nearer and nearer. I psyched myself for the jump, as I tried to prepare my horse. "Come on, Sasha, come on boy," I crooned above his streaming mane. "We're going to jump, Sasha. Jump with all your might!"

As if in slow motion, Sasha's forelegs arced, driven by the force of propulsion from the strong hind legs. For an interminable moment, we hung suspended, stretched tight in the air. I tensed to cushion the impact of the landing, giving Sasha his head, then breathed a sigh of relief as my mount regained his nimble footing and scrambled to safety just inches clear of the bank.

But I was not safe yet. Uncle Hunter bore relentlessly down from behind. He meant to cross the bridge and head me off. Sasha was losing momentum. It would take a miracle now to save us. I could hear the clatter of Goblin's hooves on the wooden planks of the bridge.

"Sasha, Sasha. Just a little longer, boy. Please. Faster! Faster!"

A scream tore the air and echoed through the woods. I looked back to see Goblin reared on his hind legs, forelegs scraping the sky. My uncle hurtled through the air, over the bridge railings, to land with a sickening thud on the rocky streambed below. Something had frightened my uncle's horse.

I brought Sasha to a halt. Shaking with dread, I sat for a long time. Though I strained my ears, there was only silence.

I trotted the heaving Sasha back through the trees toward the bridge. My heart rasped in my throat and nausea churned in my stomach. I forced myself to look. Uncle Hunter's body lay splayed on the rocks, his face just under the water line. The body was still as a mannequin, the neck bent at an odd angle. Goblin stood solid only inches away from where the bridge boards had been recently replaced. Slipping numbly from Sasha, I walked mechanically toward the chestnut, which had not budged from his stance on the bridge.

The story would be that Hunter Overton, as was his habit, had been riding Goblin at a furious pace when the steed shied and threw him off, possibly because of a loose board in the newly-repaired bridge. It would be suggested that the villainous Night Riders were, no doubt, at fault for vandalizing the bridge in the first place. It was unlikely anyone would question the circumstances of the accident.

But, I knew better. I had the evidence—the soft, fresh rose petals scattered over the new boards, red as blood.

****

The gentle night air fell around our shoulders as we strolled along the stone wall over the rolling acres of Overhome. The twilight was mellow, pastel. Stroking the cool surface of the ancient wall, I could not repress a tiny shiver.

"My father will be trustee until my twenty-first birthday, and Jeff and Aunt Monica will live here as long as they like. Miss Emma's coming around, thank God. Dr. Ross says she'll be up and about within a week. Miss Emma and Abe are beginning a well-deserved retirement, which I hope both will plan to live out here at Overhome. When I am twenty-one, the estate will be mine." I turned to my companion. "I still can't believe it, Luke. Any of it."

"The police inspectors? They're satisfied?"

"I told the truth. I said my uncle and I were having a race on our horses and that when his horse shied on the bridge, it threw him off. The rest was pretty evident."

"So, you, Miss Emma an' I—we're th' only ones who know what th' horse race was all about?"

"Yep. I'm sure Monica has no suspicion about Hunter's intentions. And Miss Emma told her she'd fallen and hit her head in Hunter's office. Also true."

"Sounds like th' case is closed then. Now, tell me again about th' slave graves," Luke said. "It's unbelievable."

"Well, yes. I agree. Rosabelle left me a—a final memo, I guess you'd say. The rubbing Jeff and Hunter did of the ancestral tombstones. I'll have to show you. It's kind of creepy, actually, to think that it was waiting for me in my room, after…"

Luke put his arm around me. "Hang in there, Babe."

I took a deep breath and went on. "After my uncle fell over the bridge, I went back to my room and, on my bed, was the rubbing, a rose beside it. 'Free the slaves' was scrawled on the back."

"Seems pretty random. I mean even more random than usual for Rosabelle."

"You know, I agree. I suppose she felt some kind of strong connection with the Overton slaves. Did you know she was enslaved in Africa herself for five years, when her ship from Scotland was pirated? I mean, who knows? Maybe she felt a special kinship with the Africans she knew there. And, then, she must have considered herself lucky that, as an indentured servant, she could live a free life, after the required seven years of labor. The slaves never had a chance to be free." I smiled weakly at Luke. "My theory is Rosabelle was a full-on abolitionist."

"So, you figger that was all a part of the FREE message she left on your computer?"

I nodded. "Why else would Rosabelle leave me that message about the slaves on the back of the tombstone rubbings? I'm getting good at reading between the lines."

Luke nodded.

"Aunt Monica is determined to find the slave grave markers my grandfather threw away. She's hired people to scout out the whole estate, including divers for the lake, if it comes to that. Unfortunately, right now there is no technology for reclaiming the bodies buried under the lake." I took a breath. "We have some experts looking at old maps that show the exact location of the original slave cemetery located on the old estate. The Historic Preservation Society, no less, is involved. Maybe someday the bodies can be retrieved and given a proper burial, or re-burial, in a church yard."

"I expect that will make a lot of people happy," Luke said. "A lot of people and one stubborn spirit."

"It will give Aunt Monica something else to think about."

"How're they takin' it all? Monica 'n Jeff. What a shocker…Hunter dyin' like that." Luke's drawl was as soft as the summer night.

"It will be a real adjustment for them, for everyone. But you know, Monica seems to be more concerned with being a good mother to Jeff. It's like, when my uncle died she knew the responsibility for Jeff would be on her shoulders now. 'I've finally grown up, Ashby,' she told me. 'I know what I have to do and I know how to do it, to be a real mother.' I know it sounds cheesy, but I think she's going to be a lot better off without someone as manipulative and condescending as my uncle hovering over her."

"Well, I feel for Jeff. His father was his idol. I know what it's like t' grow up without a dad."

"Roger that. But, you know, Jeff had an unhealthy fear of his dad, too. Unhealthy but understandable." I sighed. "He and Monica are seeing a counselor to help deal with…with everything." I leaned against Luke's chest. "And Jeff does have another father-figure he looks up to. You, Luke."

We stopped to sit atop the stone wall where I reflected on the solid, enduring feel of the aging structure. Built by slaves hundreds of years ago, it was not going anywhere any time soon. I liked that feeling because I planned to stay around for a long, long time myself. Overhome was my home now.

"So, I'll go off to college in th' fall while an estate manager runs Overhome. At least that's th' plan as of now," Luke said.

"You'll be happy to hear I've asked Eddie Mills to work the stables."

"No way!" Luke winced.

"Way. He's as eager as a schoolboy. And he's promised to sever all ties with the Night Riders."

"Well, Eddie'll give Abe somethin' to complain about, even if Abe does retire. It'll keep his mind off my leavin' for college, maybe." Luke put his hands on my shoulders. "What about your college education, Ashby?"

"I still plan to take my year off—my gap year—and to spend it here at Overhome. Now that I know there will be no problem with money for tuition, I hope to get busy writing the novel I've been composing in my mind all summer. I mean, there's enough raw material for a saga, at the very least. A trilogy. I figure next year my muse and I will find our way to the University of Virginia or some other nearby college with a good writing program."

Hopping from the wall, I grabbed Luke's hand and

pulled him to his feet. "Let's walk to the bridge and—" I stopped, remembering with a lurch the whole awful scene. "Oh, Luke. It was horrible. Terrible. A nightmare I can't get rid of. But if it hadn't happened…" I buried my face in my hands.

He put his arms around me and stroked my back. "Don't dwell on it, Ashby. Think about how you've grown to love this place and the people in it. The current stable boy, for example." He bent to kiss me.

"Wait. Smell the air. The perfume."

He lifted his face to the breeze. "Trees, grass, horses. Country air." He smiled. "Beautiful 'n sweet."

Throwing back my hair, I looked at the stars low on the horizon, rising to meet the night. "Yes, trees and grass and horse smells. But there's more, Luke. Roses. I smell roses."

Then, I heard it, as Luke enfolded me in his arms. Soaring high on the breeze, ricocheting from mountain to lake and back to me, a jubilant voice crying, "Free! Free! Free!"

And with that, Rosabelle's presence left me, probably forever. Vindicated at last, she was gone, free to cross over to the other side. Now, Overhome was rid of the malignancy of Hunter Overton. And one day, the slaves' spirits would be free again, to rest in a legitimate graveyard. The bluebirds had deserted my balcony; they had no reason to return. The spirit driving them had fulfilled her needs.

"Y'know what this means?" Luke gave me a playful look. "Y'know what y'are now?"

"A damn Yankee," we said at the same time, laughing.

A word about the author...

As a freelance writer, Susan has written for magazines, newspapers, chambers of commerce and professional journals. She also writes for several organizations at Smith Mountain Lake, Virginia, where she and her husband live. She is a member of Authors Guild, Virginia Writers, and Smith Mountain Lake Writers.

A career educator, Susan has taught students from seventh grade through college-level. She has a BA degree from Carson-Newman College and a Masters from George Mason University. She is listed in several volumes of Who's Who in Education and Who's Who in Teaching. One of her favorite activities is to talk with budding writers at schools, writers' conferences, and workshops.

Susan has long been interested in Southern concerns about culture and society, as hard-felt, long-held feelings battle with modern ideas. She was able to explore these ideas in her cozy mystery/Southern Gothic *A Red, Red Rose*, whose fictional setting is based on Smith Mountain Lake in Southern Virginia. The ghosts slipped in, to her surprise. Susan is also the author of an award-winning young adult novel.

When she is not writing, Susan enjoys boating, kayaking, golf, and yoga. She and her husband love to travel, especially when grandchildren are involved.

Visit Susan at:

http://www.susancoryellauthor.com

Thank you for purchasing
this publication of The Wild Rose Press, Inc.
For other wonderful stories of romance,
please visit our on-line bookstore at
www.thewildrosepress.com.

For questions or more information
contact us at
info@thewildrosepress.com.

The Wild Rose Press, Inc.
www.thewildrosepress.com

To visit with authors of
The Wild Rose Press, Inc.
join our yahoo loop at
http://groups.yahoo.com/group/thewildrosepress/

www.ingramcontent.com/pod-product-compliance
Lightning Source LLC
Chambersburg PA
CBHW070906180626
46817CB00003B/931